# VIRGINIA KING

# The Third Note

*The Secrets of Selkie Moon*

CELESTIAL
hedgehog

First published by Celestial Hedgehog Pty Ltd 2017



This novel is entirely a work of fiction. The names, characters and incidents portrayed in it are the work of the author's imagination. Any resemblance to actual persons, living or dead, events or localities is entirely coincidental.



First edition

ISBN: 978-0-9945923-8-5

This book was professionally typeset on Reedsy.
Find out more at reedsy.com

*If we shadows have offended,*
*Think but this, and all is mended,*
*That you have but slumber'd here*
*While these visions did appear.*

— *A Midsummer Night's Dream*
William Shakespeare

# Contents

# Books by Virginia King

The Secrets of Selkie Moon

The First Lie
The Second Path
The Third Note
The Fourth Door
Laying Ghosts (Prequel)
Leaving Birds (Short Stories)

# Glossary

*Selkie* – sea creature from Celtic folklore that takes the form of a seal in water but can take human form on land.

Hawaiian words
    *Kahuna* – wise person, sorcerer.
    *Lanai* – veranda.
    *Lei* – garland of flowers or shells, worn around neck.
    *Lolo* – crazy.
    *Tutu* – grandma.
    *Umu* – earth oven.

Irish words
    *Bealtaine* – festival held on May 1.
    *Bodhrán* – shallow, one-sided drum.
    *Boreen* – country track.
    *Cashel* – megalithic ring fort.
    *Ceili* – social event with singing and dancing.
    *Eejit* – idiot.
    *Earwigger* – eavesdropper.
    *Faerie* – mythical being.
    *Poteen* – alcohol distilled in a pot, often made from potatoes.
    *Rath* – megalithic ring fort.
    *Sheehogue* – mythical being, another name for a faerie.
    *Souterrain* – underground passage or structure.

# Chapter 1

The parcel arrives at two o'clock. I've been waiting for it. Pacing this tiny flat and wondering what the hell it's going to contain. A parcel from my great-grandmother, delivered to me all these years after her death.

She lodged it with her lawyer just before she died with instructions for me to get it on my eighteenth birthday, but his son, a lawyer too, has only just found it. I've just turned thirty-five, so whatever she wanted me to do with it, I'm only seventeen years too late.

When the lawyer couldn't find me, he rang my family home and almost got caught in Stella's clutches. My stepmother. Why not give the parcel to her for safekeeping till I turned up? My sister Gretel overheard the conversation and volunteered my address.

As the courier watches me sign for it, my phone rings. "Have you got it yet?" Stella asks.

Stella never calls me Selkie. My mother was in love with the selkies of Celtic folklore, the seal people who peel off their skins and dance in human form. I'm afraid of the sea so I'm a selkie in name only, but Stella has always hated its magical connotations. The timing of her call unnerves me. She always suppressed my imagination as a child, but lately she's been showing signs that she might be psychic herself. That's almost as creepy as the parcel in my hands.

As I wave off the courier and tell Stella I'm holding it, she applies her usual stepmotherly wiles from the other side of the world: "I forbid you to open it." This tactic hasn't worked since I was little.

"It's addressed to me, Stella."

"Please."

It's a word that's never passed her lips before. Now my interest is really piqued.

"What don't you want me to know?" I ask. "Whatever's in here, it's ancient history."

"Nothing like that. But Granny Ryan was ... eccentric."

"Eccentric old ladies can be fascinating." I'm thinking of the *kahuna* who lives in our local bus shelter. Coral. Sometimes I consult her when things get weird. "Especially when they leave you a mysterious parcel."

Stella snorts. "Not that kind of eccentric. Dangerous eccentric. At the end she kept talking about spells. Your father said she insisted on seeing you minutes after you were born, then fell off her perch."

"She died the day I was born?"

No wonder I'm feeling spooked.

"She was nearly a hundred and she was in the same hospital, after a fall. She got a nurse to wheel her around to see you, chanted some incantation, then dozed off. They left her in the chair and a nurse found her later. *Dead.*" She drops the word like a grenade in a pond.

"What kind of ... incantation? What did she say?"

"I wasn't there of course. Your father never said—and I never asked."

I wonder if Dad would remember. Even if Stella knew the details, I couldn't trust her. Our relationship has always been strained, and she hasn't forgiven me for escaping to Hawaii.

"There must be something specific you're worried about, Stella."

A secret. My family's good at secrets.

"I'm worried it will ... unsettle you, that's all."

Unsettle. An interesting choice of word. Ever since I ran away from Sydney, from my charmless ex-husband, Andrew, and from Stella herself, I've been wanting to settle, to make a new life. But life has intervened.

"The lawyer said her name was Bridget," I say. "Bridget Ryan."

Stella's never told me anything about her family.

She sighs. "Everyone called her Bridie."

"What else can you tell me about her?"

She hesitates. "She was born Bridget O'Connor. Irish. Back then, every second Irishman was emigrating to somewhere."

"When was this?"

Another pause. "Your grandfather was born in Melbourne in 1920, so before that."

I get up the courage to ask the next question. "Why was Bridie so interested in me?"

Silence. She's not going to give me anything useful, not when I'm refusing to leave the parcel untouched.

But as she rings off, she says, "Bridie *doted* on your mother."

My mother. Stella's younger sister, Prunella. If Bridie and my mother were close, perhaps this parcel just contains a keepsake from their grandmother-granddaughter bond.

Still standing at the open door, I hug the package to my chest and watch the familiar cavalcade of tourists and beach babes and students three floors below, just a few blocks from Waikiki. It's odd enough receiving it out of the blue, but Stella's call has aroused my curiosity. And my fear. There's something in here she wants to bury. Out of genuine concern for me? More likely out of a desperate desire to control me from the other side of the world.

Leaving the door open for some air, I put the package on the bed and stare at it.

I'm still staring at it when Wanda arrives. My flatmate waves her hand in front of my face. "Great zombie impersonation, Selkie."

When I bring her up to date, she's astounded that I haven't opened it. "Are you letting your subconscious do a little digging first?"

Wanda knows about my so-called psychic 'gift'. The one she hasn't got herself even though her grandmother was a *kahuna*.

"Not really," I say. "But my great-grandmother was Irish, and she must have been born in the late 1800s. Maybe … she gave birth to a baby out of wedlock and moved to Australia to escape the shame, then spent her whole life trying to track down her lost child."

Wanda likes it. "And she didn't want her children or grandchildren to know, until the generations had moved on and wouldn't care about the scandal. The parcel could hold clues to their whereabouts. Photos? A birth certificate? You might have another family somewhere."

"It's the kind of thing that Stella might have sniffed out." It's impossible to keep secrets from my stepmother. "And if it was scandalous she'd want to suppress it."

But what would be the chances of finding my long-lost

relatives after all this time? And would I want to?

"So your great-*tutu* might want you to do something for her," Wanda says. "Being her descendant comes with obligations, right?"

"I hope not. If it had to be buried until I was an adult then it's big, and I don't want to do big any more."

Ever since I won a green card and escaped to Hawaii, I've been caught up in mysteries that have taken me on a wild ride. But after my very strange adventure to France—strange but enlightening—I've finally got my head on straight.

But Wanda knows how to press my buttons. "What exactly are you afraid of?"

I pull a face, then rip the parcel open. Torn newspaper tumbles out. We rifle through the pieces but find nothing else.

"Why pay a lawyer to keep a parcel of shredded newspaper?" Wanda asks. "Was she a trickster, your *tutu*?"

"I don't know and I don't care. She died the day I was born so I owe her nothing. I've just wasted a bucket-load of emotional energy on this ... hoax."

I stuff the newspaper into the bin—relief mixed with the anger.

"She died the same day you were born?" Wanda asks.

Here it comes. "Don't go all woo-woo on me, Wanda."

"Did you know?"

"Not till Stella told me."

"So it's a message after all. She sends you a package to let you know your spirits passed each other."

Shit. It fits with what Stella said about Bridie's incantation. If she put a spell on me, has opening the parcel just activated it?

"What's the date on the newspaper?" Wanda asks, pulling a few pieces out of the bin. "March seventeen."

"My birthday."

"Saint Patrick's Day," she says, winking.

"I know that already."

"Wait a minute. Add the numbers up. Seventeen for your birthday is one plus seven. Makes eight. And the parcel's been missing for seventeen years. And you're now three plus five. That's spooky, everything adds up to eight."

I'm not buying it. "Bridie didn't know the parcel would be late. And she couldn't have been into numerology. She was Catholic."

"And Irish. They do a line in everything from Christianity to faeries. I'm not saying Bridie planned this," she continues. "It's just more than a coincidence that the numbers add up to eight." She starts retrieving more pieces from the trash. "This is what she was sending you—the newspaper from the day of your birth and the day of her death."

"So why is it in pieces?"

"It's a puzzle. She's not giving you the secret on a platter. It's some kind of test. You should be asking what's in this paper that she wanted you to see."

I sigh. "OK, but that'll take ages. I'm going out with Alister tonight. I need to get ready."

Wanda raises her eyebrows. "Is tonight *the night?*"

She means am I going to spend the night with him. After all these months of foreplay.

"I don't know. I'm terrified I'll make a mess of it."

Wanda nods. "It means more than sex."

"Yeah. We'll be consummating something huge."

Like how I feel about him. It's something I've never done

before: sex that means more than just sex. Not with my ex. Not with any man. What if it's more than I can handle?

"Think of it as 'just sex' then," Wanda says. "That's how it happened with Lew and me. There was attraction, and the stirrings of love, but we didn't let it complicate the sex."

Lew rents Wanda her art studio, and one thing led to another.

"Sounds easy," I say. "But we're eating out tonight so going back to Alister's place will be a deliberate decision."

Just the thought of it robs me of breath.

"Why aren't you eating at his place?" she asks. "He likes to cook, doesn't he?"

"He wanted to cook. The restaurant was my idea."

"Wow, you are afraid."

"Yeah. What if making love to me is like doing it with Doris?"

Doris is Wanda's shop dummy. She sits on a stool at the end of her bed, headless and draped in sun hats and *leis*. Our third flatmate, solid and undemanding. Someone to vent to when life does its worst, or to share a toast with when things are going right.

We laugh, and I give Doris a hug, avoiding the nails protruding from her chest where Wanda hangs her jewellery. "Sorry, old girl. My panic attack doesn't give me permission to question your prowess in the cot."

As I take a lukewarm shower, my thoughts veer away from Alister's no doubt king-sized bed and return to Bridie. Wanda was right about obligations. It's why I've always hated the word 'family'. My family expected me to be who they wanted me to be, even renaming me Elkie—a kind of identity theft at the hands of my own flesh and blood. It was only a few months ago that I had the courage to break free. Is that why Bridie's parcel has been buried until now?

When I emerge from the bathroom, Wanda is standing beside the table where the newspaper pieces are now stacked. I notice her body language: hands on hips again.

She smirks and points to a bundle wrapped in newspaper. "A parcel within a parcel." She's managed to stop herself from opening it.

I race over and pick it up. It's longer than my hand and heavy for its size. "How the hell did we miss this?"

"What's the first word you think of?" she asks.

"Buried."

"It's a puzzle. It's buried. If she'd sent you a hammer she couldn't have hit you harder with the message."

Wanda can't stop grinning. She loves this stuff.

"What if I'm ... unleashing something?" I whimper.

"Your great-*tutu* sent you a gift and you're going to throw it away without opening it?"

I tear off the wrapping and the contents fall to the floor, landing with a thud on my bare foot. A necklace. In the dim light filtered through the venetian blinds it appears to be gold—a pendant studded with coloured stones hanging from a chunky chain. It's unusual. An antique.

We stare at it, unable to move, as if something about its history has made us mute.

"Rub your foot over it," Wanda says, "and say the first word you think of." She's big on the sentient powers of the sole.

I do as she says and one word pops out. "Murder."

# Chapter 2

Instead of picking me up, Alister's asked me to catch the bus downtown. Very mysterious. I know we're not dining at Jimmy Ho's, Honolulu's poshest restaurant. Alister can afford it—and sometimes I let him pay—but tonight we both want somewhere more relaxed. Not the Pearl either, my favourite noodle bar in Chinatown and my second home since I landed here friendless from Sydney. I know the couple who run the Pearl so well that eating there would be almost as intimate as Alister's penthouse. Intimate and claustrophobic. No, it needs to be somewhere ... anonymous. Hard for Alister, with the paparazzi always on his tail, but he's assured me he has his ways.

On the bus, I'm overdressed amongst the shorts and flip-flops in my killer heels and little black dress. The dress Davina made for me—Davina Kennedy, the psychic seamstress. She and I share an Irish heritage but it's Hawaii that breathes 'psychic' into everything, even fashion, and the dress gives me a surge of energy whenever I pull it on.

At the thought of my heritage, I finger the necklace around my neck. Even though it looks stunning with my dress, I wasn't at all sure about carrying its history around with me, especially after the murder message.

But Wanda reminded me how precious it is. "Don't leave anything valuable in this flat," she said. "Besides, if you wear it you might get another vision."

That's what I'm worried about. It's already more than hinted at the baggage it's carrying. But when I put it on, it seemed to make a claim on me. It's hard to explain, but just like my little black dress fits me like a skin, the necklace created a kind of unbreakable connection with its wearer. Me.

Now, as I look down at the pendant resting against my chest, it feels creepy with symbolism: long and thin, shaped like bamboo in three segments, with coloured stones forming a line like buttons down its length. It was competing with my glass heart on its ribbon, but I won't go anywhere without my heart, so I've clipped it onto the antique catch on the chain beside the pendant. Their shapes complement each other.

At a busy bus stop a gaggle of tourists climbs aboard and suddenly Alister is sitting beside me. He didn't warn me that he'd be joining me and his light brown curls and broad smile catch me unawares. His proximity does what it usually does—causes a rush of desire—and I can't help grinning back. He's looking relaxed, and blending with the tourists in a stylish blue and red Aloha shirt teamed with chinos and loafers.

"Pretend you haven't seen me," he jokes, pleased that he's given the paparazzi the slip.

The passion behind his eyes washes over me. He's besotted for reasons that still astound me: Selkie Moon, Aussie seminar presenter and trouble with a capital T. But none of my hard-to-bed antics or my mythical mysteries have dampened his ardour. Yet.

I ignore the fear that's mingling with my desire; and luckily my stomach chooses this moment to rumble.

"This cloak and dagger stuff better be good, Alister. I'm starving."

"It'll be good enough to eat. Like a certain woman in my line of sight. But that's all I'm saying till we get there."

"I hate surprises."

He chuckles. "That's what inspired me."

He asks me what's new, and part of me wants to tell him about Bridie and her gift, because I don't want to keep secrets from him, my almost-lover. But I decide to wait until I've scoured the newspaper and found out if it tells me more about the necklace. If Wanda's right and it's a puzzle, maybe Bridie completed the crossword minutes before she died and I'll have to analyse every clue. Or worse: I'll find nothing, then get one of my midnight messages. That voice in my head always freaks me out.

"There's something you're not telling me," he says as he watches the thoughts dance behind my eyes.

"Like you're withholding the location of dinner?"

But the clandestine venue is adding an extra frisson to the chemistry between us.

He leads me off the bus in downtown Honolulu and onto another, taking us back in the direction of Waikiki.

"Hey, not Koa Avenue," I say. "My fridge is empty."

"Relax. Enjoy the ride."

Then he's taking my hand and we're alighting at yet another bus stop and getting into a waiting cab. When it heads towards Kaka'ako, the industrial area where Alister lives, I worry that he's luring me to his place by stealth.

The cab speeds along between low-rise industrial buildings, all closed at this hour. The district has become a hub for street art and there are quirky murals on every vertical surface, but if it's become a dining precinct too it's the first I've heard of it.

I'm about to protest when the cab stops outside a dilapidated two-storey building on a narrow block between two factories. It looks like an old house that got swamped by warehouses but is managing to cling on. The era is faded colonial with peeling paint, while the island-style thatched roof has seen better days. I gaze at the façade with dismay. Wherever we're going I'm overdressed. A sign announces a mechanic's shop, and the number of cars in the parking lot suggests they're reinventing stolen vehicles after hours.

"Easy-over eggs straight off the bumper bar?" I quip.

Alister winks, pays the cab and leads me down the side of the building to a rear staircase with a lattice rail. We avoid a few holes on the way up—me on tiptoes in my heels—and arrive on the second floor, where an open veranda is full of diners.

"Welcome to the underground," Alister whispers. "Tonight's host is an up-and-coming chef showing off his new cuisine."

I stop myself from saying 'Wow' and pretend I'm savvy about pop-up eateries. I've read about them in London.

Alister guides me to a table with a view across the rooftops to the sea. It's far enough away that it doesn't activate my sea phobia—always a problem on an island. Instead this feels clandestine and daring. He produces a bottle of wine from a bag on his shoulder while I peruse the menu handwritten on the wall.

"Aren't you going to ask me how I discovered Club Sub?" he says. "Subversive Supper Club for the uninitiated."

"Your penthouse is just down the road?"

"Walking distance. But the venues change every time—so

it's fun and mysterious. It keeps the number of diners intimate, too."

"And the health inspectors guessing? I'd like to avoid a screaming case of salmonella."

He chuckles. "They get a temporary licence to serve food at each venue. But as a person who lives on rewarmed Chinese leftovers, I'm surprised that health risks bother you."

"You're right. Starvation always makes me game."

I should apply that wisdom to my sex problem.

Platters of assorted appetisers are delivered to a long serving table by a large woman who might be the chef's mother. Variations on degustation with little parcels of dumplings, sushi and sashimi. We join the other diners and help ourselves.

"Tell me what's bothering you," Alister says when we're sitting down again. "I can feel the tension from here."

I don't want to get into the big issue—how close we are to his bedroom and how far away I feel from the carefree lover we both want me to be—so I spill the beans about Bridie. He's intrigued. Who wouldn't be? Sometimes I'm so intriguing I could scream.

He admires the chain and pendant. "I noticed it on the bus. Do you think it's more than an heirloom?"

"There was no note, just the newspaper. It might just be padding for the necklace, but I won't be sure till I put the pieces together. If there's a secret here and Bridie wanted to wait until I was eighteen to share it, then it must be big."

Like a murder, but I'm not going to mention that.

"Or she thought it was big," he says. "A scandal perhaps. It might seem tame after all this time."

"Stella begged me not to open it. She doesn't do begging so she must suspect it's something about her."

"It looks like an Albert chain," Alister says, reaching across and brushing his fingers against my throat. Did someone just turn on the air conditioning? "From an old fob watch judging by the style of the catch. It hooked through a buttonhole in a waistcoat. And the pendant looks like one-of-a-kind, added later to turn it into a woman's necklace."

He removes his hand, along with the sparks from his fingers.

"It's much older than Stella," he adds. "What do you know about her past?"

"Nothing from before she married Dad and became my wicked stepmother. She's always been a closed book. Only lately she's started to let a few glimpses of her hidden side slip."

"She might surprise you, Selkie."

"I prefer the Stella I know."

He laughs. "You hate surprises."

We work our way through the main course—a Japanese-style seafood marinara on a bed of seaweed noodles—and he admires my tiny glass heart, a special gift from an artist we both met in France. Its vibrant red planes catch the light.

Then he springs another surprise on me. "I'm off to San Francisco. Only for a few days but it might be longer. It's about Deshi."

The son he hasn't seen since he was a baby. Almost thirty years ago.

"There was a promising response to the advertisement. And now—a DNA match."

"A match? That's fantastic." While I've been dominating the airwaves, he's been sitting on this.

"It's the closest I've ever got to him," he says. "A match to his baby hair. It's all I've got—a lock of his hair." He pauses.

"A relative on his mother's side came forward."

"Wow. A cousin?"

"Looks like it. She's living in San Francisco, where some of Fleur's family still live. She agreed to the DNA test—and it's a match. Now she's just got to agree to see me."

"Why wouldn't she see you? She knows there's a reward, doesn't she?"

"That might be her only motivation. But if she leads me to Deshi …"

He doesn't need to say more. It's huge.

I reach across and squeeze his hand as his eyes tear up. It reminds me how soft he is on the outside, with a core of steel that's kept him on the search for Deshi for most of his adult life. It's a quality I want to emulate: to lose my crusty shell of fear and embrace life with all its joys and hurts.

We change the subject so he doesn't start bawling in public.

"How are the plans going for your next seminar?" he asks.

Alister's a seminar tycoon himself, but I haven't joined his stable of presenters. My independence is important to me after years under Andrew's thumb.

"So far I haven't found a venue around here until well into next year. Everywhere's booked with a waiting list. I might have to do something overseas to keep some money in the bank."

"That shouldn't be a problem. Your reputation must be spreading."

He's right. After the notoriety around my disappearance a few months ago, and the success of my seminar in France, offers from around the world are still coming in. My seminar, Being Sleek, is based on the wisdom of seals and it's attracted a corporate audience looking for something fresh and, dare

I say, quirky in their business training. I vowed I wouldn't succumb to 'quirky' just to turn a buck, but I've slipped into it like a selkie slips into its skin.

"The world's at your feet, so where would you like to go?" Alister asks.

One place pops into my mind—Ireland—but that must be the influence of my new necklace. If that's where the murder happened, it's a great reason to stay away. And anyway, I haven't had any offers from the Emerald Isle—perhaps because a seminar about seals run by a presenter called Selkie might offend the locals and their folklore.

"Nowhere," I say. "I want to settle down and get on with life here."

"A lot of people would envy you, having a career where you can travel."

"I hope it becomes a career." Based in Hawaii.

"It will."

There he goes again. Being more sure of me than I am of myself.

* * *

Later as we return to the street, just a stroll from Alister's penthouse, the butterflies in my belly start up again. But he remembers the wine bag slung on the back of his chair and returns to the rear of the building, leaving me alone.

One moment a cool breeze is caressing my skin; and the next I'm screaming. What starts like an avalanche crushing me from behind becomes sharp nails at my throat and a laboured breath in my ear. He's tugging at my chain, and in a desperate fight for air I try to stop it from choking me.

In the scuffle I catch a glimpse of him: moustache, full-sleeved shirt, waistcoat. Then he's vanished, but I can't stop screaming.

Alister comes running.

"Bridie's necklace," I gasp. "And my glass heart. He was killing me, Alister. He was choking me to death."

The guy's disappeared, so instead of giving chase Alister wraps me in his arms and presses my trembling body against his. I can't stop crying. I can feel the burn marks already at my throat.

"He wanted the gold," he says. "Since the gold price soared there've been a lot more muggings."

When I stop shaking, Alister crouches down. "Your heart might have dropped around here."

My heart … I'm lost without my heart.

"But the necklace is gone. I'm sorry, Selkie."

Now I'm crying in earnest, the depth of my emotions overwhelming. As soon as I put it on, the necklace became mine and now it's been torn from me. So much for the trust Bridie placed in me. After waiting in a vault for thirty-five years, it's gone after a few hours in my care. A surge of anger mixes with the other emotions. Of all the gold chains in Honolulu, why this one? And how the hell am I going to get it back?

As I suck in deep breaths and weep, Alister is circling me looking at the ground. It's dark now, with only the streetlights for illumination.

"We'll have to come back in the morning," he says.

After we've spent the night at his place, making passionate love for the first time.

"I need to go home, Alister."

He stands up looking resigned. "Of course. This shouldn't have happened. I should have been looking after you."

He calls a cab and we travel in silence to Waikiki. The driver waits while Alister walks me to my door.

"I'll report it to the police," he says, pressing his lips into my hair. "And I'll look for your heart in the morning. Promise."

* * *

Wanda is spending the night with Lew and I'm afraid to go to bed. The violence of a stranger's hands is giving me living nightmares. He was only after the chain so why did it feel like murder?

There's a bottle of wine in the fridge but it's almost empty. I squeeze out a quarter of a glass, remembering something that Keith, my blind psychologist friend back in Sydney, said about the power of a few sips of alcohol to arouse your intuition. I usually go way beyond intuition to the other 'i' word, impairment, but tonight the near-empty bottle is on my side.

My loss has exposed my attachment to the necklace. Acute. Letting Bridie down feels like a tragedy, but losing the necklace and my sense that I was being murdered are more than coincidences. They're another message. The murder might have happened in the distant past, but the mugging has brought it into the present. *My* present. And whatever this puzzle is, it suddenly feels urgent.

What did Bridie sense about me as I took my first baby breaths? And what did she incant over my tiny body when we passed each other into life and death on St Patrick's Day thirty-five years ago? It might be fanciful, but I sense she planted some kind of psychic seed, to be activated by the arrival of the parcel. It would explain why the responsibility she's put on me feels so personal.

But my glass heart has got nothing to do with Bridie, and losing it is serious collateral damage. A heart with no value to the mugger but so special to me, made by Fabienne, an artist who became my friend when I stayed with her in France. Losing the red heart ... is another symbol of murder. Because without my heart, I'm ... dead.

These thoughts are freaking me out.

I turn to Doris but she's no help, draped in Wanda's necklaces and looking smug. My eyes move past her to my Shona sculpture on the shelf behind my bed. Shona comes from Zimbabwe and she's my 'rock' in times of trouble. She's just a bust with a fierce profile, but she reminds me to stay grounded when I lose perspective, to call on my inner strength. And as far as wisdom goes, she's got a quality that Doris lacks: a head. The sight of Shona calms me, and an insight comes: I've lost precious things before and they've always turned up after a struggle.

There's a pattern here—the losing and the finding take me on incredible journeys of discovery. Things I need to know about myself. It's what happened when I lost my memory and had to travel across the world to get it back. I mustn't forget what I discovered then: that the answers are in my own heart.

It's time to get to work on the newspaper. I look at the stack of pieces on the table and the roll of sticky tape that Wanda's left. But sticking them back together will take hours. If I'm going to act on this urgency I feel, then there must be a quicker way.

I decide to trust my intuition for a change—to glance at each piece and see if anything jumps out.

It's a local paper from back in Sydney: *The Manly Daily*, dated 17 March, my birthday. On the lower half of the front page is an announcement about the St Patrick's Day celebrations that night—Irish bands marching down the Corso to the beachfront, pubs selling Guinness, food stalls offering potato pancakes. I laugh. It's hard to come up with Irish cuisine that you can eat off your lap.

The top half of the front page seems to be missing. It would have the newspaper's masthead but I can't find it. The word 'buried' pops into my head again.

At last I see a reference to the front-page story on page 35, where the remainder has been printed. Ignoring the fact that three plus five add up to eight, I note that the new maternity wing at Manly Hospital had just opened and the first baby born there had been featured on the front page. My stomach gets one of its peptic twinges. Was that baby me? I imagine a huge front-page image of my raven-haired mother showing off her new baby, captioned with the usual cooing details. But after going through both sides of every piece again, I can't find the headline article.

I return to the rest of the story. There's no photo but there's a summary paragraph my subconscious must have seen: *Bouncing baby Selkie, born to Prunella Ryan, and given a Celtic name in honour of St Patrick's Day.* Then I read something that takes my breath away.

*If the name Prunella Ryan rings a bell, it might be because the now sixteen-year-old mother was the toddler who went missing for three days when she was just three years old. At the time of her disappearance, The Manly Daily covered all sides of the distressing story. Here's a photographic extract of our exclusive coverage after Prunella was found, hungry but unharmed, by her older sister, Stella. To this day, no-one knows how the three-year-old managed to fall into the drain under a service road behind Wakehurst Park not far from their Manly Vale home.*

This story is news to me. But when I first arrived in Hawaii I got a psychic message that led to revelations about my mother, so the possibility of more secrets doesn't surprise me. I find the other half of the page and scan the black and white photographs with an unhealthy fervour: a row of police, some with dogs, scouring the local bushland; the dark stormwater drain under the road and a close-up of the entrance grate pulled partly aside. The caption suggests that the heavy grate must have been moved by someone unknown, creating a hole for three-year-old Prunella to fall down, but the police ruled out foul play. I move on to a photo of the relieved family. My mother, her face tear-stained and smudged with dirt, is being cuddled by her haggard but beaming mother, the grandmother I don't remember. Beside them my grandfather, Bridie's only son, glares at the camera. And, partly obscured, Stella, the thirteen-year-old heroine of the day, is frowning. Even after fifty years that frown hasn't changed.

Is this what I'm supposed to find out—that Stella saved my mother's life? If my mother had died in that drain, then I wouldn't exist. Bridie couldn't know that my mother would die early anyway and that Stella would become my stepmother, but it looks like she wanted me to know this story and be grateful. It also explains Stella's need for a little appreciation. By saving Prunella's life she saved mine.

I imagine telling Stella that I know the story, but any words of gratitude stick in my throat. And then the questions return. Why wait so many years to tell me? And where does the necklace fit in?

The wine glass is empty and the evening's events have caught up with me. I collapse into bed, too exhausted now to have a nightmare about the mugging. But the old story from the newspaper visits my dreams.

A drain appears. Like the one in the paper, but this one is lined with stones, wet and glistening. If there'd been a storm when my mother was in the drain she would have drowned. Drowning is one of my nightmares. But this drain has a magical quality, until I see what's painted in green across the grate. The slits in the grille make it hard to read, but I know what it says. *Murder.*

# Chapter 3

When I'm on the bus to the office, Alister calls. The sound of his voice takes me back to last night, and the mugging shocks me all over again. Then I remember his arms around me.

He's been for a run and found my glass heart right there in front of the mechanic's. That's the good news.

"The bad news is it's broken," he says.

A broken heart.

"No," I wail, getting looks from eavesdropping commuters.

"But fixable, I think. Let me show it to a jeweller I know."

"OK," I whisper, trying not to cry. "And Alister? Thanks."

He's also reported the theft to the police.

"The police," I say too loudly, getting more looks. After only a few months here, I've already got history with them.

"You might be lucky," he says. "They might find the necklace."

"But they'd need proof it's mine."

"I took your photo at Club Sub," he says. "It's right there on your neck."

One of those cheesy dinner shots. I'd forgotten that. Me making the most of the buffet, the necklace only just visible as I dived into a mountain of seafood.

We say goodbye and hang up. For the rest of the journey I push images of broken hearts from my mind and try to think about nothing but seminars.

At my office, in the ugliest and cheapest building downtown, Derek surprises me by being at work before midday.

He comes out of the cubicle next to mine and gives me a lopsided grin. "Just landed a part-time gig as a reporter." He puffs out his chest.

Derek Delaney is a freelance writer who does anything that pays—travel articles, corporate stuff, even local ghost stories—but I'm surprised he'd stoop to playing journalist. They're not his favourite people.

"There's been a spate of muggings," he explains, "and they need extra writers to cover it. I'm interviewing victims."

"I don't believe it."

He misunderstands. "I haven't sold out, Selkie. It's just for a few days. The editor actually pleaded with me after a bunch of his reporters went down with salmonella. An *umu* gone wrong—they stuffed the pig with chickens, didn't cook them long enough."

"It's your fault then." I got attacked so my best friend could break into journalism.

He looks offended. "I wasn't there. As if I'd undercook an *umu*."

"Your fault I got mugged."

His eyes widen as I start my story, then he's pulling out his phone ready to hit the record button.

"No publicity," I say. "Some guy crept up behind me and got his hands around my throat. It hit me like a truck. I thought he was killing me, DD. Seriously."

Derek looks at the marks on my neck and frowns. He knows

my jewellery isn't valuable. "Why choke you? Why not snatch your purse?"

"I got sent a gold chain yesterday. From my great-grandmother." The loss brings on a new rush of tears. "And now it's gone. And Fabienne's heart is broken."

Derek wraps his arms around me. "The cops will get him, Selkie. Word on the street is there's an operation to catch these gold thieves when they try to fence the booty. If you had to get mugged, last night was a good choice."

"Just lucky then." I try to smile.

"You might get the necklace back."

It feels like my life depends on it.

I bring him up to date on the whole Bridie story.

"You're at it again," he says.

"What?"

"A magnet for the paranormal." He starts ticking things off his fingers. "A gold chain that leaps off your neck the first time you wear it; old drains with dark interiors full of secrets; numbers that keep adding up to eight; and the word 'murder' everywhere you turn. Then there's the Irish connection, including your birthday. I bet you end up going there."

"I lost the necklace here, DD."

He throws me one of his all-knowing looks, then goes back to his office.

I push the mounting coincidences out of my mind and concentrate on finding a local seminar space. It's already late May, and the winter months are always booked way ahead as patrons from the mainland seek out the sun. I send out enquiries to the other islands but I'm not hopeful.

By day's end, I'm overdue for a bowl of comfort food. Time to saunter down the well-trodden path to Chinatown. If Nigel's working tonight, Derek might come with me. I could use the company.

But a phone call changes that.

"Selkie Moon?" a strange voice asks.

"Speaking."

"Detective Nakano, ma'am. Honolulu CID, Robbery detail. I'm following up a report that you were the victim of a robbery last night."

"Yes."

"I happen to be just outside your office, ma'am. Mind if I come up and run through the details, get you to sign an incident report?"

"Of course. Top floor."

Detective Nakano arrives—a chunky guy with old acne scars, and a junior officer in tow. The kid looks like a teenager with a face that flushes easily and I don't catch his name. They run through the details that Alister provided and I sign it as a true statement of events.

"Did you get a look at him?" Nakano asks. "Hair colour? Height? Clothing?"

I tell him what I saw. The mugger's outfit is not what people wear around here and my credibility takes a dive.

"A moustache, OK. But a long-sleeved blouse and a waist-coat? Some kind of steam-punker?" He looks at his notes. "Doesn't match what your friend saw, ma'am. A baseball cap and running shoes."

"It was dark."

"And you were scared. Makes sense you'd get mixed up. But the MO's one we're familiar with. This guy loiters with intent, spies something shiny, then strikes. We've got someone on

CCTV near another incident, but we're not sure it's him till we get some corroboration. Doesn't look like the guy you saw. No, ma'am."

As he shakes his head and suppresses a smile, I suspect he'll be sharing my description at the station for a few laughs.

"We do have something we'd like you to see." He's grinning openly now. "A bag full of stolen gold was found in a dumpster. A miracle it got handed in."

"You're kidding. You think my necklace might be in there?"

"Your friend provided a photo. We've got a new website for stolen property," he says proudly. "Jace here went through the bag and posted photos of each item—that's why it's up already. But I need to warn you," he adds, "it's damaged. Where he ripped it off your neck."

My pulse is racing. "Of course."

The kid pulls out a tablet and scrolls to a photo. He turns the screen towards me and I gasp. "That's it." The twisted wire of the links is unmistakable, even though one of them is broken.

"And the pendant?" I ask, my voice shaking. "It was hanging from the chain. Shaped like bamboo."

Jace shrugs. "Nothing like that in the bag."

"Maybe it dropped when the chain broke," Nakano says. "Go back and look for it. Might be another miracle." They get up to leave. "Come in tomorrow and sign for the chain."

He gives me the address but I know where it is.

"Why did he toss the loot in a dumpster?" I ask.

"Can't go into that, ma'am. It's an ongoing investigation. We need to keep the details under wraps."

As soon as they've gone, I call Alister.

"It's pretty rare that they connect stolen property with its owner," he says.

"Thanks for taking the photo and reporting it."

"It's the least I could do. I guess the rumours about a police crackdown meant that anyone finding that bag would have to be pretty savvy to make money out of it." He pauses. "You said one of the links is broken. My jeweller friend can look at it."

"And the pendant's missing." My voice catches.

"The most interesting part, I thought."

"Yeah." It means something, that pendant. I had to lose it to find out. "The detective thinks it could have dropped when the chain broke. But you would have found it this morning."

"I was looking for the red heart. And that pendant was slim enough to drop into a crack in the concrete. It's worth a look. Let's go back tonight. With a flashlight, we might see it shine."

Derek's been listening in from next door and invites himself along.

*  *  *

Derek can't believe the dilapidated building was the venue of a classy underground restaurant. "It looks haunted."

While I do my best to re-enact last night's drama by standing where I was mugged, Alister marks out a rough grid on the concrete apron with some chalk. Then he and Derek wield flashlights and we follow the beams obliquely, looking for anything that glints.

Plenty of bottle caps tucked into cracks, but otherwise the concrete is clean.

"Maybe they swept it this morning," Derek suggests.

"Why would they bother?" I ask.

But Alister is hitting his forehead. "A young guy started

sweeping right after I found the heart."

It's a blow and I feel the loss rise up again. But Alister and Derek have moved to a strip of sand at the end of the concrete where a vine is growing along a wire fence. I'm about to exclaim that you couldn't find an elephant amongst the sweepings when I see it. Coloured stones winking at me in the torchlight.

I shriek and drop to my knees. Now the dusty gold tube is sitting in my palm and something wells up in my chest—relief, pride and something else. Something ... hidden.

I stare at the pendant, trying to pick up more. What's hidden? Something that's been hidden for a long time. A murder. But why my sense of urgency after all these years? A crime that was never solved? A crime that concerned my great-granny. And now me.

Alister notices I'm shivering and puts his arms around me.

Derek begins a jig and a chant, mimicking a leprechaun. "Three things lost and three things found. The heart, the chain, the pendant on the ground. You're the one who lost them, Selkie Moon, so you're the one to find them, not late but soon." He adds with a final bow, "Our little psychic metal detector."

Alister laughs. "This calls for a celebration. Where would you like to go, Selkie?"

Derek turns to him. "Have you treated her to cocktails at La Mariana Sailing Club?"

Alister looks a tad insulted. "I don't take Selkie to waterfront venues, DD."

There's not a resident of Honolulu who doesn't know about my sea phobia. Not after it was splashed all over the tabloids when I went missing for two weeks and turned up on the beach with no memory of where I'd been, wearing a girdle of seaweed like a stranded mermaid. I finally discovered the secret of my disappearance, but it's too personal to share even with Alister or Derek. And Derek, despite his insatiable curiosity, has been careful not to ask.

"We'll get a table inside," he's saying. "You don't mind a view of bobbing masts, do you, Selkie? Come on. I'm buying." He's already striding to his car.

"You've got a lot on your mind," Alister says as we follow. "That pendant means something to you. And the chain."

"Family baggage," I say.

"Baggage can be a burden or a gift."

"Or both."

He waits but I don't know what else to say. My sense of what I'm dealing with is still so vague.

La Mariana is right on the waterfront; a bar that's stayed unchanged since the fifties. With decor that's heavy on polished wood and bamboo, it reminds me of the pendant. Why would an Irish pendant be fashioned in the shape of bamboo?

As Derek and Alister share insider gossip about the mugging spree, I reflect on my elation at getting Bridie's gift back. Losing the pendant and finding it has highlighted the deep connection I felt when I first put the necklace on. I'm hooked into something I don't understand, and the old combo of curiosity and fear seeps into the edges of my consciousness.

# Chapter 4

Derek can't resist a mystery. He's at the office early enough to come with me to the police to collect Bridie's chain. Then Alister meets us outside the jeweller's on Fort Street Mall. We're buzzed into a compact space with leather armchairs beside a long glass cabinet. The decor is understated, with not even a potted palm to suggest we're in Honolulu.

A woman in her late fifties emerges from a backroom and Alister introduces her as Erika. Something about her puts me at ease straight away. She's tamed her grey hair back into a sleek pony tail, but the inkling that she used to be a hippy remains, that under her stylish suit she hasn't lost her free spirit.

"OK," she says, getting down to business. "The glass heart." Alister dropped it in to her yesterday. "It's a nice piece of hand-blown glass and it broke cleanly right through the middle."

I swallow.

She flips open a small box and there's the heart nestling into a piece of velvet. "I could have glued it but I had a better idea." She slides the two pieces apart from the loop at the top. "A locket. I've added a tiny catch at the bottom to keep the pieces together."

Sudden warmth races through me. "It's amazing."

She beams. "I thought you'd like it. I'm kinda fond of lockets myself."

"But you'll see whatever's hidden inside," Derek says.

Hidden. The word's following me.

"Yeah," Erika says. "I like that too. Put something there you want to show. A photo, a pressed flower. This catch will hold it firm. Or keep it empty if you want. Waiting to be filled." She laughs. "And I can always glue it back together, if you prefer."

"No, no. I love what you've done. I'll find something to keep in there. Thank you."

Alister moves onto the chain. "Erika, we've got the antique chain I mentioned on the phone. A gold Albert, I think. Damaged at the same time as the heart, when Selkie was mugged."

Erika pulls a face. "I'm glad you're unharmed. A chain can be repaired. Unlucky that you were targeted."

Not unlucky. A magnet. I touch the bruises on my neck. They're more obvious today in shades of purple so I'm wearing a scarf.

"Let's take a look," Erika says, and I give her the chain. "Albert fob watch chain. Named after Albert, the prince consort and husband of Queen Victoria. Mid to late 1800s. Broken here when he pulled, but why? Some Albert links are hollow, but these twist-style links are strong. If it hadn't broken ... he might have garrotted you trying to get it off."

Alister stiffens beside me.

Erica is peering at the broken link. "Just as I thought. It's been broken before and repaired, creating a weak point where it pulled apart."

"You mean this repair probably saved Selkie's life?" Derek asks.

Erika looks up and nods. I feel sick. Alister puts his hand on my shoulder.

She shows us where gold solder has mended a break. She can mend it there again. "You'll never see it," she says, as if that's what the emotions in the room are all about.

I've put the pendant on the counter, even though it isn't damaged, and now Erika picks it up. "Wow. If this is what I think it is, I've never held one before. Not an antique one."

Derek can't contain himself. "What?"

She turns the bamboo tube around so the row of coloured stones is against her palm. At the top, a loop links the pendant to the catch on the chain. There's also a tiny hinge. She turns it over again and lifts the top to show it's a lid. "It's been a secret compartment. See?"

She holds it so each of us can look down the tube. It's empty, but the backs of the coloured buttons are visible inside. A secret compartment. What used to be inside? Something ... hidden.

"What kinds of things were kept in compartments like this?" I ask.

I'm feigning a casual interest but the secret is wrapping me in its spell. When I felt the necklace had a hold over me, I was afraid of getting caught up in a family mystery. Now I can't get enough of it.

"It might have been part of a chatelaine," Erika says. "In the 1800s women carried useful things on chains attached to their belts. Keys, matches, a button hook to do up your shoes, a perfume bottle, a thimble. These days you can buy smaller modern versions of long thin compartments like this online.

For a dagger. Hang it from your key ring."

The warmth I've been feeling turns cold. There's death here too. Murder.

"What about these buttons down the front?" Alister asks.

They're not evenly spaced, making the pendant look home-made.

"You've got me there," Erika says. "Decoration, I guess. Although some of the stones are precious. In fact ..." She picks up her eyeglass. "This white one looks like ivory. And this is a diamond. The green is an emerald, roughly cut. They're not high-quality stones and it looks like an amateur job with the different colours and sizes ... and the uneven spacing. That happened a lot in the nineteenth century. Jewellery was made by amateurs from found things."

"Is it gold?" Alister asks. "It's a different colour from the chain."

"Brass," Erika says. "But it's not a bad match for colour—the rose gold in the chain gets its pink tinge from a mix of gold, silver and copper."

"So none of it is worth much?" I ask. "Even the stones?"

"The mugger took a big risk for not much gold. But an Albert chain is worth something as an antique. Hundreds, though, not thousands. And it's been damaged. The pendant might appeal to a collector, and if you know where it came from, the provenance adds to the value. But if it's a family heirloom, it's priceless, isn't it?"

And I did my best to lose it.

* * *

I leave the chain with Erika, and when we're back in the mall it's almost lunchtime.

"We're not far from Merchant Street," Alister says. "Have you eaten at Murphy's lately?"

The Irish pub just down the road from my office.

Derek's been hovering but suddenly he's got a deadline. As he makes a discreet exit, he winks at me and I want to punch him. I know what he's thinking: it's Irish all the way from here.

"Never," I tell Alister. I always head for Chinatown.

He's doing a little mind-reading of his own. "Murphy does a good Asian salad."

The pub has a great buzz. I go for the shepherd's pie just to show I can consume other things besides dim sum. When we've ordered and are seated under the ceiling fans, I pull out my red heart and stare at it, imagining Fabienne's approval of what her work of art has become.

"Thanks again for finding this," I say. "And for introducing me to Erika."

"You're thanking me after my choice of dinner venue nearly got you killed?" His voice wavers so he rushes on. "I'm glad you like the locket. She's creative like that. What will you put inside?"

"I don't know."

"Something you love."

An emotion I'm afraid to talk about. I change the subject. "Did you see they've arrested a pawnbroker?" Derek was full of it this morning.

He nods. "Trying to buy stolen gold from an undercover cop."

"I hope my mugger wasn't a cop getting into character with too much gusto." It might explain the costume.

Alister pulls a face. "I shouldn't have left you vulnerable like that. It's my neighbourhood and I should have been more protective."

"It's not your fault. It could have happened anywhere to anyone." Except Erika's word returns: *targeted*. "And the last thing I want is for you to protect me."

He waits a beat. "What do you want from me, Selkie?"

Shit.

The food arrives and rescues me from answering straight away.

The mugging has distracted us from the bigger issue. And I can't blame Alister for wanting to know if he should hang around any longer waiting for me to declare how I feel—and show it. Or if he should let me go and set us both free. I'm desperate to tell him the truth—that he's the man I want to be with—but the words have turned to stones in my throat.

The waiter moves away and I stare at my plate wondering where my appetite has gone. "I ..."

Alister watches me. He doesn't touch his food.

Now the words come out in a rush. "I know how I feel. I just can't say it. Or show it. Not yet. I know it's pathetic and I don't want to be like this, but – "

He touches my hand. "It's OK. I just needed to know." Then he picks up his fork and gives me a half-smile "Eat. Before it gets cold."

I don't deserve his patience. Or his love. I reach for my fork and sink my teeth into a mouthful, bringing new meaning to the term 'comfort food'.

A noise at the bar gets our attention. Murphy himself is frogmarching a guy with a camera out the door and yelling after him.

Then he comes over to our table. "Sorry about that. I've given that eejit a warning."

Ever since a paparazzo snapped us together right after my disappearance, there've been rumours that the eligible tycoon Lester Sloane (known only to his friends as Alister) might be dating the Aussie nobody-turned-mermaid Selkie Moon. This one's probably stationed himself outside with a long lens, but Alister doesn't look concerned, and the guy missed the moment of tension between us, so I relax for the first time in quite a while.

On a whim I ask Murphy if he spent much time back home before he settled in Honolulu.

"All my formative years," he says in his unmistakable accent. "It's why I'm mad as a brush, then went troppo for good measure."

I laugh before pulling the pendant out of my pocket and flipping open the little lid. "Any idea what this is? It might be Irish. And over a hundred years old."

"A little before my time." He winks. "And I can tell you there's not much bamboo in Ireland."

"That's what I thought."

"I can't help you with what it's been turned into," he says, "but I do know what it used to be."

"Really?" I can hardly breathe.

"I know a knife handle when I see one. That's why it's hollow." He picks up the knife I've been using and points to the place where the blade meets the handle. "A rod that's joined to the blade goes inside the hollow handle, then held there by a tiny screw."

I wrap my fingers around the three bamboo segments and see what he means.

"Bamboo-style cutlery goes in and out of fashion," he continues. "If it's as old as you say, and Irish, they might have thought it was exotic. A taste of the Far East. Then some tinker found it broken in a rubbish heap and turned it into a piece of jewellery for his ladylove."

For the first time since its arrival the pendant makes me smile. "Thanks," I tell Murphy.

"The Irish love the East and the islands, they do. Even got some old songs about Hawaii." He grins and throws a napkin over his shoulder, then wanders back to the bar singing, "*Since our Finnoula learned to hula hula, Ireland has never been the same ...*"

# Chapter 5

The next two days disappear as I try to find seminar space. By Wednesday morning I've schmoozed every hotel events manager in the whole Hawaiian archipelago and got myself onto every cancellation list. They all tell me the same thing with varying degrees of drama: trying to book something six months out is '*so last minute*'.

After my success in France I'm fine for money for a while if I'm careful, but getting some seminars scheduled here is more about putting down roots in my new home. Without roots I'm … drifting. The sea analogy isn't lost on me.

By midday I'm ready for a change of scene. The Swap Meet is open till three and I'm desperate to catch up with Davina. It's been ages since we've seen each other—she lives on the other side of the island—but her fashion stall at the Aloha Stadium is only a bus ride away. When she hears about Bridie's gift and the psychic messages it's inspired, she'll have some wisdom to impart.

I could use some. My own intuition is screaming 'Ireland', but I suspect that's just an unacknowledged wanderlust. Since I ran away from Sydney I've been backwards and forwards and around the world all in less than a year. And what would be the point of going to Ireland? If there was a murder, it happened a long time ago. And I've got nothing to go on but a psychic message. If only Bridie had sent me a letter with a list of instructions attached. In her mind, the necklace and the newspaper article might have been tangible clues, but to me they're cryptic.

If I take the chain with me to show Davina she might be able to do a reading. I phone Erica and discover it's fixed, but I'll need to move fast if I'm to pick it up and get to the Swap Meet before Davina packs up for the day.

I send her a text to let her know I'm coming.

*That's grand. I'll wait. Bring POG*, she texts back. Pineapple, orange and guava juice.

Walking to Fort Street Mall, I pass the coffee cart. Curtis the barista gives me a wave and points to his neck.

"Wearing your *lei* too tight," he quips. "Loosen up already."

If I didn't like him and his coffee so much I'd wrap a *lei* around his cheeky neck.

Erika shows me the repair. Almost invisible.

I put the chain on and clip the pendant back in place, and suddenly the hands at my throat are back, along with abject terror as I fight for air. I clutch the glass display case so I don't swoon, and a name pops into my head. I catch it just before it disappears, a name I've never heard before: *Keira.*

Erika steadies me and leads me to a chair, where she frowns and suggests a doctor. The episode has passed as quickly as it came and I shake my head. Then, over glasses of iced water, I tell her the whole story.

"It's like getting a heart transplant," she says, her eyes dancing, "and inheriting some character traits from the previous owner."

The previous owner. Was it Keira?

"At least I can take a chain off," I say. "And put it in a box with a brick on the lid."

Or throw it in the ocean—somewhere I'll never find it—and get on with my life.

Erika laughs and it helps me see the funny side.

"Have you heard of psychic jewellery before?" I ask.

She thinks about it. "Not from a reliable source, but folklore attributes qualities to certain gems, and some fortune tellers ask for a ring or a necklace to read your future. If the chain was used to garrotte someone, at least it's already happened. That takes the pressure off, even if it does make you behave oddly in public." She pulls a face so I don't take offence. "But for psychics who predict something *before* it happens, that must be a terrifying responsibility."

She's right. At least this murder was in the past, but the vision is bringing some kind of responsibility. What am I being asked to do?

"If you want to sell the chain," Erika says, "I can find you a buyer. The provenance might double the price."

"No. Thanks for the get-out-of-jail card, but I'm committed now."

Whatever that means.

* * *

Even though I keep wearing the necklace the vision doesn't return, and soon the bus is dropping me at the Aloha Stadium, where Derek first introduced me to the Swap Meet and Davina. After several visits, the avenues of stalls are familiar to me.

As I stop to grab the POGs from a juice bar, I'm startled by a group of novice nuns gliding by in their white habits. Doing the rounds of the handicrafts I suppose and falling in love with Hawaii and its artefacts like anyone else.

It reminds me that Wanda's stall is around here somewhere. She fashions garish resin plaques from dead fish. There are dozens of them adorning the walls of our flat so I've never felt the urge to visit her stall, but almost every tourist who comes across it goes home with at least one decorative mullet. Wanda makes each fish unique, with character oozing from the colours and expressions. The nuns might find one with a beatific smile or a devilish grin, depending on their take on Christianity.  The thought of Wanda's fish as religious artefacts makes me chuckle.

When I get to Davina's stall, a young novice is lurking behind the racks of slinky handmade garments. She's very young so I guess she's taking a longing look at some of the things she's given up for God.

Davina hasn't noticed me; she's intent on a tall woman draped in gold chains who's clearly trying to bargain.  Her accent is upper-class English, her manner imperious. She's met her match with Davina who remains calm and unmoved. For her tribal-chic one-off originals Davina has one policy: the price is the price. I stand under a neighbouring awning and watch the show. The woman tries flouncing off, which might work in a Hong Kong market, but when Davina doesn't call after her with a lower price, she storms back, snatches the dress off the hanger and scowls into the mouth of her enormous purse.

"Another satisfied customer," I say as the woman stalks off.

Davina laughs. "The fabric's hand-woven in a fair-trade co-operative in Senegal." She usually screen-prints her own or uses local designers, so this is new. "Most of my customers like that they're giving something back, but this one wanted to know if my garments are available online, thinking she'd use my stall as a change room then get it cheaper somewhere else."

"Cheaper than the Swap Meet? In her dreams."

"I said it's on my website, same price, but she can add postage and packaging—and tax depending on where she lives."

We giggle. I love Davina's confidence. I should have taken a video for sales training.

She invites me behind the counter to two fold-up chairs and a tiny table. She takes the cup of POG gratefully, but before she sits down her face turns dead white and her jaw sags. She's staring at something over my shoulder.

"What?" I say, putting her cup on the table before she drops it.

Her eyes are wide, and I'm turning to see what's startled her when her legs give way and she falls against me. Just as I'm grabbing her and getting her into the chair—like Erika did for me not long ago—I catch a flash of white disappearing from behind the clothing rack. Thieves come in all costumes it seems. Not just waistcoats.

"That bloody nun," I cry. "Has she run off with a frock?"

Davina is ashen-faced. She's shaking so much that I push her head between her knees. That's when her whole body starts to shudder. She's sobbing in total silence. From the depths of her soul.

I lower the awning at the front of the stall so we're out of sight of gawkers. Then I sit down beside her again and rest my hand on her hunched back. It's a while before her body stills. When she sits up I'm shocked by the toll the tears have taken on her beautiful face. She's a different person. Something inside her has shrivelled and whatever is left is as wispy as smoke. And the same colour. Even her wild red curls have turned to string.

When I offer it, she takes a sip of the juice. I wait until a little colour returns to her cheeks. It's not much but it's better than the mortuary pallor of a few minutes ago.

"You're not dead," I say, the thought coming from somewhere.

"Not *yet*," she whispers.

As stalls around us begin to pack up, we finish our drinks in silence. The last time we saw each other, Davina confessed that she was sitting on a secret. Something life-threatening. But I was so distracted by my own secrets it wasn't the right time for her to tell me. She's going to tell me now. I won't leave until she does.

At last she speaks. The flatness of her voice is completely out of character. "I've dreaded this moment for twenty years, but I should have known it would track me down."

"What?"

"It won't make any sense unless you hear the whole story, Selkie." She looks around for eavesdroppers but the Swap Meet is almost deserted. "It started when I was studying in Paris. Twenty years ago. I've never told you, but I got into that fashion course under ... false pretences."

It's not at all what I was expecting. "You faked your credentials?"

"Worse than that. I said I was someone else. Dervla Kelly."

The same initials as her own, but I don't understand. "Why did you make up a false name?"

She shakes her head. "I didn't invent the name. I *stole* it.

From another girl. We looked alike, Dervla and me, so ... I borrowed her name and took it to France." She drops her voice. "I was desperate to study in Paris, and I wouldn't have got into that design school on my own. I was artistic but I hadn't finished school. Dervla had her Leaving Certificate."

"How did you get away with it?"

"It was easy back then—with some calligraphy skills, a glue stick and a photocopier you could fake just about anything."

"Identity theft and counterfeiting," I murmur. If it was anyone else I'd be judging her, but Davina's my friend and I trust her. "Go on."

"I've never told anyone the next part. And telling you may be my downfall, but ... I can't deal with this on my own. Not now."

She looks like she's going to cry again and I'm reminded how changed she is. Davina's always been the strong one while I've blubbered.

"I was doing so well in Paris," she says, "making a name for myself."

*A name for Dervla.* But I don't say it.

"I had a stall like this in a market, selling my frocks. My fashion label was Dee Kay, and I called myself Dee so I didn't have to answer to Dervla. It was grand."

"But you were someone else, Davina. You were living a lie."

She doesn't have to put a spin on it for my sake. I let Stella and Andrew rename me Elkie and then spent a lifetime calling myself that, until a green card gave me back my birth name and my identity.

"I was young and ambitious," she says. "I had something to prove, but I hadn't thought it through—that if I was successful, I wouldn't be me, I'd be *her*. And then I saw something in the market that scared me out of my wits. I ran away. I never finished the course."

"What did you see?"

"A fetch," she whispers. "There it was, just staring at me. It was twenty years ago but I'll never forget it. It was like looking in a mirror and seeing ... my own death."

She waits for my reaction, but I don't know what a fetch is.

"Do you mean Dervla came to fetch you? Is that who you saw just now? Dervla's come to seek her revenge?"

She shakes her head. "A fetch is a double. It looks exactly like you but has the qualities of a ghost. Not quite real. The thing I saw wasn't Dervla."

"The thing. It's ... supernatural?" I'm going pale myself.

Davina nods. "If you see your fetch it means ... you're going to die."

I try to sound wise. "We're all going to die."

"It means your death is *close*. When I saw it the first time, Selkie, I was barely twenty years old. I didn't want to die."

I'm still trying to get my head around it. "A double that's not real—isn't that a doppelganger?"

"It's the same. I saw a fetch who looked like me." She drops her voice. "Or ... Dervla."

"So it could have been Dervla's fetch," I cry. "And you've been hiding away for nothing."

"I've wondered about that for twenty years, Selkie. Because I'm still alive. Right up until a few minutes ago, I've wondered if the fetch was for her."

"What happened to Dervla after you saw the fetch? Is she dead?"

"I don't know. I've tried to find her online, but she's nowhere. No evidence of her death either. She's just ...

disappeared."

This explains why Davina grabbed back her own name and took off to a Pacific island, where she's been hiding out ever since. She could almost pretend the whole episode in Paris never happened. But what about the real Dervla?

"Why did you think you could outrun the fetch?" I ask. "If it's an omen, then hiding away in Kailua Bay wouldn't defy the prophecy, would it?"

"I had to take the chance that it might."

I recall the flash of white when Davina saw the fetch. "What did it look like just now?"

"She … *it* … was dressed all in white. Even its hair. Like something surreal."

"The novice." I thought that nun was up to no good. But I saw her too. "There were a lot of novices in the Swap Meet today. She was just like the others."

"They always stick together like a flock of geese. This one was *alone*."

"And she looked exactly like you?"

"I couldn't look at her face. Not again. As soon as I saw her halo of white, I knew who she was."

I didn't notice whether she was a dead ringer for Davina or not. Dead ringer … I'm glad I didn't say that out loud.

"You've been thinking that Dervla's dead and you caused it, haven't you?" I say. "By masquerading as her, you think you tricked the doppelganger and Dervla died."

She nods. "Or I … *inspired* it."

"What do you mean?"

"Stealing someone's identity is like stealing their soul. If your soul is compromised, you're vulnerable. You're more likely to attract the notice of a fetch. You're more likely … to die."

"That's pretty far-fetched," I say and we both laugh, breaking the tension for a moment.

The story makes me realise how strong Irish folklore is. Davina might have left her homeland more than twenty years ago, but the superstition is still flowing from her elfin slippers to her wild red curls.

"What if she was just a nun?" I ask. "I saw her too."

"Other people can see a fetch. Sometimes it's someone close who sees it first. They think they see you walking down the street then find out later it wasn't you. Then you know your number's up."

Nothing I say is going to shake her. She isn't in the right space to discuss this rationally. It reminds me of 'pointing the bone': a psychological death warrant meted out as punishment by some Australian Aborigines. If you believe that having a bone pointed at you can cause you to die, then it does.

"What will you do?" I ask. Not that she's had time to decide.

"Run. It worked before. It might work again."

She's probably had her escape plan ready for years. "Where will you go?"

"I can't tell you."

Bloody hell. She really believes she has to 'disappear', even from her friends. And whose name will she take this time? She's already worn out two.

My next words come out of the blue, but my voice is strong and clear. "You've got to go back to Ireland."

"Don't you know I've thought about doing that, Selkie. I've thought about it every day for the last twenty years. Instead I've waited for the fetch to show itself again so I'd know if it was for me or Dervla. I thought a little deception didn't matter, but I was wrong. Identity theft is powerful magic. I can't stay here and I can't go back to Ireland, not now. If I seek Dervla out, if I show myself back in Ireland ..." Her desperation is palpable.

"What if you could heal the past?" I say, surprising myself with my wisdom. Since I came to Hawaii it's what I've been doing, in my own chaotic way. "Heal the past and live to tell the tale? Then you could come back to Hawaii ... a free woman."

She starts to cry again. She's afraid, but the chance of freedom is like a lifeline.

It takes a while, but when the tears finally stop, her expression has changed and her old voice is back. "You're right. I can't live in hiding any longer. If I'm going to die, then it's my time. I have to know the truth. When I borrowed—*stole*—Dervla's identity did I help her die?"

"And if she is dead?"

"I can only take it one step at a time. Just going back is a bigger step than I ever thought I'd take. Thank you, Selkie."

As we sit in silence her decision feels like the right one, but my involvement frightens me. What have I done?

When Davina speaks again, it's a change of subject. "I had a strange dream about you last night. So I wasn't surprised when you turned up today. You were digging in a rubbish heap and you found a gold charm. It seemed to be hot because you dropped it, and then you couldn't find it again. You were digging in the rubbish, digging and digging, and all the time you were crying because you'd lost something precious."

I say nothing for several minutes, reminding myself it was Davina's dream, not mine. But it mirrors what happened with Bridie's pendant. Davina's up to her old psychic tricks and turning my fears into reality—that the necklace has a mission for me.

"Why have you gone pale?" she asks.

I sigh and tell her the story that brought me to the Swap Meet—Bridie's parcel and the 'chain of events' it's generated.

"You witnessed a murder," she says.

"I witnessed my own mugging." I pull back the scarf and show her the bruises.

"When he had his hands around your throat you got a telepathic message. He wasn't trying to kill you, Selkie, he was after your chain. But the chain is telling another story. It killed ... someone else."

Bridie lived till she was nearly a hundred, so it wasn't her.

"I haven't told you the end of my dream," Davina says.

Do I want to know the rest? "It wasn't my dream so it doesn't count."

"Don't be so sure about that. You know we have a psychic connection. In the dream, you were digging and digging for the lost charm. Then you started screaming. But you hadn't found the charm. You'd found ... a human finger."

That's when the name returns. Into my head and out of my mouth. "Keira."

It confounds me again. I'm still wearing the necklace. Does that mean it wasn't Bridie's, that it belonged to someone named Keira? Or maybe it's just my famous imagination 'carrying me away' to quote Stella.

I touch the chain as if it might speak to me. It doesn't.

Davina's watching me. I tell her that I first sensed Keira's name at the jeweller's. "But nothing else has popped." My word for a psychic seizure, if that's what it was.

I take off the necklace and hand it to her.

"What did the jeweller say about it?" she asks. "If we know

what the pendant was used for, you might see something."

"A secret compartment with a lid. Homemade out of an old knife handle, according to Murphy at the Irish pub. It might have hung on a chain from a woman's waist with something useful in it. They wore things called chatelaines in the 1800s when Bridie was a girl."

"And these buttons down the front?"

"Just for decoration, the jeweller thought."

Davina hands the necklace back and we sit in silence, feeling overwhelmed by everything that's happened over harmless cups of POG. Was it my presence in the Swap Meet this afternoon—what Davina calls our psychic connection—that aroused the fetch from its twenty-year slumber? A chilling thought to add to the knowledge that Davina is going back to Ireland because of me.

"Keira," she says. "It's an Irish name, you know."

"Is it?"

Does this mean I have to go to Ireland too? I don't want to follow a psychic hunch across the world, but cryptic clues have a way of leading me on.

Then my mind latches onto something and I laugh out loud with relief.

"My mind's just been playing with the letters. I sensed the name Keira when I was at the jeweller's. Her name is Erika, with a 'k'. I saw it on her business card."

"An old Norse name," Davina says. "I forget what it means."

"And an anagram of Keira."

* * *

As Davina drives me back to Waikiki we both stay off the Irish subject, but I sense she's sitting on something.

"Out with it," I say.

"Sorry, Selkie. It's just a mad idea. Selfish."

"What?"

"Come with me," she whispers. "I can't do this on my own, I just can't."

"But how could I help? I don't know anything about Ireland. My great-grandmother was born there, but that's where my Irish links end."

"I'm asking you as a friend ... a friend I trust."

Shit. At the mention of the word 'trust', I realise my problem. Davina's been an amazing friend to me, but after hearing what she did to Dervla, I'm questioning her integrity.

It's in the space between us so I have to say it. "And I've always trusted you, but ..."

She keeps her eyes on the road. "But now you know I compromised Dervla's soul?"

"Forget the fetch for a moment. You stole Dervla's identity for personal gain. I know you've paid the price with twenty years in hiding, but it doesn't change what you did. The person you were."

The silence is uncomfortable.

"Telling a painful truth to a friend is an act of trust," she says eventually. "I've exposed my shadow side to you and I'm not proud of it, but I won't ask you to trust me in return. That's for you to decide."

It's the right thing to say, and it helps me get things clear.

"My trust has been shaken, but you've been a friend when I needed one. I know that's who you are."

She exhales loudly and we laugh.

"But as much as I'm your friend," I go on, "your past isn't

mine to sort out. I've also got a business to run."

"Are you booked up with seminars here?" she asks, and I suspect she knows I'm not. "They'd adore Being Sleek in Dublin, you know—a little magic with their corporate training. And then there's your own unfinished business."

"Like what?"

"That murder was never solved, Selkie. Or it wouldn't be sending you messages."

After deciding that Keira is an anagram of Erika, I've pushed the murder from my mind. But Davina's held onto it for me.

"I didn't murder anyone," I say. "Unless mean thoughts about Stella count, like they do in the Bible. So it's not *my* unfinished business."

"You're not the murderer, you're the detective. Bridie sent you the first clue."

It's not the first time Davina's called me a detective—a spiritual detective, responsible for delving into the mysteries of the soul. It's a role that's clear to her and a total mystery to me, even after my other escapades and insights. It's as if each time something amazing happens, I gain a higher understanding, then in a flash I turn back into ordinary Selkie. I remember the insights but they haven't transformed me into a mystic.

"You're just saying that," I tell her, "because you want to drag me off to Ireland on another psychic goose chase."

"And the last journey was a goose chase, was it?"

She knows it wasn't. She pushed me to go in a certain direction and I resisted, then the universe intervened like her lap dog and suddenly I was fighting my way out of a pit full of cryptic clues.

"I did learn a thing or two," I concede. "About myself." And they opened me up to my feelings about Alister; feelings I still haven't consummated.

Davina nods at the road ahead. "Of course you can refuse to take up Bridie's challenge, but I don't think you will."

"I've got no idea what the challenge is. And the timing sucks. Sorry. I want to stay put." Book some seminars. Get up the courage to make love to Alister. Live a simple life revolving around money and sex.

"You're going to ignore the woman called Keira?"

"My mind reassembled the letters in Erika."

"Is that so? That's not the Irish spelling, you know." She spells it. "C I A R A."

"I didn't know that so it doesn't count."

"If you're so sure about that, test your hypothesis."

"How? And don't tell me to wait for one of my dreams to scare me half to death."

"Ring that lawyer and ask him if he's got anything else for you from Bridie."

"You don't think he sent me everything?" My mouth's gone dry.

"You're the great-granddaughter Bridie never knew. You might have turned out to be as capricious as your mother. She's testing you. From the grave. Sending you a teaser to see what you do with it."

I shiver. It's entirely possible there's more to come. Then there's the whole incident in the newspaper—Stella rescuing the little sister she hated.

I tell Davina about it.

She sniffs the air in that way I call her psychic olfactometry. "It's relevant but it's not the main story," she says. "Knowing what happened with Stella and your mam will help you solve the other mystery. The murder of Ciara."

Davina isn't infallible, but the statement has the awful ring of truth about it.

I look at my watch and see there's still time to phone the lawyer in Sydney.

"If you call him," she warns, "there'll be no turning back."

I dial anyway.

"I've got something to ask you," I say when I've introduced myself. To maintain some credibility, I decide not to mention psychic twinges.

"Anything," he says. He's got me on speakerphone and I can hear him rustling papers on the desk.

I take a breath and look across at Davina. "Who's … Ciara?"

"Shit." He's dropped something by the sound of it. "Sorry, sorry. Very unprofessional. I've knocked over my drink—hang on."

I hear more swearing and more rustling papers and mopping-up sounds. It's a while before he's back.

"I've made a hell of a mess. But I really wasn't expecting the question. How could you know?"

"There is a Ciara then?"

"Bridget Mary Ryan nee O'Connor instructed us to send the parcel to you, her great-granddaughter Selkie, on your eighteenth birthday.  Then it all got mislaid in the back of Dad's vault, which made it awkward to follow your great-grandmother's instructions to the letter, but I'm doing my best." He clears his throat. "After you received the parcel, her instructions were that if you called and asked about someone called Ciara, we were to ask you to spell it. Get that right and we send you something else."

Something else. I swallow and give him the Irish spelling.

"Same address as last time?" he asks.

"Is it another parcel?"

"An envelope."

"It's a photo isn't it?"

An image of a family portrait just popped into my head. An old image I've never seen before, everyone posed and stiff.

"I don't know," he says. "It's sealed. But ... you're the psychic."

# Chapter 6

While I wait for the next offering from Bridie, my mind keeps reliving the mugging. The visions take me beyond my own experience, my surprise and shock descending into panic—and terror. I've tried not wearing the necklace but I get the visions anyway. It's as if I've uncorked some kind of dark energy that's now flowing through me.

As I was going for a run this morning along the Ala Wai Canal, I stumbled and suddenly someone was on top of me. There was no-one there, but when another runner stopped to help me up, I thought he was murdering me and screamed my head off.

The bruises on my neck seem to trust what I'm sensing, taking an age to fade and making me self-conscious. Coral, the *kahuna* who lives in the bus shelter, has noticed them while I've been waiting for the bus and mimed a choking action with her hands.

When the package arrives there's no cataclysm. Just a large envelope with a stain on one corner, stiffened with cardboard to prevent bending. As soon as the courier's gone I take it straight down to Coral, so I've got a witness when I open it.

Coral grins her bare gums at me, then eyeballs the chain and the pendant for several meaningful seconds until I distract her by opening the envelope. The photo inside could be the one I saw in my vision, but these sepia family portraits are always similar: the men standing to attention in stiff collars, the women on chairs in their high-neck blouses and full skirts, their severe expressions making them look like they're perched on milk bottles. This one's a little different. Five people are posed around a piano. Two men, one older, one younger, stand behind an older woman, and there are two girls who look about sixteen, one sitting at the keyboard and looking over her shoulder at the camera, the other standing beside her.

Coral and I look at the young women.

"Shit," I cry.

They could be twins. They look exactly alike, right down to their high foreheads and rosy cheeks. But that's not why I swore. They also look like … me.

Coral looks at me and back at the photo, then she points to her feet. They're resting on her large check bag, ready to engage with her next client. Coral does her psychic readings using the soles of her feet—'sole to soul' as Wanda calls it. I've worn shorts in case this happened and she's soon pushing against my bare thighs. I wait while she closes her eyes and hums to herself.

Then she speaks. "*Hokio.*"

I'm getting used to these one-word pronouncements in a language I don't understand. I think I can actually spell this one so I text it to Wanda.

*Whistle*, she texts back. I can sense her laughing. *Not enough music in your life, honey? :-)*

If she knew the word was in response to Bridie's photo she

wouldn't be so flippant. Coral is always accurate even when she says something totally bizarre, so I won't ignore it.

I look at the image again. The reference to music resonates with the piano even though it's got nothing to do with whistling. When I show Coral the photo again, she points to the twin at the piano and repeats the word. "*Hokio.*"

Is one of the girls Bridie? I turn the photo over and find names written in faded copperplate behind each person. The older couple are Orla and Thomas, the young man is James, and the twins are Bridie and Ciara. Bridie is at the piano, the one Coral just pointed to. I peer at the bottom corner: *Tralee, Co Kerry, 1896.*

Bridie had a sister, Ciara. I didn't make her up. My great-great-aunt. A young woman who, if my visions are right, was strangled with the chain I'm wearing. It's shocking to look at her face—my face—knowing that I've witnessed the last moments of her life.

I stare at her, trying to learn more from this picture that gives very little away behind the schooled masks and rigid poses. But I sense a slight smile around Ciara's lips. A childlike joy about having her photo taken? Or just fanciful conjecture?

Bridie sent me the chain that killed her sister. Why?

There's nothing else in the envelope—no note—so even with this photo I've got no idea what's expected of me. Except Coral thinks all I have to do is whistle. Bloody hell. It's as clear as mud. And I've never been good at whistling.

I call for a pizza delivery to thank Coral for her wisdom.

Back in the flat, I prop the photo against my Shona sculpture, then pour a glass of wine and think about phoning Sydney. It's not too late to call the lawyer again to find out if there's anything else. Derek has taught me about the rule of three, which means there's one more parcel. Has to be.

There's someone else I could call in Sydney, my only living link to Bridie, but do I want to talk to her? Stella has to know more about the family history than she told me last time, even if it's just gossip. Gossip can be gold. And she's been leaving me messages and texts demanding to know what was in the parcel. That decides me. We can do a swap. I'll tell her what Bridie sent me, on the condition she spills everything she knows about her grandmother.

"I wondered when you'd call," she says. "I wasn't holding my breath."

"I need some family info, Stella. Everything you can tell me about Bridie. In exchange I'll tell you what was in the parcel."

The first parcel. She doesn't need to know there's more than one.

I hear her exhale the breath she hasn't been holding. "You go first."

That makes me laugh. I look over at my Shona sculpture and strengthen my resolve. "You can trust me, Stella."

But I can't trust her and she knows it.

She sighs. "You always were Little Miss Manipulative. What do you want to know?"

I haven't prepared any questions but one pops into my head. "Why did Bridie leave Ireland? And don't just say everyone did back then. She must have had a reason."

Because Ciara was murdered?

When Stella replies she sounds relieved, as if there's something she's been hoping I won't ask. About rescuing my mother from the drain?

"She ran away from the convent with Patrick Ryan, my grandfather."

I'm shocked. "Bridie was a nun?"

"I don't think she'd taken her final vows, but the story goes that she was cloistered away in Dublin, leading a chaste life as a bride of Christ."

Dublin must have been a world away from Tralee where the photo was taken. Why was she so far from home?

"The convent caught fire," Stella is saying. "It was one of those old buildings with several floors. A death trap. The nuns were asleep upstairs and they had to be rescued by ladder. Suddenly a fireman was wrapping Bridie in his arms and carrying her to safety. For a career virgin—she was over thirty—you couldn't get more intimate than that. It was love at first sight apparently."

In spite of Stella's harsh tone, the image moves me. The romance of a lightning bolt to the heart. Or was Patrick Ryan, my great-grandfather, just the first man who'd ever held Bridie in his arms?

"I gather the family wasn't too pleased that she was turning her back on the Church," Stella says.

I stare at the austere couple in the photo and sense the courage it must have taken to defy them. Even at thirty Bridie would have had zero power.

"Why weren't her parents happy?" I ask. "Didn't they want grandchildren?"

"I only ever heard about the romance. He swept her off her feet—and over his shoulder."

"Why did a healthy young woman like Bridie go into the convent? It's akin to prison."

"I'm the last person who'd know the answer to that, but I imagine sometimes they were 'called'. And sometimes they were ... sent."

Something about that word snags my attention, but I've got more questions before Stella clams up. "What else do you know about her? Or her sister?"

"What makes you think she had a sister? There was only Bridie."

So she doesn't know, and thankfully she's too distracted by finding out the contents of the parcel to quiz me.

"You told me she dabbled in spells," I say. "Did you ask Dad what she said over me in the hospital?"

"Nothing that made sense, he said. Just that she talked about spells. All the time when she was old. If I think of anything else," she adds, "I'll phone you." We both know she won't. "Your turn."

"OK. There were two things," I tell her. "A *Manly Daily* from the day I was born, and an old fob chain with a pendant on it."

"A newspaper. What was in it?"

"An article about my mother and baby Selkie, and a summary of an incident that happened when Prunella was a toddler. When she disappeared and her big brave sister found her in a drain."

Silence. Meaningful silence. I sense her relief. Why?

"A lot of fuss about nothing," she says.

"Being trapped in a drain for three days isn't nothing. If you hadn't found her, she could have starved to death, or drowned when it rained."

"It's a long time ago."

"Is that why Bridie sent it to me? So I'd know you were a hero?"

"Stop quizzing me. It's not part of the deal."

"I'm trying to understand Bridie, not you. She was your granny so she'd want to sing your praises."

"I doubt it."

"Why not?"

"I'll tell you," she snaps, "but this is the last conversation we have about this, understood? Bridie lived in Melbourne when I was growing up. I stayed with her sometimes but it wasn't a proper relationship. After Prunella was born, Bridie couldn't stay away. She moved to Sydney, but I was at boarding school by then."

"Boarding school? Why?"

She's trying to keep it matter-of-fact, but boarding school isn't all that different from the convent. There's a secret here, I can feel it.

"I wasn't happy ... at school. I needed a ... fresh start."

Was she bullied? It's hard to imagine. Expelled more likely. Or was she unhappy *at home*?

"Where was the school?" I ask. A picture of an austere institution in the Australian outback pops into my mind.

"None of your business. That's all I'm saying, so you understand why I can't tell you more about Bridie. We barely knew each other, OK?" Then she hangs up.

The conversation unnerves me. Not long after saving my mother's life, Stella was in some far-off dormitory while Bridie cooed over her other granddaughter. And Stella showed no interest in the necklace. So what's the link between the necklace and her rescue of my mother? There's got to be one.

I return to the photo and take another look at Bridie and Ciara. Something about sisters ...

My eyes wander over the picture and stop at the piano. It's a significant element in the photograph, and by their positions Bridie and Ciara appear to be not only twins but a duo. My knowledge about the late 1800s comes only from movies, but these teenage girls could have entertained the family with parlour music. It's what young women did, trussed up in their corsets and bored to death with needlework; music must have transported them beyond their narrow lives. While they waited to marry. Or to give themselves to God.

It's something I've never understood, young women choosing a saint's name and a convent over a life. But then it's not that different from me being renamed Elkie and imprisoned in a marriage with Andrew.

Stella's comment comes back: 'Sometimes they were 'called'. And sometimes they were ... *sent.*' Bridie was being punished, I'm sure of it. Then a candle ignited a curtain and she got her chance to escape. No wonder she ran all the way to the other side of the world. Just like I did when I won a green card—I ran as far as I could from Andrew Tabrett.

I pick up the phone again. The lawyer is on his way out but he confirms that there's one more parcel.

"What's the password?" I ask. "Last time I had to spell Ciara."

He laughs. "You just ask for the final package and it's yours."

Because that means I'm hooked? Is that what I want?

While I'm hesitating he's got something to tell me. "This is highly embarrassing after our firm mislaid your great-grandmother's instructions for so long. But there's been another ... mishap."

Bloody hell. I'm glad this guy isn't handling my other legal matters. "What?"

"When you called the other day and asked about Ciara, I knocked over my drink. Your parcels were on my desk, and the third one—another envelope—scored most of the spill."

"Is it ruined?"

"I haven't opened it of course. But it's … heavily stained. The contents may be too."

"Send it anyway," I say, and give him the address of my office so I don't have to wait at the flat.

* * *

Wanda makes one of her flying visits to stoke herself up with a smoothie. She's larger than life in her cut-offs and headband as she sweeps into the tiny space we share and catches me with the photo in my hands.

"Taken up whistling yet?" she asks, remembering Coral's advice.

"Are you sure *hokio* doesn't mean anything else?"

She throws fruit into the blender and talks over the noise. "It can be a noun or a verb, but whichever way you spin it, *hokio* still means whistle."

She's in a hurry but on her way out she takes a peek at the photo. She whistles and we both laugh.

"Will the real Bridie please stand up? Tell me all tomorrow night." But it's her departing comment that floors me. "The old dame looks like a jailer with all those keys at her waist."

I take a closer look at the woman who must be Bridie's mother. Orla is standing at the side of the girls in all her finery, including several chains hanging from her waist. What did Erika call them? A chatelaine. She thought the pendant might have been part of a chatelaine. Did Bridie inherit the pendant from her mother? I inspect the tiny silver objects hanging from each chain. There's a hook of some kind, several keys of different sizes, and some mysterious cylinders. Each item is decorated with fine etched patterns, making a matching set. Nothing like the brass pendant with its bamboo segments and coloured buttons.

As I polish off another glass of wine I gaze at the photo until my vision blurs. When I tumble into bed, my dreams keep looking into empty tubes that turn into dark tunnels. At each fork I have to choose which way to go, but the tunnels become a labyrinth that never ends.

# Chapter 7

On his way to the airport, Alister meets me for lunch at Murphy's pub. It's got the potential to become our special place since neither of us has frequented it with past lovers. These things are important when you've been around the block a few times—creating a shared history to build on.

This time I indulge in the Asian salad and Alister has the Irish stew.

He's got some news about Deshi's cousin.

"She's agreed to meet me." His eyes well up. "When I arrive in San Francisco she'll tell me where. Somewhere neutral. Not Chinatown."

"So her family doesn't know she's contacted you?"

"They've spent thirty years making sure Deshi doesn't even know he's got a father. They don't want me to find him."

"Brave of her to defy them."

He nods and says he'll let me know how it goes.

I tell him about Bridie's photo and my call to the lawyer for the last parcel.

"Will you go to Ireland?" he asks.

"I feel like I'm being dragged there by wild horses."

He chuckles. "If Bridie was still around I'd put her in charge of my advertising. Send out the right emotional teasers, then watch as you reel yourself in."

I think of Stella's name for me—Little Miss Manipulative. Just like her grandmother? Is that why I look like Bridie? Like her and her murdered sister? The thought makes me shiver as if someone just stomped over my grave.

"Davina's going back to Dublin to catch up with her past," I say. "And she's putting out her own emotional teasers for me to go with her."

"Why not? You'll get plenty of takers over there for Being Sleek. After the financial crisis they're pretty much back on their feet and every big company on the planet is using the place as a tax haven. What a hub for corporate training Dublin must be. But if you go … just remember where your heart is."

We both look at Fabienne's heart nestling beside Bridie's pendant, but there's a deeper meaning to his comment.

I open the heart and ask him to press his finger to the inside.

"A fingerprint," he says. He presses his lips to the tip of his little finger and makes his print on the inside of the heart.

On the opposite side I do the same.

"I might be mixing my Chinese and Japanese folklore," he says, "but there's a legend in the East that the lunar matchmaker ties an invisible red cord to the little fingers of two people who are destined to be lovers. They're joined no matter where they are in time and space. The cord will stretch, even get tangled," he laughs, "but never break."

While the magic of the story stuns me, Alister leans across the table. Without thought to lurking paparazzi he kisses me deeply on the lips. I've never been pashed in a restaurant before and I give myself up to it, thrilled and embarrassed all at the same time.

Then he's gone, out of the pub and into a taxi, leaving me gasping.

As I watch him drive away, I can feel the invisible thread connecting us. Its ability to stretch and never break is a comforting image, but I wonder if it's my tentativeness that's stopped him from inviting me to share this journey with him.

Then I remember that his search for Deshi is so personal and so linked to his private tragedy that he needs to do it alone.

My phone chirps.

*Touching your heart*, he writes.

*I know*, I write back. *I can feel it.*

*And getting tangled in that bloody cord :-)*

* * *

When I ring Davina to fill her in on Bridie's photo, she invites me over. I don't mention that we're both dealing with look-alikes because I want to surprise her. Davina and Dervla; Bridie and Ciara—and me. The fact that I'm a 'dead ringer' for my ancestors is an unexpected—and creepy—twist. It's as if when Bridie gazed at my crinkled newborn face, she knew.

It's always juice for the soul to walk through Davina's vibrant living room, filled with art and ethnic fabrics, to her private *lanai* beyond. She pours glasses of chilled white wine, then looks at the photo. I had copies made today, and the original is in my filing cabinet—where nothing can be spilled on it. I dread to think what the lawyer's little accident has done to the third clue.

As Davina looks at each face in turn, I say nothing and wait.

"I'd like to see the original," she says. "But it could be carrying too much emotional memory of the photographer.

Creative individuals can interfere with the message."

"They look like there's not an emotion between them," I say.

"Don't be so sure about that. They might have had a fight about who was going to stand where, then pasted on those stern expressions."

"Their faces clash with the setting around the piano. Surely parlour music was joyful?"

Davina is pressing her nose to the photo. "These girls are sure to be more than just sisters—twins. And of course they look like you. But reading their faces, Bridie's the sharp one. Ciara's just as pretty but not as clever. Look at their eyes."

"Bridie was the pianist," I say.

"And if Ciara could sing by ear, she didn't need to be quite as clever. The parents aren't used to having money, I'd say. They're still very conscious of their social status. He probably made his money in some kind of commerce. Middle class and climbing. She's wearing that apron of tools like a badge of honour, and he's been practising his expression in the mirror."

Davina might be all bullshit, but I love this stuff.

"And who's this red herring in the hand-me-down jacket?" she asks.

She means the young man. "James, it says on the back." I've forgotten to write the names on the back of this copy so Davina's been working from intuition. "Why is he a red herring?"

"He's not part of the family. Different colouring. They're all dark and he's fair. He's tried to copy the old man's moustache, but he's a redhead by the looks of those freckles. The old man's lent him a waistcoat and a jacket, probably just for the photo.

They've seen better days and they don't quite fit."

"So why is James in the family portrait?"

"Adopted? That was always going on. Some third cousin twice removed made an orphan when his parents were killed by a runaway horse and cart."

I tell her the date of the photo: 1896.

"Too late for the potato famine," she says. "He looks about twenty, but I can't tell where he blew in from just by looking at a photo—a *copy* of a photo. I don't like the look of him though. Dodgy. And he can't take his eyes off those girls."

I stare at the image and notice the slight inclination of his head in the twins' direction. "Maybe the jacket's giving him a kink in his neck."

"And maybe the wind changed while he was peeping around corners to spy on them when he was supposed to be doing his chores. They're good-looking girls, and if I'm not mistaken that's a bulge in his pants."

We both look at what we can see of his crotch and burst out laughing.

"He probably borrowed the pants too," she says, "and they're too tight to contain his manhood. He needs a tailor to ask him discreetly whether he keeps his crown jewels on the right or the left."

We're both crying now, rocking back on our floor cushions and spilling our wine.

Davina composes herself and says, "I shouldn't be drinking and intuiting. I've broken my own rule. It makes me talk nothing but gibberish."

"Some of it sounded spot-on to me."

"A load of rubbish. Show me the real thing when I'm sober."

I let it go and she asks me for any updates on the necklace.

"Whether I'm wearing it or not," I tell her, "I keep thinking of Ciara. And reliving her murder."

Every time I get the vision, I sense a little more. I'm sure she didn't scream. When I was being mugged, the screaming was mine. Ciara died in silence. Was that because she knew her murderer and couldn't believe he was killing her?

"It's strong then, the memory," Davina says. "A murder would do that. And if the emotions embedded in an object are strong enough, you don't even have to be psychic to feel them. Just ... sensitive."

No-one's ever accused me of being sensitive so I'll have to settle for psychic. I pick up the photo again and the men's waistcoats suddenly make sense. I tell Davina about the guy I thought was mugging me.

"No-one around Honolulu dresses like that," she says. "You saw Ciara's murderer, Selkie. It fits with the power of the vision."

But the memory of real hands on my throat hasn't faded.

"I think she knew her murderer," I say, and tell her about Ciara's silence. "So it could be one of these two—Thomas or James."

"Or a boyfriend. These girls would have had lots of suitors, I'd say. Pretty and charming, a father with money. Don't rush to conclusions because of a waistcoat. Do you recognise his face from your vision?"

"Only the moustache."

"They all wore facial hair and waistcoats back then. Even labourers. It could be anyone. And if she was a well-brought-up young thing—which it looks like from this photo—that mother of hers –"

"Orla."

"Orla, she would have put the fear of God into her daughters that a young lady *never* screams."

It's becoming almost certain that I actually *saw* Ciara's murderer. Saw him at the exact same moment that the mugger was choking me. In the face of these shocking revelations the wine is keeping me calm.

A new question pops into my head. "Why was a well-brought-up young thing like Ciara murdered?"

"If it wasn't theft," Davina says, "then the next most likely reason is –"

"Rape." I spill my drink. "What other reason could there be?"

And what the hell will the visions show me next?

The possibility it was a sex crime quietens us for a while, then I tell her about the third parcel.

"The stains from the lawyer's coffee aren't a coincidence," she says. "If the contents are smudged and obscured in some way they're adding another layer to the mystery."

Just what I need, another layer. She hasn't mentioned her Irish trip yet, but she's already posted on Facebook that she's taking a break for a month, closing her shop and her market stall.

"Where will you start looking for Dervla," I ask, "if you haven't found a trace of her online? It's easy to find both the living and the dead these days, so why has she vanished?"

Davina shrugs. "I can only think she's changed her name."

"Then there'd be a record of her wedding. Or her deed poll."

But Davina has something else on her mind. "I've had another dream," she whispers, as the pink drains from her cheeks.

"Not the bloody fetch?"

"They don't do dreams. No, ironic as it is, you only see a fetch in the land of the living. But if I was thinking of backing out of the trip, I can't now. I think your lawyer spilled his drink on my dream."

She takes a sip of wine and I wait, sensing that she's tangled in a web she can't see her way out of.

"I saw a name in big letters ... it might have been carved on a gravestone, or printed on paper, I'm not sure. I could only see the initials 'D' and 'K'."

"Davina Kennedy, or Dervla Kelly?" I ask.

"In the dream I was confused about that because the other letters were smudged. And whatever was smudging them was red. Like ... blood."

"Not coffee then."

"Did he say it was coffee he knocked over?"

I try to remember. "Is it important?"

"I don't know. In my dream it looked like a stain blurring the letters, and then you turn up with a story about a stain."

"What do you think it means?"

"What does it mean when someone's name is smudged out?"

"Shit." Again I wonder: Davina or Dervla?

"And there was something else that wasn't smudged," she says. "It looked like the number eight."

I'm remembering what Wanda said: everything adds up to eight. "Does eight mean anything to you?"

"I don't know," she says, "but I've got to go to Dublin. I can't live like this, Selkie. Not a minute longer."

That's when she refills our glasses and tells me the rest. The story of how she met Dervla.

* * *

"I grew up outside Cork," she begins. "They told me I was adopted as soon as I could understand what that meant. My birth mother wasn't married—a mortal sin—and I was supposed to be grateful to have a roof over my head. My stepdad used to come into my room most nights so I could show my gratitude. My stepmam never lifted a finger to stop him. She must have heard me. He put his hand over my mouth while he was doing it—but afterwards I couldn't help crying."

She's never told me this shocking story.

"Why adopt a precious baby," I ask, "if she was going to stand by and let you be abused?"

"I've wondered that for a lifetime, Selkie. I was an innocent child. It was a criminal offence she was party to. But she couldn't have kids herself, and now I think she resented me for being someone else's daughter, someone who could get pregnant by accident and then give me up like I was nothing special. She wanted me to carry the shame for my unmarried mother."

The inverted logic resonates with Stella's attitude to me—her sister's wayward offspring.

"You told me once that your mother was a witch," I say.

"My stepmother. That's how I thought of her."

"Did you ever look for your real mother?"

She shakes her head. "My stepmam convinced me she was worthless, that she tossed me away because she didn't care about me. Then later when I thought about finding her, my heart wasn't in it. What if my stepmam was right?"

It feels like unfinished business. And if her mother had her as a teenager, she could very well still be alive.

Davina continues with her story. "As soon as I looked old enough, I ran away from that house of horrors. I was lucky—it was an old truck driver who picked me up. If he'd been young it might have been out of the frying pan into the fire for me, but he was old enough to be my grandfather and he could see what was going on without asking. He gave me some money and told me where I could get a bed and a job in Dublin. It gave me a start and I got by, working at McDonald's of all places. I'll bet those golden arches are still there on Grafton Street.

"Dervla Kelly had the opposite life to me. Her parents had loads of money and they spent it all on her, their only child. She went to a fancy private school. I went to look at it once—a big house on the south side: Ashford College. Her friends used to come into McDonald's after school and hang around. It was cool in those days."

We laugh.

"I told you I looked like her," she says. "Like her twin, it was that uncanny. Well, her friends saw me serving behind the counter and they thought it was a grand joke—a scruffy runaway the spitting image of the princess of Ashford College. One day they dragged her in to meet me. She wasn't the type to be caught dead or alive in McDonald's so they must have told her a good story, but there she was standing in the queue, waiting for the surprise they'd told her about. I didn't notice her until we were face to face. We couldn't believe it. It was like we connected instantly: two girls with nothing in common but our faces. Our hair was different, but I found out later she'd coloured and straightened hers and underneath we were the same. I stood there gaping like a goldfish, but she was as cool as you like, pretending it was nothing, while her friends taunted her about being separated at birth from an urchin."

"But you got to know her."

"A few days later she came back. Without her friends this time. She was waiting for me when I finished work. That was a shock, and you couldn't imagine how mesmerising she was."

"Because she looked like you?"

"She looked like me, but she had something I didn't have … magnetism, charisma. Except I didn't know what that was then. I let her take me to a little pub where they didn't ask your age. She bought me drinks and asked me questions. She wanted to be sure I was … suitable."

"Suitable?" My skin starts to prickle.

Davina laughs. "She was always after the main chance was Dervla. After she'd quizzed me and found out I was all alone in the world—no complications—she made me an offer on the spot. Her parents were really strict, she said, never letting her out of their sight. She'd been caught in bed with the boy next door when she was fourteen, so they had a meltdown, moved house, put her into Ashford College and watched her day and night. Just to meet me, she'd had to lay a false trail and bribe a friend to cover for her. She couldn't do that more than a few times. Too risky. They'd threatened her with the convent if she ever stepped out of line again."

The convent, just like Bridie.

"She needed a decoy," Davina says. "Someone to sleep in her bed in case her mam came in to check on her."

"Bloody hell. How could you get away with that?"

"Dervla had it all worked out. We met again so she could give me a couple of her nightdresses—I was to wear them under my own scruffy clothes on the bus. The first time we did it, I was scared out of my wits, but excited. And after what had already been done to me, what was the worst that could happen? Dervla had lots of money so she was paying me well, I made sure of that.

"They had an outside loo for their garden staff, so I waited in there, freezing half to death, until she came and got me. Her parents were in bed or watching TV, and she let me in after I'd stripped down to the nightie and she'd changed into my clothes. Then I crept up the back stairs to her bedroom and slept, while she went out the way I'd come in through the garden."

"But her mother would know her own daughter," I say. "What about your hair?"

"Dervla paid for me to get mine done like her. And each time I went straight to her bed and slept until she came home at about five, before anyone else was up."

"My god, you were audacious, both of you. I could never have got away with something like this with Stella." And I wouldn't have had the nerve.

"We were young," Davina says. "Invincible."

"What if her mother had caught you together?"

"After that first time, we made sure we were never in the house at the same time. She'd knock on the toilet door and I'd be waiting. I'd slip out of my clothes and go up the back stairs. Her mam did see me once, in the upstairs hall, and I froze. Dervla had warned me never to speak if this happened, just to act sullen. My accent was different, not posh like hers. I stood there trying not to panic, then had the presence of mind to yawn and go back to Dervla's room. Why would she think I was anyone but her daughter?"

"What was Dervla up to while you were sleeping in her bed?" I ask.

"Meeting the boy next door from her old house? Shagging

married men? She was almost seventeen by then so she could have been up to all sorts. Sex. Drugs. She was fearless. She never said where she went because it was none of my business. And I couldn't tell if I didn't know."

"When did she sleep? Didn't anyone notice she was tired?"

"We only did it twice a week. Weeknights, when her mam wouldn't be so suspicious. At the weekend she studied like an angel. She was clever at school so she got away with it."

"And when she got her certificates?"

Davina takes a breath. "I borrowed them and copied them. I was in her room for hours at a time so it was easy. I took my photo in a booth and sent my application off to Paris."

"I know you wanted to study design and this was your big chance. But why do that to Dervla? She was like your sister."

"Was she? Everything was always about her, you know. I was nothing but her decoy. And when she was off to her Swiss finishing school, she tossed me aside like a blow-up doll with a puncture."

A thought pops into my head. "That's why you saw the fetch."

"What do you mean?"

"You conjured it up. When you were in Paris, you wished in your heart you were Dervla because she had everything you didn't have. And for you to be her, she had to be dead. But you were masquerading as her already, so that's why you're not sure who the fetch came for. You or her?"

She frowns and tilts her head, considering what I've just said. "I've never thought of it that way. I just thought the fetch was doing its own business, heralding a death. It's not a vendetta they're on, you know—the fetch is just the messenger of what's foretold. But if my craving to be Dervla put a hex on her, or on me pretending to be her, then why did I see the fetch at the Swap Meet? I haven't been Dervla Kelly for twenty years."

"I'm still not convinced that wasn't just a harmless nun who reminded you of the fetch. But it was almost a repeat of last time—in a market again where you're selling your frocks—so that suggests it's about you, not Dervla. But if it was the fetch this time, turning up again after twenty years, it could only mean one thing."

"Something's changed."

I nod. "You've just travelled for the first time, thrown off your 'cloak of invisibility', and you went back to France. That's a big change."

"I knew that trip was a mistake. I've stirred something up."

Our dispassionate talk has been treating this like another psychic puzzle, but now we're staring down the barrel of the truth. Is Davina about to die?

As tears prickle the backs of my eyes, another thought pops. "This is about twins, Davina—two women who look alike. Bridie's parcel with its messages about Ciara have collided with the sudden reappearance of the fetch. I was there when you saw it. So this isn't just about you, it's got to be about your 'twin' too. You've done something big—you've come out into the open after years of hiding—so something equally big must be happening to Dervla."

"Something big like ... death?"

"Maybe, but it doesn't feel like that to me. Death would feel like an end, and this feels like a beginning, something else that's momentous. Yours was winning the design award that took you out of hiding to New York. Dervla might be having success or notoriety in some way too. And I think when the fetch appeared to you the first time, it must have overlapped with something big happening to Dervla. It makes sense. The two of you are linked by your faces, and then by your identities when you became her."

Davina is crying, but she's smiling through the tears. "I've never shared any of this with anyone and look what's happened, Selkie, you've cracked it open. I was totally stuck in fear and I'm ashamed that all I could do was hide. You've reminded me how much I want to ... live." She throws her arms around me.

It's the first time I've been a model on how to live, but I accept her thanks and hug her back. *Just don't go dying on me, OK?* I say to myself, hoping she's too distracted by the light shining on her problem to read my thoughts.

* * *

The state of the envelope makes my heart sink. The stain is red. Just like Davina's dream. That day I called him, that bloody lawyer was balancing a glass of wine on his desk surrounded by his clients' files. No wonder his company archives were in disarray and Bridie's instructions were mislaid for seventeen years.

Derek is just next door and hears the courier. He hovers as I open the envelope.

"This should be the clincher," he says.

"If we can read it." I explain about the stain.

There are two sheets of paper, both heavily affected by the wine. A piece of music. And a folded newspaper article. The lawyer was 'too professional' to open the envelope and try to minimise the damage, so the wine soaked through every layer then stuck them together as it dried.

I hold the music up to the light. It's a song but the words are almost unreadable. Is this what Coral meant by *hokio*—a tune for me to whistle? I was hoping for a letter explaining the whole mysterious business. Instead I get a song that I can't read, and I'm furious.

"It's another piece of the puzzle," Derek says. "And you haven't looked at the newspaper yet."

I'm trying to unfold it but the layers are stuck. "I'll have to steam it open with the kettle."

"What was in the second parcel?"

Derek hasn't seen the family photo yet. I point to the copy on my desk.

His assessment is similar to Davina's. "The girls must be twins, and they look like you. It might be a celebration—they're all dressed up. A portrait to mark the occasion."

"What do you think of James?" I ask, indicating the younger man.

"Uncomfortable. He's trying to model himself on the old guy. I don't think he's their brother, but he's not much older. Who is he?"

"I don't know, and this bloody sheet of music isn't going to tell me."

"There's a book of songs on the music stand," he says.

Sure enough, perched above the keyboard behind Bridie is a leather-bound book. Derek ducks next door and comes back with a magnifying glass and I peer at the title: *Irish Melodies* by Thomas Moore. It gives me a sense of Bridie's joy in music. Maybe Ciara's too. Before the tragedy that surely followed.

I sigh. "All the clues are linked."

"But neither of the girls is wearing the chain. Their necks

are bare."

"It's a fob chain," I say. "For a watch. Weren't they worn by men?"

The same man who killed Ciara with it? I touch the place on my neck where the bruises have finally faded.

"We can't see if Thomas is wearing one," Derek says. "And James isn't. But wait a minute." He grabs the magnifying glass, then points to something peeping out from the side of Bridie's bodice, almost covered by the arm that's resting on the keyboard. "She's wearing it like a watch chain."

I peer closer too. The links are the same as my chain. Is the pendant on the end, hidden in her pocket? But why hidden? It's the word that's popped up before. The chain killed Ciara, but the pendant hides a secret.

"Ciara's not wearing a fob chain," I say.

It's another clue: she wasn't killed with her own chain, but with Bridie's. And now it's mine.

Derek is still using the magnifying glass. "Ciara's wearing a sweet little bird brooch on her collar."

He turns his attention back to the song sheet. "There are marks in pencil making changes to the words. Is it torn from the book?"

The edges of the sheet aren't jagged from tearing, and the paper and print seem too modern for 1896. I turn it over and see that it's printed on both sides. At the top, the title is visible and my energy comes back in a rush. 'Two Sisters'.

"We have to decipher the words, DD."

Using the magnifying glass, I dictate the song while Derek types them onto my laptop. Here and there he helps me figure out a word. A few stanzas in, we know what we're dealing with.

"It's a murder ballad," he says. "They're like fairy tales,

they go back so far they're in the folklore. And sometimes they were inspired by real murders."

He gets onto Google. 'Two Sisters' first appeared in the 1600s, and other versions have been found all over Europe, even played by folk bands right up to the present day.

We finish transcribing, and Derek reads it aloud as waves of emotion wash over me.

*There were two sisters who played in the sun*
  *When a miller came vowing to marry one.*

*He gave her attention, the love of his life,*
  *Before he asked her to be his wife.*

*But the other was angry, bitter and vexed.*
  *How could he love her sister the best?*

*Envy and hate in her breast they did dwell*
  *Till her sister's joy was her living hell.*

*The jealous one to her sister did say,*
  *'Come take a walk with me today.'*

*Then down to the riverbank they did go*
  *Where the water flowed by, deep and slow.*

*The jealous one said, 'Lean your foot on that stone*
  *And wash your hands in the river foam.'*

*As the sister leaned over the river rim*
  *The envious one pushed her in.*

*'O sis,' cried the drowning one, 'lend me your hand*
*And I'll make you the heir of my house and land.'*

*'Pulling you out again wasn't my plan.*
*I'm after your miller to be my man.'*

*'O sis,' cried the drowning one, 'lend me your glove*
*And I'll make you the lady of my true love.'*

*'Sink on without hope for my hand or my glove.*
*Without you he'll better become my love.'*

*Sometimes she sank, sometimes she swam,*
*Until she arrived in the miller's dam.*

*The miller was standing there at his door*
*And watched as she floated down the shore.*

*'O no,' he thought, 'I see a white swan*
*Or else it must be a drowned woman.'*

*He caught up her petticoats in his long crook*
*And hooked the fair maid out of the brook.*

*He wept for his lady love, laid her to dry.*
*Then a famous fiddler came riding by.*

*When he the drowned maiden did come near*
*Her ghostly spectre did appear.*

*'Take you my fingers and locks of my hair*

*To make pegs and strings for your fiddle there.'*

*He did as she asked, removing her rings.*
    *Then left the miller to keep her fine things.*

*The very first time that the fiddle did play*
    *It sang of the murder that happened that day.*

*'My sister killed me,' is the song that it sang.*
    *'She is the one who surely should hang.'*

*But the song came too late, the miller was dead.*
    *The sister never lay in his wedding bed.*

*The rings in his pocket pointed the blame*
    *And the murderous sister lived with the shame.*

"These ballads often include a musical instrument," Derek says. "A harp or a fiddle fashioned from the dead person's ribs or hair and pointing the finger at the murderer when it's played."

He's talking as if this is a fascinating exercise in musical folklore and not the story about a murder—two murders. This version of 'Two Sisters'—some of the words are rewritten in the margin in a shaky hand—tells a particular story: of one sister killing the other to claim her sister's lover for herself, then the lover taking the blame. I'm telling myself it's not literal. That a dead girl's fingers and hair can't become part of a fiddle. It's folklore, springing from emotions, not facts. So why did Bridie send the song to me? There can only be one reason.

"It's a form of haunting," Derek goes on. "The soul of the dead sister is embodied in the musical instrument, unable to rest until it sings the truth."

Until it sings the truth. What is the truth here? When I first sensed that Ciara had been murdered with the chain, I thought Bridie must want me to find out what happened. That the truth of who killed Ciara was what was 'hidden'. If I could find out the truth, it would be too late for Bridie but at least it would lay the past to rest. I had no idea how I might do that over a century later, with only a chain and a photo as clues, but now the song suggests that Bridie knew what happened to Ciara.

Davina said such good-looking girls would have had lots of suitors. The song says they both wanted the same man, but he only wanted one of them. And the other one was jealous enough to kill. My head is spinning. If the song mirrors the real-life murder, then it was Bridie herself who killed Ciara. It explains why she kept it all hidden, and why I had to be an adult before I could hear it. It also explains why Bridie was sent to the convent. If Ciara's lover had already been executed for the crime he didn't commit, the family might have meted out their own punishment to Bridie.

*The murderous sister lived with the shame.* Not only the shame of killing her sister, but allowing the man she wanted to marry to be killed in her place. What if I'm descended from a murderer?

Derek has put the kettle on.

"Thanks," I say. "I could use a cup of tea." Or a stiff drink.

"I'm not making tea. Aren't you going to steam open this newspaper article?"

I've forgotten about the newspaper, all stuck together and unreadable. It must hold the final piece of the puzzle.

Although the article from *The Manly Daily*—unstained and legible—hasn't enlightened me.

Or has it? Shit. Two sisters. I remember the frown on Stella's face after she found my mother in the drain. It happened again. And afterwards, just like Bridie and the convent, Stella was sent away to boarding school—to keep her away from the sister she hated, the sister she'd tried to hurt, if not kill. No wonder she was relieved that article had called her a hero.

The kettle's produced lots of steam, and Derek returns from his office with a ruler. He slips it into an opening in the matted mess of paper and we take turns holding it over the steam. Slowly the layers of newspaper peel apart until we can open the final fold.

It's a single page of newsprint, but another sheet is folded inside. It looks like notepaper; once a cream colour, now stained in shades of red to brown. We have to hold it over the steam again to separate the two folded halves. But as it opens up, I can see that the ink has run.

I'm crying. I know it's a letter from Bridie. She never intended to leave me a puzzle to solve from cryptic clues. But her handwritten words have formed an ink-blot pattern where the folded halves touched.

"Fountain pen," Derek says. He takes it away, and I hear the hand dryer in the toilet at the end of the corridor. The letter was already ruined but the steam made it damp. He returns and lays it on the table.

"I know what Bridie did," I cry. "She killed her sister. With this chain. The letter was a confession, and she wanted me to read it, to acknowledge her crime. And now I can't."

Derek lets me cry, and when I'm done he turns me back to the newspaper. It's ruined too, but phrases are readable in places where the print from the reverse side hasn't leaked through. The masthead is still visible: *The Kerryman*. And a blurred date in 1896.

"The same year as the family portrait," I say.

The headline states: *Missing Girl Murderer Charged*.

Now Derek is pointing to three phrases from the lead paragraph that the soaking wine somehow missed.

*… of Miss Bridie O'Connor, the sixteen-year-old … satisfied that the missing girl met with her death last … charged Br … with murder.*

I scan the rest of the page, trying to make sense of the odd word: *bloodstained, musicians, trace, hair*. It's useless.

Derek makes me sit down and hands me a cup of tea.

"*Charged Br … with murder*," I say. "So it's true. Ciara must be the missing girl and my great-grandmother killed her. This is all about sisters. And in a bizarre rerun of family history, Stella tried to kill my mother by pushing her into a drain."

I take a sip of tea and it burns my mouth.

"Sorry," Derek says, taking it back. He blows on it as if I'm a child. Then I drink. It soothes me.

He's bending over the article. "From what we can read, the murdered girl might have been Bridie herself."

"What?" I look at the words again and read them aloud: "*… of Miss Bridie O'Connor, the sixteen-year-old … satisfied that the missing girl met with her death last … charged Br … with murder.* I see what you mean, DD, but Bridie wasn't murdered. She ran away to Australia and became my great-grandmother. So the 'Br' who was charged with the murder has to be Bridie."

"That doesn't fit with the song," Derek says. "One sister kills the other one, and the wrong man is charged. Why send you the song if it doesn't mirror what happened?"

I'm crying again. The song doesn't fit with my visions of a man in a waistcoat bearing down on Ciara either. And it doesn't fit with the convent. If Bridie was found guilty of murder in 1896 she would have gone to the gallows, not the nunnery.

"Curse that lawyer and his drinking habit," I wail. "Now I'll never know what happened."

Derek puts his arm around me. "Put the letter under your pillow. You might see the message in your dreams."

It's not as woo-woo as it sounds. I've had nocturnal messages more than once. I watch him staring at Bridie's letter, knowing he's looking for meaning in the pattern of blurs.

"It might even be why these clues are scrambled," he adds.

"What? The lawyer spilled the wine to keep me guessing?"

"Serendipity at work. If you could read this stuff you'd only know what they were telling you. Now you've got to dig beneath the surface. That's where the real truth lies."

And it's doing my head in.

* * *

After a restless night trying to make all the clues fit—and failing—I arrive at the office feeling wretched, and find Derek is already there. He's got subscriptions to all kinds of archives that ordinary mortals only dream of, and he's found *The Kerryman* article online.

"I tracked it down by keyword since we didn't have the full date," he tells me.

"You're an angel, DD. I put the letter under my pillow last night and got nothing but confusion. Thank God I don't have to do that again."

"Don't get too excited. The article's embargoed."

"What? Why would they do that?" I start pacing. "This murder happened over a hundred years ago. And if the song is right and someone was executed for it, then it's not even a cold case."

"The embargo states that *The Kerryman* article—and several others—play a central role in a major exhibition at the Kerry Museum. It's called *Murder Victorian Style*."

I don't believe it. "An exhibition of Victorian murders? And this article is part of it?"

"It's in Tralee," he says. "You can pop over to Ireland and read the article in the display cabinet. Or you can wait until the exhibition closes and they lift the embargo, then read it online."

Excitement trounces my frustration. "But that means this murder is part of the exhibition. The curators will have collected evidence and artefacts that may never be in one place again. Maybe they'll solve the mystery of who killed who and who was executed." And why Bridie wanted me to know about it.

"It closes in ten days," he adds.

"Shit."

The Kerry Museum's website is coy about giving sneak peeks into an exhibition that has perfectly judged the modern-day fascination with anything Victorian and ghoulish. There are no photos of any of the exhibits, not even a list of the victims featured. But there is a photo of a queue of visitors stretching down the steps and along the road.

I try googling Bridget O'Connor to see if anyone's written a travel blog about the exhibition, but nothing relevant comes up. If I want to know more, I'll have to get on a plane.

I pick up the phone and find out when Davina's leaving. The day after tomorrow. After checking my bank account, I book a seat on the same flight.

* * *

Gretel, my own sister, needs to know about all of this. She heard about the first parcel when the lawyer called Stella. It's time to fill her in on what's happened since then.

"Are you sure you're not making too much of this, Selkie? Mum says Bridie was weird, especially at the end. There was some spell she wanted to remember—it was the only thing she talked about. And now you're telling me that my mother tried to kill your mother, and that our great-grandmother might have been a murderer herself. None of this is trustworthy."

Stella has been sandbagging Gretel before she heard the other side from me. I'm not surprised.

"Look," I say, "Stella's your mum so of course you're not going to believe she tried to kill her little sister. But don't take Bridie's word for it. I'll send you the piece from *The Manly Daily.* You can judge for yourself and ask Stella about it. She won't talk to me."

"But why did Bridie send you this stuff? It's a huge burden to put on a newborn, even if she did get them to hold it until you were an adult."

I can't really answer this question yet.

"She knew she had a great-granddaughter," I say, "and maybe she wanted to come clean about the past. It might have helped her die in peace."

"Good thing these parcels didn't land on you when you were

eighteen," Gretel says, and laughs for the first time. "Andrew would have used your evil ancestors against you."

She's right. My ex-husband is older than me and a master of emotional abuse. It was Gretel who encouraged me to finally walk out on him. Less than a year ago.

"This is about you too," I say. "You and I are the next generation. Two sisters."

I read her the murder ballad. Twice.

"Wow. And you think this is Bridie's story?"

"That's what I'm hoping to find out at the exhibition."

"Two sisters. You're not planning to kill me, are you? History repeating itself. That spell she kept talking about wasn't a death spell, I hope. She didn't include it with the song?"

"No instructions. Or the ink ran and I can't read them. If you get too annoying, I'll just have to wing it."

We laugh.

* * *

Before I leave, I give Derek my *Celtic Folktales* book for safe-keeping. His eyes light up and he promises to read it, then send me any insights into Irish folklore that might be relevant to my quest.

"It's not for research, DD," I protest. "I just don't want to leave it to the cockroaches in the Waikiki flat. And Ciara was murdered by a living person. She wasn't stolen by the faeries."

"An Irish mystery without any faeries?" he says. "Fat chance."

Bridie's blue ink smudges go under my pillow again the night before we fly out. They didn't produce any visions last time but my intentions were too vague. Now I've got a goal. I don't know if the letter's responsible for my dream, but human fingers appear. They're sticking up out of the ground, a circle of standing stones pointing to the sky. On each finger an eternity ring dotted with diamonds sparkles in the light. I'm not sure if I'm looking at a cemetery of headstones or a gruesome version of Stonehenge.

When I wake, the visuals fade but a phrase lingers in my mind.

*Ring of truth.*

# Chapter 8

We're on our way to Dublin. For the first couple of nights Davina and I have booked a B&B. Then, while Davina starts her search for Dervla, I'll travel down to Tralee near the Atlantic coast in time to catch the final days of the murder exhibition. We're both paying our own way, so we'll share everything we can. Then there's the moral support—heaven knows we both need it.

My decision to accompany Davina was so last-minute that I didn't get to organise a seminar tour, but I sent off some emails, hoping the notoriety from my disappearance a few weeks ago hasn't completely faded and will get me some work while I'm away. Bridie might have left me a suitcase full of clues but they didn't come with an inheritance.

It's a long flight and there's too much time to think. This is my first visit to the home of my ancestors, but the excitement of the trip is dampened by the event I'm investigating. While Davina dozes beside me, I pull out the song and read the words again as if I don't already know them by heart. I keep hoping to see something I missed. Something that lets Bridie off the hook. But the story it tells chills me to the bone all over again, especially the aftermath of the murder when the apparition appeared.

*'Take you my fingers and locks of my hair*
  *To make pegs and strings for your fiddle there.'*

*He did as she asked, removing her rings.*
  *Then left the miller to keep her fine things.*

*The very first time that the fiddle did play*
  *It sang of the murder that happened that day.*

*'My sister killed me,' is the song that it sang.*
  *'She is the one who surely should hang.'*

*But the song came too late, the miller was dead.*
  *The sister never lay in his wedding bed.*

*The rings in his pocket pointed the blame*
  *And the murderous sister lived with the shame.*

The dead sister's fingers and her rings must be what inspired the circle of finger stones in my dream. Does the dream foretell that my journey will reveal the 'ring of truth'?

I wonder if anyone in Bridie's Australian family ever suspected that she was sitting on such a dark secret. Stella didn't know about Bridie's sister, but did Bridie ever come clean to my great-grandfather, Patrick Ryan?

And Stella called Bridie 'dangerous', so she must have had an inkling of her grandmother's character. Then there was Bridie's constant talk of spells. Maybe sitting on this degree of guilt for a lifetime pushed her over the edge.

* * *

We arrive in Dublin on an overcast spring day and share a taxi from the airport. On the way, Davina points out places she knows.

"If the sun comes out, they'll be talking about it for months" she tells me, finding something for us to laugh about. She hams up her accent. "Oh, remember that day when it was so hot our freckles fairly sizzled on our cheeks."

The B&B is an old two-storey house on the north side of the river. The street is lined with similar brick buildings in various shades of grey. It's not far from Davina's old boarding house, but being so close to the city centre the whole area has been gentrified and commercialised. A bubbly woman called Kathleen mothers us into our shared room at the top of the stairs. An ensuite bathroom has been retrofitted into the corner of what must have been a grand room in its heyday, with a large picture window looking onto the narrow street.

We take it in turns to shower, then fall into bed. After a couple of hours I'm wide awake, so I leave Davina sleeping and pop downstairs. It's still daylight so I take a chance that Kathleen's around and knock on the kitchen door. She might be able to tell me something about convents. It's the one fact I've got that I can investigate in Dublin—Bridie being rescued from a fire.

Kathleen's been baking and her hands are covered in flour, but she's as gregarious as I'd guessed. "Your great-granny, was it? And a convent in Dublin that caught fire in the early twentieth century. Didn't Mr Google give you a hand at all?"

"I've searched for hours," I say, "but there are so many religious sites listed that don't exist any more—too many to track down why each one closed. And I don't know if the convent I'm looking for was in Dublin, near Dublin, or if the family gossip is all wrong."

"Gossip wrong?" She chuckles. "Now don't go spoiling my fantasies, will you?" She wipes her hands on her apron and picks up the phone. "I'll just ring my hairdresser. What Maggie doesn't know about the Church isn't worth knowing. Hasn't she told me a hundred times that her mam's sister was a nun."

Someone answers at the other end.

"Ah, Maggie, I've a question for you. I've a good friend with me." She turns to me. "What's your name, darlin'?"

"Selkie."

Her mouth falls open. "Yes, my dear friend *Selkie*," she says to Maggie, "needs to find the convent where her great-granny was. It burned down about a hundred years ago give or take. Somewhere in Dublin." As Kathleen listens, she rolls her eyes and moves the fingers on her free hand to form a yapping mouth. "This one burned down and they rebuilt it? You're sure about that now, Maggie? Saint Scholastica's. Fine. Yes, I'll send her around for a trim, sure."

I can't keep the excitement from my voice. "What did she say?"

"The building was destroyed, Maggie says. But the land was so valuable close to the city and all, that they've turned it into apartments."

My excitement deflates.

"But she says you can go there and see what's left of the perimeter wall."

"Oh."

"Now, it's your turn," she says. "Tell me about this name of yours."

* * *

According to Maggie, the apartment block that's replaced St Scholastica's is called Convent Gardens. Clever. But when I slip upstairs again to view the building online, the name is too grand for the functional block of flats in grey brick with white trim. I see what else I can find about Convent Gardens and a real estate advertisement pops up. One of the studio apartments is open for inspection this afternoon.

I don't know why I decide to go along. Whatever's left of the convent's original wall isn't going to turn up any secrets about Bridie, but I've decided not to question my urges on this trip.

When Davina wakes, she's got a plan of her own. To visit Dervla's old house. "Her parents might still be there," she says.

I'm horrified. "But they're not going to talk to you—a stranger who looks like their daughter. They could be hostile, especially if she … dead."

"I'm not going to knock on their door and tell them I'm Dervla's long-lost decoy, am I? I just have to go there, Selkie."

Like a pilgrimage. I understand.

Davina comes with me as far as the old convent site, and after a hug continues on her own. We picked up some pre-paid phones at the airport so we can keep in touch without roaming costs.

I follow the signs up the stairs to the open house, where a real estate agent is greeting the few people viewing what turns out to be a small modern apartment with little ambiance. It's ridiculous, but in each corner I pause in case there's some presence there. What was I expecting? A resident ghost who relocated after the fire and wants to chat after a hundred years?

I ask the agent, who's standing by the door ready to pounce, what he knows about the old convent.

"Not a thing," he says. "Will you be making an offer?"

What a waste of time.

As I leave, an old woman who's watering a pot plant outside another flat stops and stares at me. Her white hair is permed within an inch of its life.

"What do you want to know about the convent?" she whispers.

Perfect, a nosy neighbour.

Her name is Molly. She invites me in, and over a cuppa and homemade scones, we make each other's day.

"There's a museum, you know," she tells me.

"A museum of things from the old convent?"

She nods. "Tiny it is, but it tells the story of Saint Scholastica's."

"Really?" I can't believe my luck. I imagine the nuns gathering precious artefacts and record books and carrying them down the ladders under their habits. Except they were in their nightwear if Stella got the story right. "Where is it?"

"At Saint Scholastica's, of course."

For the first time I wonder how legit Molly is. "But Saint Scholastica's ... burned down," I say carefully. "And now it's been replaced by this block of flats."

"I know that. Don't I live here? And haven't we just been talking about the fire?"

"I'm confused."

"The *new* Saint Scholastica's," she says. "After the fire they moved to Ballyknock Castle outside the city."

* * *

After I leave Molly, I google St Scholastica's Ballyknock Castle, and the scale and grandeur of the place where the nuns ended up is astonishing, like something out of a fairy tale. The photo on the homepage shows sweeping lawns and a turreted building, not unlike a French chateau, overlooking an ornamental lake. There are also old photos of the original convent—prison-like by comparison—and a history of the order, including a personal account of the fire by Lady Abbess Mary Margaret:

*It was the early hours of January 15, 1917. A calm moonlit night, cold and frosty. Inside the convent our community of thirty-seven was sleeping in their beds. At about two in the morning I was woken by the sound of cracking. Thinking it was frozen snow falling off the roof, I was about to go back to sleep when my door burst open. We were on fire.*

The story tells about the rush to wake everyone and count heads, the fire brigades that attended, how the nuns had to be carried down long ladders from the upstairs dormitories, how the fire was thought to have started from a candle igniting a curtain, and how the building couldn't be saved. But the few items that were saved, wrapped in a hurry inside waterproof capes, have been preserved in a tiny private museum that can be visited by appointment.

Before I can wonder how far away it is and what purpose it will serve, I've completed the online request form, stating as my reason: *Great-granddaughter of Bridget O'Connor, member of the community at time of fire; have travelled from Australia to track down Irish roots.*

Almost totally true.

Then I have the urge to touch base with Alister.  I write him a text: *Making an appointment at Bridie's convent.* Then I realise that under the circumstances he may not be amused by references to chastity, so I change it to: *Still touched.* And, inspired by the fairy tale castle, I sign off: *Your finger-princess, S xx.*

The reply from St Scholastica's is quicker than I expected. I'm in. Someone will meet me at 11 am tomorrow at the main entrance.  They remind me to bring ID and direct me to the page on their website that's devoted to how to get there by every form of transport, including helicopter.  I'll be taking the bus—a series of them, then a taxi.

# Chapter 9

When Davina and I catch up late in the day, she's as upset as I'm excited. Dervla's family has moved. Although Davina told me she just needed to see their house again, she was obviously hoping for more. She knocked at the houses on either side, but a maid sent her away from one; and on the other side, the woman was happy to chat but hadn't lived there long enough to know anything about the Kellys.

"It's a dead end," she says. "I tried the local corner shop, but it's been taken over recently by an Indian family. Then I went to Ashford College, Dervla's old school, but they don't give out private information about former pupils and the secretary threatened to call the guards if I didn't leave."

"Guards?"

"The Garda Síochána, the Irish police. I was so desperate, Selkie, I even wished I'd pretended to *be* Dervla. Put on a posh accent and charmed the woman."

I've never seen Davina in such despair, and I realise just how much of herself she's invested in this trip, in making peace with her past.

"Did Dervla ever mention her parents' professions or interests?" I ask. "Did you see any golf clubs? Maybe her mother did charity work."

She shakes her head. "I don't even know their first names. And Kelly is hardly uncommon around here."

As I rack my brain, desperate to get her a lead like Kathleen gave me, an idea pops. "You know their old address! Let's see if we can find them on the electoral roll. There must be archives for that kind of thing."

We huddle over my laptop. There are electoral archives from 1908 to 1915, and from 1938 to 1965. For some reason no other years are even listed, and the ones that are have been moved from a searchable format. We have to send an email enquiry to the city archives.

Davina's reluctant. "I don't have any right to enquire about them."

"Not them, *Dervla*. Say you're searching for your birth sister. Give them your name, your last address in Cork and the date, then do the same for her. It'll probably take weeks for a reply, but it's *something*. Action stirs things up."

She agrees it's better than feeling stuck.

While she sends the enquiry, I go downstairs and get the address of Maggie the hairdresser from Kathleen. But as I suspected, her salon is north of Dublin's River Liffey and the Kellys lived on the more expensive south side. Without more information, Dervla and her family are still invisible.

"I don't know what else to do," Davina says.

"Go back tomorrow and ask around again. Try a local hairdresser—you might stumble on another Maggie. Or a real estate agent might know when they sold the house. And the library. Librarians know a lot about the locals. You might get lucky."

Over dinner in a pub that Kathleen recommends, Davina is

unusually quiet and picks at her food. The disappointment of her first investigations is weighing on her and I hope tomorrow brings a breakthrough to her search.

*　*　*

As the taxi sweeps up the long driveway of Ballyknock Castle, my anticipation mounts. At the commanding front portico with its marble pillars, there's a bell to ring. While I wait, I take in the grounds. Hedges clipped into topiary angels—by a nun with too much time on her hands?—divide the lawns that descend in terraces to a lake dotted with ducks. The rich green of the grass looks unreal.

The door creaks open, and the nun who greets me introduces herself as Sister Bridget.

"My great-grandmother's birth name was Bridget," I gush. "Bridget O'Connor."

"So you said in your enquiry."

She's somewhat terse, but I remember this is a convent and she might just be shy talking to a woman wearing a red power suit and matching lipstick. It was that or skin-tight jeans. I left my convent-visiting outfits behind in a previous life.

I try to make polite conversation but she puts her finger to her lips. She leads me through a maze of corridors lined with fabulous portraits of haughty personages or tall windows that look onto several inner courtyards. If she leaves me alone, I'll be lost.

When we stop outside an enormous oak door, she fishes a large key from a chain at her waist. She's wearing a chatelaine.

When I gasp she looks at me sharply. "I'll stay with you while you look."

"Of course. Thank you."

As we enter a tiny room dwarfed by a soaring ceiling, it's clear there's not much to see and I'm already disappointed. Under glass, there's a huge book, a register of names. They must have thought it was precious to carry it down a ladder. Good for me that they did.

"There's only one O'Connor," she says. "I've opened it at that page."

She's a woman who likes her keys—she's already locked the glass lid again. I want to protest that my hands are clean, but instead I scan the page.

The list of first names doesn't include Bridget. Moving to the surnames, I run my eye down the list until I find O'Connor. I stare at the lettering written with a nib dipped in ink. It states that a Ciara O'Connor entered St Scholastica's in April 1897, adopted the saint's name Sister Cecilia, and remained a member of the order until the fire in 1917. For almost twenty years she was an inmate in the old building until the fire released her.

It was Ciara who entered the convent, not Bridie. The shock knocks the breath out of me.

There's a small hard chair in the corner and I flop onto it and inhale deeply. I've been hoping this visit would corroborate what I know, not tighten the mystery with an unexpected twist.

Sister Bridget is watching me with veiled interest, as if I'm a specimen to be locked under glass. "Not the person you were looking for?" she asks. Her expression reminds me that not all nuns are saints.

Without replying, I get up and move around the few relics, candlesticks and statuettes, looking for I don't know what. In another glass case there are photographs. The light isn't very bright—just a bulb dangling at the end of a long rod from the ceiling high above—and I pull out my phone.

"No photos," my warder says.

"May I use it as a light?"

She hesitates, then nods.

About thirty nuns, their individual identities hard to distinguish under their wimples, are standing in a group and staring at the camera. If the Ciara O'Connor in the register is my ancestor, I'm determined to find her.

My phone lights each sepia face, old and young, but before I recognise Ciara something else makes me stop. A large cross is hanging against one woman's chest—two tubes that have been twined together. The main tube is the pendant Bridie sent me—three segments of brass looking like bamboo and dotted with coloured stones. I look at the frowning face of the nun who's wearing it and see myself staring back at me.

"I've found her," I say, feeling a strange mix of emotion and confusion. "Ciara O'Connor was Bridie's sister. The family story about who was here must have got mixed up. Let me take a photo. Just of her."

My warder gives a sharp shake of her head.

I'm about to say 'please' but change my mind, guessing there's another word she'll warm to. "If I zoom in," I say, "you can *supervise* what's in the photo."

It's a moment before she nods and moves to my side. She doesn't unlock the case but the close-up on my screen is good enough, and when she sees Ciara, how alike we are, she gasps herself. She knows I'm telling the truth.

Making sure the photo also includes the pendant, I press the shutter. "Thank you."

There's nothing else to see, so I step into the corridor and she locks up.

Then a thought pops into my mind. "I'd like to meet the abbess. I have a question for her."

Really? I have no idea what the question is. Unless I think that after a hundred years she can tell me why Ciara was here and not Bridie.

Sister Bridget is already doing the head shake. Her default action. "You don't have an appointment and ... she's away. In Rome."

"Who else can I see? Someone senior," I add before she suggests herself.

"You'll have to make another appointment."

"I've come a long way," I remind her. "All the way from Australia."

She's unmoved. Against house rules she let me take a photo, so all favours have been dispensed.

"Then I'll request the appointment and wait," I say. "Show me where I can sit."

She's not happy as she leads me back the way we came, to a tiny office just inside the front door. It contains a small antique table, a hard upright chair and a large classic-style painting of the Virgin providing beatific surveillance.

Sister Bridget doesn't offer me a paper form of any kind, so I pull out my phone and start typing an email asking for an audience—if that's what it's called—hoping by then I'll know what the hell my question is. My warder's mouth is a line of irritation. She doesn't want to stay with me but she won't leave me alone either.

I hope the pressure might make something pop, and it does. A noise at the front door indicates that a car has pulled up and my guard hisses, "You can't stay here. Come this way."

She bundles me back into the entrance hall, then through a side door onto a narrow exterior walkway bordered by pillars. I've just been shunted out of the way of whoever's arriving, but from behind a pillar I can spy on the proceedings. A grand-looking nun in burgundy robes is emerging from a car driven by another nun in a plain habit. Others are swarming to unload her suitcases, all in total silence. This must be the abbess returning from Rome.

As I watch, she turns to go inside and the sight of her face causes my legs to start running and my voice to start shouting, "Wait!"

The sound breaks the peaceful scene. The abbess looks towards me, the interloper, but before I reach her I'm held captive within a circle of habits.

Sister Bridget has emerged and is tossing me her finest frown. "So sorry, Mother Clare," she says to the abbess. "She's *Australian*. I've told her to make an appointment if she wishes to speak to you."

"Selkie Moon," I say, extending a shaking hand to the abbess between the shoulders of my captors. I can't believe my eyes.

"Miss Moon is just leaving," says Sister Bridget.

"No, I'm not." Not now.

The abbess has fixed me with the greenest eyes. They sparkle with interest from a face I know well.

"I was making an appointment," I say, "but now that I've seen you, it's more urgent that we speak. I have some important news about ... an old friend of yours."

"I doubt it, Selkie Moon." Her voice is like music. "I've never been to Australia."

I'm aware of the audience, all ears flapping. "She lives overseas these days but she knew you when you were both

... in your teens."

She pauses, then dismisses me with her hand. "Make your appointment then."

I pull out my last card. "Her name is Davina. Davina K–"

"Take Miss Moon to my private reception room," she snaps, losing the music. Then she recovers and smiles. "We'll be able to talk there. I'll join you when I've freshened up. Lovely to meet you."

A silent nun escorts me past a glaring Sister Bridget back into Ballyknock Castle and up a sweeping double staircase. As my head spins from my encounter with the abbess, progressively narrower corridors lead us finally to another oak door and I'm shown into an elegant room lined with books. There's another antique table similar to the one downstairs, but the tub chairs look comfortable.

Another nun arrives before this one has left, the tray of tea and sandwiches she's carrying suggesting some kind of telepathy. They say nothing and leave me to my refreshments, but after the discovery of Ciara and now this, I'm so flustered I can't eat or even sit down.

Why did the abbess have me whisked up here with such haste? I know their history might be difficult for her in her present position, but I only want to tell her that Davina is looking for her. And do I text Davina now and get her hopes up, or do I wait until after I've talked to Mother Clare?

The abbess keeps me waiting for a while, perhaps to give us both time to compose ourselves. By the time I've succumbed to the aroma of the sandwiches, I've calmed down. What I've discovered makes sense of Dervla Kelly's disappearance. The fact that she's now Mother Clare explains why Davina wasn't able to find her. Hidden away in a convent with a saint's name is as close as you can get to dead without a death certificate.

But when the door opens and she greets me in a different robe, her dazzling presence reminds me that she's very much alive.

"Sorry to keep you waiting," she says. "I had some urgent business to attend to on my return."

"Of course. Thank you for seeing me."

"You didn't give me much choice."

"Sorry if I embarrassed you."

"You didn't."

Because she interrupted me before I could?

She gestures me into a chair, before walking to the long narrow window, where she stands with her back to me, looking out at the grounds.

Then she turns and speaks. "I don't know who you are, Selkie Moon, but you've got the hide of a rhinoceros."

I laugh. "I'm more of a unicorn person."

She doesn't join in. "Turning up here out of the blue and making veiled threats about my past."

"What threats?"

"Tell me what you want, then get out."

Whoa. I feel like I've been slapped.

"Davina Kennedy is a friend of mine. She's looking for you."

"So you deny that you're a journalist?"

"I'm a friend of Davina's."

"OK, let's assume that's true and you're Davina's spy. What does *she* want? After twenty years."

Her manner reminds me that she's used to power and she's got a position to protect. I reassess the interview. If she really suspects that I'm here to expose her sordid past, there's only one way to play it: straight.

"OK," I say, matching her tone. "I want two things."

"Only two? I'm not promising anything. Even God doesn't do that."

"One," I say. "Listen to the whole story about how I came to be here today. Nothing to do with you. Or Davina."

I'm hoping she really does believe in divine providence. Or whatever she might call my psychic connection to Davina. If I hadn't come to Dublin with Davina, if I hadn't thought my great-grandmother had been a nun in this order, if I hadn't had a hunch to visit the new St Scholastica's, if I hadn't seen Ciara's name on the list and delayed my departure to ask a mysterious question, Dervla Kelly would have remained undiscovered. Forever.

"And two?" she asks.

"I'll tell you the second one after you complete the first."

Making a bargain is something she understands. And she's obviously wary of journalists. If she sends me away, I could do anything with what I might know about her relationship with Davina.

She looks at her watch. A fob watch on a chain. "You've got ten minutes."

Taking a deep breath, I tell her everything. She could just tolerate my story so we can move on to my next demand, but instead she allows herself to be intrigued. Or pretends to. I haven't forgotten what Davina said about how manipulative she was as a teenager.

She sits beside me and looks at the copies of everything I've got, including the murder ballad, then asks, "What do you hope to discover by tracking down an old murder? If that's what this mystery is."

"I don't know. I'm drawn to it. When I get drawn to things

...” I get into a lot of trouble.

She examines my pendant and the photo of Ciara from their own museum and agrees the cross and my pendant are probably one and the same.

“A knife handle, you think?” She laughs. “That would be right. Any old trinket could be turned into a cross back then. Or a religious relic. Especially by the tinkers.”

Then we both sit in silence for several minutes.

When she finally speaks, it’s with less acrimony and more fatigue. “I’ve heard your story. What’s the second thing?”

“Meet Davina.”

Her face is a mask, as if she expected what was coming. She misses a couple of beats, then reaches for a business card in a holder on her table and writes something on the back.

The message is brief: *For DK. Ring me.*

# Chapter 10

In the taxi back to the bus stop, I can't believe I've pulled it off. Not only stumbling upon Dervla, but getting her phone number too. I won't share the news with Davina until we're face to face. She might need a hug or a shoulder to cry on, it's that huge.

She's sent a text saying she's had another fruitless day, and I've replied that I'll meet her at the pub on the river bank not far from our B&B.

When I arrive, it's standing room only under the art-deco lighting along the bar, but the buzz of alcohol-fuelled conversation is perfect for breaking the news. If Davina starts screaming, no-one will notice.

We manage to get a table in a far corner and after we've sat down, she senses I've got something to tell her. "What are you sitting on, girl? Have you found Bridie's ghost while I've been finding nothing at all?"

I give it to her straight. "Don't die of shock. I've found Dervla."

She almost chokes on her drink. "My God, I knew you had something big sticking in your throat, but not this big." Then she thinks the worst and drops her voice. "You found her grave. She's in the ground out there at Ballyknock, isn't she? Her parents would want her buried somewhere grand."

"Nope. I met the living, breathing, arguing specimen."

"My God, you spoke to her? You spoke to Dervla Kelly?"

I hand over the business card of Mother Abbess Clare of St Scholastica's, with the simple message and private number scrawled on the back in Dervla's hand.

"She's a nun," Davina screams, drawing a few looks.

"A mother superior," I say.

Now she's laughing. "So they sent her to the nunnery after all. They threatened her with it, but now that I think about it, it'd be right up Dervla's alley—a whole bunch of silenced women doing her bidding." She shakes her head. "After her years as a teenage tearaway, it's the last place I'd have thought to look her up."

As I fill her in on the details, it's not long before she's crying into her drink. "She's alive, she's alive. My God, I didn't kill her."

She tells me over and over what a special friend I am.

"I didn't do anything, Davina. Except follow a hunch about Bridie."

My comment makes her stop. "And why would Bridie's past lead you to Dervla? Have you thought about that?"

"Because every direction we turn," I say, "we fall over a bloody nun?"

She chuckles and her cheeks glow with new colour. Dervla's not the only one who's been brought back to life.

"And while you were finding my nun," she says, "what were you doing about your own?"

"My hunch about Bridie got flipped on its head." I tell her about Ciara. "I've been trying to make sense of it. If Ciara was in this convent until 1917, she was murdered after the fire. But the murder reported in *The Kerryman* took place in 1896 so that doesn't fit. Or did Ciara die in the fire and my visions of her murder can't be trusted? And what about Bridie? When she fled to Australia it looks like she took on her twin's past as her own."

"You're sure this nun is the Ciara in your visions and not someone else? Ciara O'Connor is a common enough name."

"It's her. She even turned this bloody pendant into a cross." I show her Ciara's photo from the museum.

"Our stories might be about nuns," Davina says, looking up at me, "but they're about something much more significant as well. It's why you 'fell over' Dervla. And this photo nails it."

"What? What have I missed?"

"It's not a great photo, but look at this woman's eyes and remember the twins at the piano. I don't think this is Ciara."

I see it now. Although her body language is cowed compared to her straight back on the piano stool, the hint of a sharp intelligence hasn't diminished.

"Oh my God," I say. "It's Bridie."

* * *

We don't really get into why Bridie might have called herself Ciara because the discovery of Dervla consumes us. We drink too much at the pub, and back at the B&B neither of us is going to be sleeping anytime soon. Davina sends a text to Dervla saying she'll call tomorrow, but gets no reply.

We turn on the TV. And there on the late news is Dervla, her beautiful face filling the screen like a movie star swathed in an exotic headdress. She's surrounded by microphones after emerging from Dublin airport earlier in the day.

"Suddenly she's everywhere," I murmur. "No wonder she thought I was a journalist."

We just catch a question from an off-camera reporter: "So what *can* you tell us, Reverend Mother Clare? Surely you don't want us to rely on rumours."

"His Holiness will make an announcement at the appropriate time," Dervla says.

"So you can confirm that he sent for you to discuss a special position? Is that the announcement?"

"I'm afraid I can't comment further. Now if you'll excuse me, I'm tired."

As she turns away, another reporter can just be heard calling after her. "Is it true that you're tipped to become the most powerful woman in the Church?" But Dervla has already gone.

"The most powerful woman in the Church," Davina says, looking almost as stunned as she did in the pub. "Why am I not surprised?"

I pull out my laptop and google Mother Abbess Clare of St Scholastica's. There's lots here for Davina to look at, but a story in the *Courier-Herald* catches my eye. I read it out:

*Vatican commentators are tipping that of the three candidates shortlisted for the new position of Head of Special Committee to Investigate Child Abuse, our own Reverend Mother Clare of St Scholastica's, Ballyknock Castle, Dublin, is the most likely to be appointed. The Pope is looking to expand the role of women in the Vatican hierarchy. At almost forty years of age, Reverend Mother Clare has both youth and maturity, and her doctorate in clinical psychology boosts her credentials. There's also the rumour, which she hasn't denied, that she was taken from her mother at birth and was herself the victim of sexual abuse by her stepfather. If this is true, her background could give her the personal experience needed to bring empathy to the new position; something that's been sorely lacking in investigations into the serial child abuse by some members of the Church.*

Davina has gone pale. "I had no idea."

"She never told you about her past?"

"She wanted me to know as little about her as possible. I was her tool, not her confidante."

"If she agrees to meet you, what are you going to say? Will you confess to the identity theft?"

"I have to, Selkie. It's why I'm here. This guilty secret's been hanging over me for far too long. I have to come clean so I can get on with my life."

The fetch pops into my mind, and my theory that something momentous must be happening to Dervla for it to show up again after twenty years. But Davina seems to have forgotten it—for now. And I'm not going to remind her. But her words make me think of Bridie and the guilty secret she sat on until she could share it with her great-granddaughter. Another secret involving an identity swap ... and premature death.

As Davina is collapsing into bed, Derek rings. I take my phone downstairs to the guest lounge that's now deserted. He doesn't know what's brought Davina to Dublin so I don't share her news, but he's amazed at the turns of events in my mystery in just two days.

When he hears that it looks like Bridie took Ciara's name at the convent, he asks me to text him the photo. He compares Ciara's eyes with the copy of the family photo I left behind. "Ciara looks younger somehow. An ingenue. But this nun has Bridie's sharpness."

"You said those wine stains on the newspaper might reveal

something hidden," I tell him. "I thought you were off with the faeries, but it looks like our confusion about which twin was murdered and who was arrested was a clue."

"Wine stains never lie," he jokes, "especially when they're down the front of your shirt." He gets serious again. "So swapping identities is part of the puzzle."

"But why? Bridie turned up at the convent in 1897, a year after the murder, pretending to be her dead twin."

"Anonymity?" Derek says. "Her own name had been all over the papers so it explains why she'd want to be someone else. But if she was trying to hide, the name of a murder victim wouldn't be any better."

"Dublin's a long way from Tralee. Back then the news might have stayed local."

"And she could use Ciara's birth certificate as ID, if they had such things."

Bridie's eyes might be sharp with what looks like intelligence but I have to remember how Stella described her: dangerous.

"After getting the murder ballad," I say, "I've wondered if her family might have sent her away—as punishment for killing her sister. The old St Scholastica's looked like a prison. Maybe calling herself Ciara was Bridie's last act of defiance before the convent swallowed her up."

Derek is quiet for a moment. "Maybe we're asking the wrong question, Selkie. Not *why*, but *when*?"

I'm not sure what he's getting at. "When did Bridie start calling herself Ciara?"

"Yeah. After the murder? Or *before*?"

Shit. "Why would she pretend to be Ciara before the murder?" But the implications are creeping across my skin like spiders.

Derek isn't psychic but he knows human nature. "To get something she wants more than anything, but can't have," he says.

We're quiet for a moment as we both remember the song.

After we hang up I can't get the idea out of my mind. If Bridie and Ciara were caught up in a love triangle, the possibilities become more sinister. To get close to the man she desired but couldn't have, Bridie might have masqueraded as her twin. The song says the jealous sister killed the other one to get the man, but my visions of Ciara's murder tell a different story. Now the awful possibility hits me. If Bridie was pretending to be Ciara *before* the murder, might the deception have caused someone else to kill her? Why?

* * *

Davina tosses all night, and I know she's waiting until she can pick up the phone to call Dervla. I can't sleep either, my mind spinning different scenarios to explain why Bridie used Ciara's name in the convent register. It feels central to the mystery, and I can't wait to get down to Tralee and the exhibition.

Davina's sleepless state also wakes her sleeping demons. Over breakfast she wants to talk about the fetch, about what it might mean for her now that Dervla isn't dead, but the breakfast room isn't private enough. Back in our room she expresses her fears.

"Was the fetch always coming for me?"

"Neither of you is dead," I say, "so maybe it wasn't a fetch at all."

Before we can discuss it, her phone buzzes and she pounces

on it.

"She'll meet me at eleven," she cries. "At a pub called Eight Bells in Howth. Up north, at the end of the train line."

"A long way from Ballyknock Castle," I say. "Makes sense. No journalists. And if you turned up at the convent looking exactly like her, silent tongues might wag. But an abbess in a bar sounds conspicuous."

"She says to come alone. But I want you there."

"She won't agree to that. Lose the nosy Australian in case my recorder's running. And your history with her is private. I'm just the go-between."

But Davina is frowning and pacing. "Now that I know she's alive, I can feel the power she had over me. It's as if all the years have dissolved and I'm a timid teenager again. It's one of the reasons I couldn't sleep. I want to tell her the truth, for my sake, but when she knows what I did to her ..."

"I think you can relax about that. She's the same old Dervla you described—aggressive and manipulative—but now she's got a position to protect. If this job in Rome is at stake, exposing you would only do her damage. She'll probably do anything to keep her past hidden—even be nice to you."

Nevertheless, Davina can't shake the feeling that she's in some kind of danger. I don't say it, but I suspect it's because her fear of the fetch is back. A harbinger of death has to be scarier than facing another person, even someone as fierce as Dervla. But then I'm not the one who has to tell her that I stole her name.

I was planning to catch a train to Tralee today, but Davina's so nervous that I agree to go with her. I'll wait nearby so we can debrief after her meeting, and I can support her if Dervla lashes out.

Howth is on the coast, and the air is filled with briny smells and seagulls. We're early so we walk from the station to the village centre, passing houses and shops styled with a nautical flavour. The pub Eight Bells is vibrant in blue and white and nestled behind a church—well-located for that after-mass thirst. I spy a tearoom across the street and Davina and I part company.

Over tea and scones at a window table, I watch for the arrival of Dervla. Twenty minutes later I almost miss her because she's abandoned her robes for streetwear—and not a pleated navy skirt and button-down white blouse but denim jeans and a sporty light blue shirt. I can't see if her hair is cropped ultra-short for wimple-wear because she's covered it with a stylish scarf. Travelling incognito makes sense, but how did she smuggle herself out of Ballyknock dressed like this? I imagine a quick change in a phone booth somewhere—but what's the abbess of a prestigious convent with Vatican connections doing with jeans in her wardrobe? Although the outfit is simple, it's surprisingly modern. I wonder if Davina is right to be wary of her still.

As Dervla disappears into the pub, I return to my own quest. I need to research other avenues in case the murder exhibition offers no clues beyond *The Kerryman* article. In a small community the murder would have caused a scandal, and if the local newspaper covered it, other press clippings could be filed away in an archive somewhere. Or there could be personal accounts—letters written with ghoulish glee to family in other places; or maybe someone kept a scrapbook and their descendants donated it to the historical society.

As a start I search for historical societies in Tralee and elsewhere in County Kerry, then fire off some enquiries via their websites. But it's likely everything has been gathered at the museum. It's frustrating to be sitting in a tearoom in Howth when I'm only a train ride away from some answers. Next I search a genealogy site, figuring that twins called Bridie and Ciara O'Connor born around 1880 might be rare enough to show up. But I come up empty.

After re-checking the opening hours of the exhibition, I look up the train timetable, then find a B&B near the museum. The accommodation includes a ticket to the exhibition—seems everyone's cashing in on it. I phone the B&B and tentatively book a room, but I won't confirm until I'm sure Davina's done with Dervla. She might even want to come with me.

Something flutters in my chest—excitement mixed with expectation. Then I remind myself of the dark circumstances I'm investigating and reach for the chain at my neck. Even before my fingers touch it, Ciara's last breaths have me gasping. Every morning I consider not wearing it, but I'm afraid of losing it again and I'm committed now. Every vision is an ordeal but it takes me closer to the truth. And this time I see something else: shiny dots like stars. Pinpricks of light? I feel sick, hoping they're not the last things Ciara saw on her way to the afterlife.

A text beeps on my pre-paid phone. *DK gone*, Davina writes. *Exploding with news. Barman pouring drinks.* Dervla must have slipped out while I was engrossed.

It's midday but the interior of Eight Bells is dim, which explains why Dervla chose it for a private meeting—but how does an abbess, an abbess in line for a top job, know such a place exists? There was a number eight in Davina's dream, as if she predicted it. The place isn't very busy, just a handful of elderly patrons propping up the bar. Davina is tucked away at a table in a corner and it takes me a moment to spot her.

"We're sisters," she blurts out before I've even sat down.

"What?"

"Twins." Even in the low light, her eyes are as bright as I've ever seen them. "It's why we look the same. It's like a fairy tale, Selkie. We were separated at birth, adopted by different families. I got the poor Kennedys of Cork and she got the rich Kellys of Dublin."

"Whoa. Slow down. Dervla's your sister?"

"She thinks so. As sure as sure without a test. It's incredible. She was researching those terrible Magdalene Laundries for her psychology doctorate—the convents where single girls were locked up and their babies were snatched away. It was still happening in some places when we were born. All the records were hidden away because they were so shameful, but Dervla got hold of them because of her position and her studies. What she didn't tell anyone was that she was desperate to find her own records, hoping she might find her real mam."

Davina's been talking so fast her mouth's gone dry. She takes a huge slug of beer.

"The Kellys hadn't told her she was adopted until she defied them and went into the convent. They didn't send her there as a punishment; she had an epiphany and knew she was being *called*. So she didn't think she owed them anything after their grand deception—and her stepfather's kiddie-fiddling. Just like mine. It's the reason she went wild with boys. All those years of abuse destroyed her sense of self-worth. Imagine when she discovered that her mam ... *my* mam," her eyes well up, "had twins, and the two baby girls went to different families. She couldn't believe it, then she remembered me. She's been looking for me ever since, but I've been hiding away in Hawaii."

Somewhere in the distance one of those eight bells rings. So why wasn't Dervla delighted when I announced Davina's name? And Hawaii or not, Davina's got a website. It doesn't show her photo, but why not email her and see if she's the same Davina?

But Davina is laughing and I realise she's a little drunk. Who could blame her?

"You've had a lot to talk about," I say. "Being sisters, your adoptions, your ... mother."

"She's *alive*, Selkie."

Now she's crying and I take my first sip of wine. Bloody hell—I need a drink too.

"Dervla's seen her," she says, "talked to her. She's only fifty-five."

"Alive and well?" I ask.

I don't mention it, but I've read somewhere that mothers of stolen babies are overly represented in psychiatric wards.

She nods. "We're going to see her together. As soon as Dervla can arrange it." She starts to laugh. "I'm going to meet ... my mam!"

Davina is euphoric of course, but Dervla's reaction to first hearing Davina's name is still niggling at me. Along with her aggressive attitude towards me in private. She was anything but pleased to know Davina was back. But I suppose that could have been shock; or her fear that I was a journalist digging up dirt. And I wonder if there's a twinge of jealousy on my part—I missed meeting my own mother before she died.

I reach over and squeeze Davina's hand. "What's her name, this mother of yours?"

Her mouth drops open and she laughs again, her emotions

riding the roller-coaster. "Can you believe it? I forgot to ask."

"And Dervla didn't say?"

"No. We had so much to catch up on, we both forgot."

I'm about to say it's odd, but hold my tongue.

"It will be a grand surprise," she says.

* * *

We've got the rest of the day to kill and Davina insists on buying a new outfit.

"What do you wear to meet your mother?" she asks, looking slightly terrified.

"I'm not the best person to ask. The last time I met mine I was two years old, and besides my frilly bikini I was wearing an enormous frown after a wave nearly drowned me."

All Davina's clothes are her own tribal-chic design, totally gorgeous and unique, but when I say that her mother will adore seeing her in one of her own creations, she can't hear me. At the age of thirty-nine, she's going to meet her mother for the first time, so I'm happy to humour her in her crazy quest to look like the perfect long-lost daughter.

We do the rounds of Dublin's shopping precincts, starting near Davina's old stamping ground in Henry Street and trying everything from charity shops to department stores, many of which sell high-end fashion from Europe. Then not finding anything she can settle on, we cross the river to the south side and the George's Street Arcade. Its grand arches and pillars are chapel-like and I realise the architecture is Victorian. A plaque shows the date: 1881—about the same time Bridie and Ciara were born.

After checking out the arcade's quirky boutiques and vintage shops, we stop for a very late lunch.

"What don't you design yourself?" I ask her. "That's what you've got to buy."

"Jeans. I never wear them."

My mind flashes back to Dervla and her streetwear. "Why not dress up like Dervla? That'll surprise your mother if you both walk in on her dressed alike. Assuming Dervla wears the same thing again, but an abbess probably doesn't have too many mufti outfits in her secret wardrobe."

"I love it," she says. She tries on every pair of jeans in the arcade until she's happy, then teams them with a light blue shirt that's shaped at the waist, with buttons down the front—very similar to Dervla's. "Pockets," she cries, patting her buttocks. "I hardly ever have pockets." And she stuffs both her phones into them.

* * *

It's only much later after we fall into bed and I'm dozing off that I wonder if Davina got to come clean about the identity swap. We were so focussed on the revelations about her relationship with Dervla and on getting ready to meet their mother that she didn't tell me if they discussed it—and what Dervla's reaction was.

# Chapter 11

On a bay on the south-west coast, Tralee is the gateway to the Dingle peninsula. It's almost four hours away, including a change of trains, and Davina and I watch a wet landscape of green fields fly by. White cottages are dotted about and I wonder what it was like to live in these humble dwellings back in the 1890s. I imagine that even the middle classes must have lived hard lives.

Davina decided to come with me after a call from Dervla early this morning. Their mother is away on holidays and Dervla needs to track her down. "If she's off in a tiny cottage somewhere," Davina told me when she got off the phone, "Dervla might not be able to contact her. We might have to wait till she comes home in a week or two."

She's trying to stay upbeat, but she must be deflated after yesterday's euphoria. So close to a mother she's never thought of contacting, and now she has to wait.

There's something about travelling by train—a sense of portent—and as we get closer to Tralee my anticipation mounts. The journey also reminds me how far Bridie had to travel to get to the convent in Dublin. In 1897 by steam train it would have been an ordeal, with the air full of smoke and soot staining her face and clothes. How safe was a young woman travelling alone back then? Unless her parents went with her and my idea of a punishment is true. Were the nuns expecting a girl called Ciara O'Connor? Or did Bridie concoct the idea of an identity swap en route? And were her parents ignorant or complicit? Every question seems to take me deeper into a tunnel.

As Davina dozes beside me, my thoughts drift back to last night. We laughed and cried as she tried on her jeans again and kept checking her image in the mirror. But I could tell there was another emotion lurking below the excitement. Fear. Of course she's afraid of meeting her unnamed mother—afraid of what her mother will think of her, whether she'll compare her to Dervla, if they'll hit it off, whether she's someone to love and admire or someone to be ashamed of. But I haven't forgotten Davina's fear of meeting Dervla again—and what they've turned out to be. Two sisters.

As if he's reading my thoughts, my phone chirps with a text from Derek: *Irish band Altan recorded a version of the ballad 'Two Sisters' in 2005 with the alternative title 'The Wind and Rain'. Just saying :-)*

The B&B isn't far from the station, above a pub in a narrow curving street right in the centre of town. The buildings huddle together with common walls and their doors open straight off the pavement. Except for their vibrant colours they remind me of back streets in France.

After we've checked in and dropped off our bags, Davina is so emotionally spent that she settles in front of the fire in the tiny guest lounge and stares into the flames. She needs to be alone, and there's still time for me to grab directions from Nola our host and walk to the exhibition before it shuts for the day.

"It'll be open again tomorrow," Nola says, wondering why I'm in a rush, "and all of next week. And they say it might be fine tomorrow."

But I don't want to wait, despite the rain that's now bucketing down. There might be a cryptic clue that my subconscious can work on overnight. Or the puzzle might be solved in one visit and I can relax. I wish.

When Nola sees my determination, she insists on lending me a hooded raincoat from the row of hooks in the hall, zipping me into it until only my nose is poking out.

The museum's three-storey red brick building stands grand and alone on the edge of a park. The entrance portico is trimmed with white. I recognise it from its website but there are no queues standing in the rain today. Perhaps the photo was from the opening and the interest has dwindled.

In the foyer, I check in Nola's coat and follow the signs to *Murder Victorian Style*, past a room full of archaeological artefacts and posters of megalithic structures. At least I won't be delving back that far. At the door to the murder room, an elderly woman is checking tickets. She looks like a clichéd historical-society type—twill skirt and matching twin-set over a flat chest, a strand of pearls. Her name tag says *Mary*.

Inside the large open-plan space, I'm confronted by huge montages of old newspaper articles and photographs, mannequins dressed in period costume, glass cases of weapons and relics, even a barrel-top wagon. There are few other visitors and I'm tempted to breeze past everything and soak up the ambiance, but then I turn back to Mary.

"Can I help you, darlin'?" she asks with a thick local accent.

"I imagine you're familiar with all the murders in the exhibition?"

"Best friends with the curator, I am. Where are you from, darlin'?" I tell her. "Yes, I helped put this together. Very popular it's been too. Look how far you've come and all. Everyone loves a good murder, especially a Victorian one."

I take a deep breath. "I think the sister of my great-grandmother was murdered around here. I'm not sure of the exact date. The sisters were twins—Ciara and Bridie O'Connor."

"June 20, 1896," she says.

"You know about her?"

It's what I've been counting on but I still can't believe it.

"Bridie O'Connor," she says, startling me. "Murdered she was, but they never found her body. That's her over there. And don't you look just like her."

She points to a mannequin dressed in period costume and its likeness to me makes the room spin.

*The lights have gone out. There's only the moon. And I'm running along a path, wearing a long navy skirt and a peplum jacket. Suddenly a man blocks my way, his face a mask of rage. I'm confused, then alarm takes over when he wraps a fob chain around my neck. The chain tightens and I'm flailing my arms and gulping for air, then toppling over under his weight.*

"Are you all right, darlin'?" says a voice behind me.

I'm stumbling backwards, but I'm saved by a chair.

"Take a few deep breaths," Mary says as I look around and see where I am. "Goodness, you've had quite a shock. You didn't expect to walk in here and find her just like that, did you now?"

"No," I manage to say, the emotions of the attack still pulsing through me. As I blink the vision away, his contorted face fades. Only the moustache remains. When he was strangling me I knew who he was, but the knowledge has slipped away like a ghost.

"It's almost closing time," Mary says, "so why don't I get us both a nice cup of tea and I'll tell you what I know about Bridie. Then if you want to come back tomorrow and look at the exhibits, they won't give you another turn."

While Mary leaves me, I take more deep breaths and avert my eyes from the mannequin so it doesn't happen again. It's just an effigy so why was I suddenly *her*? I'm so relieved to be back in my own skin that a few tears escape. That was more than a vision. For reasons I don't understand, the sight of the mannequin made me lose myself and *become* my Victorian ancestor. The one being murdered. Mary called her Bridie.

With an effort I push the experience aside and try to think. The memory of the murder is embodied in the chain, which is why I'm picking it up—and maybe even more strongly because the chain is back where it happened. But I haven't forgotten that my great grandmother chanted something over my newborn body. When the first parcel arrived I feared that opening it might activate some kind of psychic seed, even though the idea seemed fanciful. At the time I thought it was inspired by my reluctance to get tangled up in my family's past, but now the mannequin's triggered something. Something that's made the psychic connection feel much more real. Too real.

I think about the psychic test I had to pass to receive the second parcel: sensing the name 'Ciara'. I've been so sure it was Ciara who was murdered, but as soon as I heard Bridie's name just now and saw the mannequin, I was *her*. Does that mean my great-grandmother was really Ciara? After looking at her eyes in the convent photo, I was sure that Bridie had taken her sister's name, but how could that be if Bridie was murdered? Unless the identity swap happened the other way round and Great-Granny Ryan was an impostor. Or this exhibition has got the name of the victim wrong.

Mary returns from the tiny office with cups of tea on a tray. She's laced mine with sugar and she watches me glug down grateful mouthfuls, still with no idea why I'm so shaken.

Then after a few minutes she begins her story. "They never found Bridie's body, but they hanged him for her murder—the tinker, Brendon Blake."

The name is new, but a tinker ... surely someone's mentioned tinkers before?

"Afterwards," Mary continues, "his people burned his wagon—just like that replica over there, only bigger. They burned it and everything in it to avoid bad luck. And to drive away his ghost."

"But if they never found her body, maybe she ran away."

All the way to Australia. While Ciara turned up in a Dublin convent—and Bridie borrowed Ciara's history for herself. It would be a relief if both sisters had lived but my visions say the opposite.

"When a girl like that goes missing, from a good family and still in her teens, and there's incriminating evidence, they didn't waste time, not back then. Three Sundays they waited, then it was the gallows for Brendon Blake."

I shiver and think of the song. "What incriminating evidence?"

"Someone saw them together the night she disappeared. That nephew by marriage who lived with them, it was, James Sullivan. The O'Connors took him in after his parents died. He was coming back late from the pub and he saw Bridie meet her tinker over near their camp. She was never seen again. That James couldn't wait to tell what he'd seen."

"*Her* tinker? Bridie and Brendon were lovers?"

"That was the gossip. A girl couldn't be too careful about the company she kept, not back then. If she passed the time of day with a young man in the street, tongues started wagging. And those tinkers were a handsome lot. Rough diamonds who could steal a heart with a wink. But no parent wanted their daughter to marry a tinker."

"Why not?" I can guess but I'm desperate for facts.

"They call them Travellers now." She pauses as if choosing her words. "They had ... strange ways. And for that they were despised. A pauper's life on the road, living out of a trailer. What's that song? 'Gypsies, Tramps and Thieves'. You didn't want your daughter to marry a tinker, to turn your grandchildren into tinkers, no, you didn't."

"If they were lovers," I ask, "why did Brendon kill her?"

"He said he didn't. Right up to his last breath. But the necklace gave him away."

"The necklace?"

Mine is peeping out of my shirt collar and I notice Mary looking at it.

"It was Bridie's necklace," she says. "But the girls were twins, so who was stepping out with the tinker behind her father's back? Maybe Bridie was killed by mistake."

"You think Brendon meant to kill Ciara?" My head is spinning as I try to make sense of her story.

"Just conjecture, isn't it?" she says. "A fob chain the necklace was, from a watch. Gold. Like the one you're wearing."

"Is that why they thought he did it—he killed her for the

necklace?"

"Who's to say? But they never could resist gold, the tinkers. They had that reputation. Thieves, for all their good work as tinsmiths. If a tinker comes to mend your pots and pans, lock away your valuables and your daughters, that's what they used to say. Still do in some parts."

"What happened to it?" I ask. "The ... murder weapon."

She doesn't notice that I've assumed Brendon killed her with the chain. "It went back to the family, I suppose. Heaven knows if they wanted it. There was blood on it when they brought Brendon in. He garrotted her with it, they said, and didn't even bother to wash it afterwards. He would have had to go to the well to do that and it was too close to the O'Connor house, I suppose."

My hand wants to touch the chain at my neck. I resist.

"But if Brendon was after the necklace," I say, "he'd be too clever to lose it surely? Why leave it covered in blood for the police to find?"

"That's what he said, but the constabulary said he must have dropped it when he was getting her body out of the way. It was found in a mound of rubbish not far from the tinkers' camp, just lying there."

"I've had a ... dream," I say, "where a young woman is strangled with a chain. A watch chain."

"The chain you're wearing, is it?"

I nod, and start to say that Bridie sent it to me, but call her my great-grandmother instead. "Along with an old photo of the O'Connor family and James Sullivan."

Mary asks if she can photograph the chain. As I unclip it, she pays no attention to the pendant. Once the chain is in her hand, she holds it like a clairvoyant trying to get a vision.

"Bridie's my favourite," she says. "She was such a beautiful girl, just like you, and the murder is still a mystery, even though Brendon Blake went to the gallows for it. He protested his innocence, they say, even as they put the noose around his neck."

The image is so shocking it silences us.

"Did you see the murderer ... in your dream?" she asks as she arranges the chain on the tray and takes a photo with her phone.

"I just remember a moustache."

She nods. "It was the fashion back then, along with those horrible side whiskers."

She asks if she can make a copy of my photo and I agree to bring it tomorrow, then she shows me to a staff exit.

In spite of the pouring rain I take a long walk through the streets of Tralee, trying to clear my head. Was my great-grandmother really Ciara calling herself Bridie? Did Brendon Blake murder one of the twins, his lover? And if he did, why did the other twin send me a song about one sister killing the other?

* * *

I want to share the latest twist in Bridie's mystery, but after her own emotional tsunami Davina's out for the count in our darkened room. I know Derek will be at the end of the phone, but first I have the strongest urge to call Alister. I dial his number and get his voicemail, and just hearing his voice makes me smile. I leave a message telling him that he's in my thoughts. He's got enough on his mind without a garbled account of my latest dramas.

Then I call Derek. He listens to the mannequin incident and when I share my fear that whatever my great-grandmother chanted over me as a newborn might have been some kind of psychic seed, he blurts out the word I've been dreading: "Possession."

"Bloody hell, DD. Now's not the time to be making stuff up as you go along."

"Puh-lease," he says. "Don't shoot the messenger. I've been boning up on Celtic folklore from your very own book and I don't need to point out that information is power when it comes to dealing with strange phenomena."

"Sorry. Thank you. But I'd know if I was possessed. I became the victim. She didn't become me."

"That may be semantic, but what's this 'psychic seed' if it isn't possession? You think Bridie might have planted a seed ... in your soul."

"I'm probably making it up as I go along," I say.

"But there's something going on. Trust your instincts, Selkie."

# Chapter 12

As Nola serves a fried breakfast that will keep us going for a week, she asks us how we slept.

"Like the dead," Davina says, pulling a face at me.

But I spent the night tossing and turning, and I show Nola what I found under the mattress this morning: a silver serviette ring delicately cut into a filigree pattern, just like the ones on the breakfast table.

"Like the princess and the pea," I say, laughing to show it's not a big deal. But I'm intrigued to know how it got there.

"That Fiona," Nola says, rolling her eyes. She's talking about her two year old, who we met on our arrival. "Doesn't she love shiny things. This must be her latest trick—hiding them under the mattress. She'll lose me all my guests if I'm not careful."

"But only *your* mattress," Davina says to me when Nola's gone.

"Fiona must know I'm a finger-princess." I show her the locket with the fingerprints inside.

Davina likes the symbolism, then she picks up the serviette ring. "A ring for a princess with giant fingers." Why does that sound familiar? "And it might be saying, don't let the finger-prince slip through yours."

I think of the text Alister sent me last night: *Just got your message, but it's past midnight where you are, so unless you're carousing in a bar with a handsome Irish musician, you'll be tucked up in bed :- ) Sweet dreams. A x*

I can't tell if he's worried that I might be flirting with other men, or if he's so sure of me that he knows I wouldn't. The thought that he's on the loose in San Francisco and might be frequenting bars himself gives me a jealous pang. We might be joined by an invisible thread but we haven't made that final commitment yet, so are we even a couple?

Davina has her own plans for the day. After breakfast she sends Dervla a text asking for their mother's name and receives a one-word reply: *Peggy.*

"Peggy's short for Margaret," I say. "But Peggy who?"

Davina isn't pleased. "I know how Dervla's mind works. She thinks if I've got Mam's full name I'll try to find her myself."

"And she's right."

"Sure, but it doesn't mean I'm going to visit her without my twin sister."

"She doesn't trust you," I say. "Is that because you told her about Paris?"

Davina nods. "Everything except the fetch—in case Reverend Mother Clare is above such pagan superstitions. If she laughed at me, I'd be catapulted right back to my teens."

"How did she take it?"

"Like a psychology textbook. She went on and on about how we'd both been abused so it wasn't a surprise that I'd acted out by stealing her name. I was trying to pick up her real reaction but she's brilliant at hiding her feelings."

Davina won't be searching any online adoption lists without Peggy's surname, so she comes with me to the museum. As we stroll along under a cloudless sky, I fill her in on yesterday's revelations. She pleats her forehead at my theory that the mannequin triggered a psychic seed from Bridie—and Derek's theory about possession.

"The psychic seed's possible, but in this case it's not the same as possession, so you can stop worrying about that."

"How can you be so sure?"

"The contradiction proves it—about who was murdered. You became the murder victim but Bridie can't be both the victim and the great-granny who planted the seed."

"Yeah, I've got that far," I say. "But maybe Bridie planted a seed that turns me into Ciara?"

Davina shakes her head. "Not possible. And if your great-granny was really Ciara, she couldn't make you become Bridie."

"Even though they were twins?"

"Being twins is a clue, for sure, but you need more facts about the murder."

My head's about to explode. "Why can't my psychic experiences be simple, Davina? I'm way out of my depth with this stuff. It's scary."

"Contradictions are the enemies of secrets," Davina says. "They make chinks in their armour. There are contradictions about the murderer too. Is the man in your visions Brendon Blake, and if he is, how does the song fit with that?"

"No idea."

"Let's think up some scenarios and see if anything has the ring of truth."

The ring of truth. It was the message from my dream. Where fingers were standing like stones wearing giant rings.

"OK," I say, pleased to get my mind out of its rut. "I'll start.

Brendon was the lover of one of the twins and he wanted his lover dead. Maybe she was becoming demanding, or she was pregnant and he wanted her out of the way. But the sisters were so alike that he killed the wrong one. Then the real twin was scared for her safety and ran away. Or she was … riddled with guilt." I stop walking and Davina looks at me. "The song might not be literal that the sister was the killer. It's about guilt."

It's another chink in the armour.

"Your visions of the killer might not be literal either," Davina says. "They might be reflecting the community's belief that it was Brendon Blake who did it. Universal consciousness can be strong enough to do that. And the sister could be riddled with guilt if she killed her twin so she could take her place with Brendon, but he was executed for her crime. In shame she entered the convent –"

"Wearing the fob chain? I keep thinking about that, Davina. Would you wear the chain that killed your sister? Unless it's a trophy and you're a psychopath." Now I'm wearing it, but I race on with another scenario. "Ciara was hiding away in the convent to escape her jealous sister, but Bridie staged her own disappearance, caught up with Ciara and killed her –"

"Then took her place at Saint Scholastica's, letting Brendon take the rap back home."

I nod. "Plenty of guilt in that one. But if Brendon was executed for a murder he didn't commit, and Bridie's set me up to clear his name so she can rest in peace, it feels way too huge. And who is there to care after a hundred years?"

But there is one person. I started to care as soon as I opened the first parcel.

* * *

At the door of the exhibition, I'm pleased to see someone else on duty. A young guy with his eyes glued to his phone. Mary was generous yesterday, but now Davina and I can move around anonymously. First she takes my arm and marches me right up to the mannequin. She warned me I had to confront her again—as a test—so I take a deep breath and look at the face. The likeness to me wasn't a mirage, but she doesn't inspire a repeat of yesterday's vision. She's just an inanimate dummy. I breathe out.

"She could be you, Selkie," Davina says. "It's uncanny. But if it's not happening again, then she didn't trigger it."

"But it happened as soon as I looked at her. The lights went out, my bodice felt tight and he was bearing down on me."

"It must be something else."

She looks at the clothes. A long navy skirt over petticoats, a short jacket shaped into the waist with a peplum, a white blouse with a high collar. It's what I was wearing in my vision. The mannequin is also wearing gloves. Without checking to see if the attendant is watching, Davina pulls one of them off.

One of the dummy's fingers is missing. I gasp.

The guy on the door walks over. His nametag says *Danny*. "Don't be tampering with the displays or I'll have to ask you to leave."

"What happened to her finger?" Davina asks.

His voice wavers. "It ... dropped off."

Davina gives me a knowing look. "When did this happen?"

"Last night, right after closing," he whispers. "Mary who works here was switching off the lights and she saw this glove on the floor. She thought it had just slipped off Bridie O'Connor here, but when she went to put it back on ... she saw that the finger was missing." He crosses himself. "It was inside the glove, so she shook it out and took it away. You won't catch me doing the graveyard shift, not after this."

"What do you think is going on?" Davina asks.

"I know Bridie here isn't real," he says, "but a dead woman without a finger ... in a murder room. It's too much like Margorie McCall—and didn't that give me nightmares when I was a boy. Margorie was buried with a ring on her finger, a valuable ring and all, so in the middle of the night a grave robber digs her up and cuts her finger off to get the ring. And she wakes up!" By the wild look in Danny's eyes, he's still having the nightmares. He takes a few deep breaths. "The robber nearly died of fright himself, and some say Margorie wasn't dead, that she was—what do they call it—a 'victim of premature burial'. Mary came in this morning with the finger and some glue, like she wanted me to do the fixing. 'Not me,' I said. 'Not after Margorie. What if Bridie ... grabs me?'"

The story of Margorie is obviously just folklore, but the injury to the mannequin happened right after I had my vision. I don't like the coincidence.

"What made you pull off the glove?" I ask Davina when Danny's gone back to his post by the door.

"Intuition, I suppose. You found that ring under your mattress and I thought she might be wearing a ring. But it's the finger. You found a finger in my dream, remember?"

And a circle of fingers in my own. I tell Davina about it.

"It's another chink in the secret," she says. "The finger falling off sounds like it coincided with your vision—and now the finger's gone, so no repeat of the vision. We need more facts."

It's a relief to move to the newspaper banners and look for the article from *The Kerryman*. There's a brief report on 'Miss O'Connor's' disappearance, then the one that Bridie sent me. Without the wine stains I can read it all, and it confirms that 'Bridie' was murdered and Brendon Blake was the 'Br' who was arrested.

*There was a sensational sequel last night to the disappearance of Miss Bridie O'Connor, sixteen-year-old daughter of Mr and Mrs Thomas O'Connor. The constabulary are satisfied that the missing girl met her death last Saturday night, and have charged Brendon Blake with murder.*

*Twenty-year-old Blake was arrested at his camp outside Dingle, Co Kerry, where members of his tinker community tried to prevent the arrest. The camp had been under observation by detectives after an informant communicated that he saw Miss O'Connor on Saturday night meeting Blake along the trail between her house and the camp. A bloodstained fob chain was found in the vicinity on Wednesday morning, leading to a widespread search of the surrounding countryside by an army of volunteers. No trace has been found of the missing girl.*

*Brendon Blake is the son of Paddy Blake, both known for their skills as horsemen, tinsmiths and musicians. Their community has been returning to the area on a regular basis for many years.*

*Mr O'Connor is highly respected as a dairy farmer and manager of the Double-D Dairy Co-operative. Miss Bridie and her twin sister, Miss Ciara, are well known for their musical duets. The O'Connor family moved from Cork to Dingle when Mr O'Connor took up the position of dairy manager. Their property in Chapel Lane on the outskirts of town borders the tinkers' camp. It appears that Mr O'Connor's generosity in allowing the tinkers to draw water from his well may have brought Blake into contact with the twins.*

*When his daughter Bridie was not in her bed on Sunday morning, Mr O'Connor raised the alarm. Blake was arrested at 7 pm and charged with murder.*

*The constabulary are inclined to think that a horse was used to transport the young woman's body along the boreen that leads to the cliff at Beenbawn, where she was put into the sea, perhaps wrapped in a rug to weigh her down.*

Accompanying the article is an enlarged mug shot of Brendon Blake. It's grainy, but his eyes are glaring at the camera with a defiance that's palpable. His moustache is unkempt and the stubble on his strong chin gives him a rakish look. These days he'd be described as 'hot'. I half close my eyes but his face doesn't look familiar.

I imagine Bridie and Ciara laughing at his jokes as they all drew water from the well. Did he want both of them, or just one of them? And did that make one of the trio crazy enough to kill?

Reading the report again, one word catches my attention: *informant.* Yesterday Mary named him as James Sullivan, the young man in the photo Bridie sent me. Nephew of Thomas or Orla by marriage, so not a blood relation. It's what Davina surmised from the photo. And Mary said something else, but it eludes me; something that made James sound eager. It fits with his wandering eye and the bulge in his pants.

I find the report from the trial that names James Sullivan as the informant. Some of his testimony was printed verbatim in the press for a no-doubt insatiable audience. I read his explanation of what he was doing on the path near the camp, which wasn't directly on his way home:

*After the bonfire on Midsummer Eve there was some good*

*fiddle-playing going on over at Feeney's ceili-house. Feeney had made some fine poteen and me and the boys drank too much and gambled too much. When Feeney finally closed the door on us, there was talk about finding somewhere to keep ceili-ing—the moon was high and we had a bottle of poteen with us. We knocked on a few doors, but people were in their beds and weren't interested in our shenanigans. Then someone suggested the ol' ruined church in the faerie ring not far from the tinkers' camp, but we'd have none of that—not with the ghosts and faeries for company—so we all decided to go home. But on the way back, I got lost. It must have been the drink and the talk of faeries made me lose my way. Next thing I'm hearing a strange rustling and moaning coming from the shadows at the side of the path. It scared me nearly to death, I tell you, thinking I'd stepped onto a faerie path after talking about them too much and attracting their attention. I pulled myself behind a tree, still as a standing stone, hoping the faeries would pass me by. That's why they didn't notice me. Not the faeries. It was Miss O'Connor. With him. Brendon Blake.*

The detail he offered surprises me and Mary's words come back: *He couldn't wait to tell what he'd seen.*

I read on. He was asked if he knew which twin it was with Brendon Blake.

*I couldn't see them, but I guessed soon enough it was a tinker up to no good with one of our Dingle girls, it being so close to their camp. There was a lot of kissing and rustling, so I knew Blake had her up against the well with her petticoats pulled up.*

I can almost hear the gasp from the public gallery. And feel them turning against Brendon.

*I didn't want to feel the tip of his knife between my ribs, so I stayed still. Then the girl spoke and I knew it was Bridie. Her voice is different from Ciara's. 'Oh Brendon,' she said, 'that tickles.'*

Her words hit me with an insight: Brendon wasn't raping her; she was willing.

Then I wonder who else was there on that path, overhearing the same words as James Sullivan. If the other sister was there, as the song suggests, James either didn't see her—or didn't tell. And after the lovers parted, she choked her sister to death in a rage fuelled by jealousy and hid the body where it was never found.

But it doesn't match my vision. And unlike the drowning in the song, a choking murder would require physical strength—and nerve—not letting go of that chain until there was no air left.

That means the killer was unlikely to be one of the twins. Unless she had help. Not from Brendon Blake ... from James. He might have caught her with her hands around her sister's throat—and finished the job for her. Was James Sullivan the man in my vision? Did he and the remaining sister collude to let Brendon hang?

# Chapter 13

After my ghoulish investigations, I'm desperate for some fresh air and Davina agrees. Nola has packed us lunchboxes and, as she foretold, it is indeed a fine day. Across the road in the park, everyone is making the most of it with picnic rugs spread on emerald lawns and squealing children chasing each other. So much vibrant life is a great antidote for murder.

We sit on the grass and eat our sandwiches. Davina checks her phone but there's no news from Dervla.

"Do you like the name Peggy?" I ask.

She shrugs. "To be honest it doesn't sound real to me—I can't match the name with the picture I have in my head. Not magical enough. I so much want her to be magical, Selkie."

I reach over and touch her hand. "Careful. Mothers are like daughters. They don't come made to order."

She nods. "I'll know soon enough what she's like. It's just the waiting that's messing with my head."

We move onto my theories about James and look at the family photo again.

"Do you recognise him?" she asks.

"Only the moustache. And Brendon's got one too. James wasn't the sisters' flesh and blood so maybe he had his own designs on one of them. Marry the boss's daughter and become the next manager of the dairy co-op?"

"If he caught one twin murdering her sister," she says, "and what you saw was him finishing the job, it would give him power. He'd help her cover it up, but he'd want something in exchange—her hand in marriage and all the trappings of a son-in-law in a family without a son."

"But he didn't marry either of them. After Brendon's execution, a girl called Ciara O'Connor took holy orders, then a girl called Bridie O'Connor became my great-grandmother."

Davina knows what I'm getting at. "The body of the murdered twin was never found, so were those two young women Ciara *and* Bridie, or just one of them playing with names?"

While I was reading the newspaper accounts, Davina was examining a display case of artefacts from the Irish Traveller community. Once known as 'tinkers' or 'pavees', they were itinerant tinsmiths and horse traders living in wagons and tents.

"What kinds of artefacts?" I ask.

"Copper tools, old kitchenware, musical instruments. I thought I might pick up a scent of something useful but all I got was alienation. There was a poster stating that these days Travellers are more settled, part of the community, but when I was growing up they were treated with scorn. I might have been a good-for-nothing, out-of-wedlock brat, but I wasn't as low as a tinker."

* * *

We return to the museum and, perhaps because of the sunshine, the exhibition hall is almost empty. At the door I stop and think about calling it a day. The whole mystery with its contradictions is exhausting and I've got the rest of the week. But Davina will be gone to meet her mother soon, and then I'll be on my own with the puzzle, and sometimes pushing through makes something pop.

Along with the Traveller artefacts there are old photos. Scruffy children are leaning out of horse-drawn caravans, while others are huddled in front of campfires circled by tents. I gaze at them, imagining how hard life must have been. What would make a young middle-class woman turn her back on comfort and choose a life on the road? Only a fierce love. But if that's what one of the twins and Brendon Blake were contemplating, what happened to turn it into murder?

An attendant wanders over. Danny has departed and been replaced by another elderly woman. She cuts a different figure from Mary, with her dyed red hair and mini skirt revealing skinny legs in striped tights. Her nametag says *Sheila*.

I nod towards Brendon's mug shot. "Brendon Blake maintained his innocence right to the end."

"There was gossip," she says. "But no evidence."

"James Sullivan?"

It's the only encouragement she needs. "Blake couldn't argue with the bloodied necklace, but what was Sullivan doing on the path that night? All that rubbish about getting lost and faeries and ghosts. He was following Bridie, more likely. These days he'd be called a stalker."

Davina and I share a look. This is the kind of stuff I'm after.

"Why do you say that?" I ask.

"It runs in the family. One of his descendants is in jail for it."

"He had children?"

"He managed to father at least two, and the girls said it was rape. Those babies were never going to amount to anything except trouble. And trouble breeds trouble."

So much for my theory that James helped one twin hide the other's body in exchange for marriage.

"They tried to make Ciara marry him," Sheila adds.

Shit. "What happened?"

"Thomas and Orla O'Connor weren't getting any younger, and she'd lost a few babies before she had the twins. They wanted a son-in-law to help in the business, but after Bridie was murdered Ciara took to her bed and refused to see anyone. So she wasn't going to find a husband in that state. And there was Sullivan, hovering like the pong of a peat bog." She wrinkles her nose.

"But they didn't marry?"

"The gossip goes in two directions. Take your pick. Ciara ran away rather than marry Sullivan—she was known for her tantrums. Or she refused to marry him and her father sent her away."

"Where did she go?"

"By the sound of your accent, Australia." At my shocked expression she points to a photo of the twins. "You're what's called a spitting image. And Bridie was murdered before she could have any children, so you must be descended from Ciara."

We're right back to the contradictions. That it was Ciara's name that came to me after I put on the necklace. Why would Bridie pretend to be Ciara—until she moved to Australia? Changing identities more than once is the only thing that fits with what I know.

"How do you know all this?" Davina asks Sheila.

"Here at the hysterical society," Sheila quips, "we're great believers in oral history. A few people corroborated Sullivan, said they'd seen Bridie with the tinker before that night. And one thing that's interesting is Ciara's testimony."

My excitement mounts. "Where's that? I haven't seen it."

"Because it doesn't exist. At the trial, her parents answered all the questions about Bridie and her movements that night, even though the girls shared a room. Ciara was described as too ill to be put on the stand." She looks at each of us for our reaction. "Suspicious, isn't it?"

"She must have been devastated by the murder," I say. "Her twin sister. It sounds like she had a breakdown."

"She's your what—great-grandmother?"

I nod. Or great-great-aunt.

"Well, pardon me for speaking ill of the dead," she continues, "but I think her parents shut her up."

"Why?"

"Ciara knew what happened. What if she felt responsible for her sister's death? What if the wrong girl was murdered? They wouldn't want her saying too much at the trial."

What was it that Mary said yesterday in her garbled account? *... the girls were twins so who was stepping out with the tinker behind her father's back? Maybe Bridie was killed by mistake.* It seems to be a favourite theory around here.

"But Ciara's testimony couldn't have saved Brendon, could it?" I ask. Unless she knew who really killed her sister—which would explain the guilt.

"What if one sister was jealous of the other?" Sheila says. "One of them was Blake's lover—Bridie they said. What if the other one wanted a kiss from the tinker? The girls looked alike but Blake would know soon enough which one he was kissing."

I remember the squeal that James heard: *That tickles.* If James was telling the truth, then Sheila's right: Brendon would have known in that moment that the woman in his arms wasn't his lover. That was the reaction of an innocent. Is that what got her killed?

"You're looking shell-shocked," Sheila says. "Get some rest and come back tomorrow. Because there's one more thing you won't have seen." She points to a printed book open in a display case just inside the door. "It's owned by the society and only a handful of copies still exist. Back in the 1930s, a journalist investigated every murder in this exhibition. His research made it possible, in fact. He tracked down people who were still alive and they told him things they didn't say at the time, mostly because they weren't asked. There's an account in there from the maid in the O'Connor house."

My heart does a little skip.

"We've been told not to unlock the case under any circumstances," she continues. "But when you come back tomorrow, you'll see that it's open at the page that interests you."

On our way out, I remember my promise to Mary about the family photo. Sheila is pleased to see it. She makes a copy and we leave.

* * *

By 10 pm, Davina and I are propping up the bar in the pub below the B&B with glasses of Guinness in front of us. Nola was determined to get us here tonight because her nephew's band is playing—aptly named Tinker's Cuss—and she thinks it'll put the colour back into our cheeks.

The band hasn't started yet, but the place is noisy with

chatter and I'm trying to get into the mood. My phones are in my back pockets and one of them vibrates.

"Alister," I say to Davina as I pounce on his text.

*Thinking of you*, he writes. *Negotiations stalled. She could be Fleur's double, only tougher. Trying to take me to the cleaners in exchange for news of Deshi. She knows I'll pay, but does she have the goods? I hope your secrets are rising like bubbles in champagne. Can't wait to share a bottle. And other things. Your finger-prince, A x*

Poor Alister. Fleur died when they were just teenagers, so her look-alike niece must be stirring up old feelings. How is he thinking straight?

*Can't wait to share a bottle ... and other things.* I stare at the creamy head on my glass of beer and remember how attuned Alister is. In spite of his quest and our distance, he's with me—joined by an invisible red cord. But I haven't even peeped into his bedroom on my way to the bathroom. Too scared. And now his text is stirring up all those dormant pheromones.

Distance makes me brave.

*Bubbly, tick. Other things, double tick. Secrets tying me in knots. Tell her you'll double the reward if her tip leads you to Deshi. Your finger-princess, S x*

The band begins, drowning out all thoughts other than being here. There's a female fiddle player with wild black hair that she tosses around in a fetching manner, two older guys playing a smaller version of bagpipes and an accordion, a stocky woman beating the rhythm on a bodhrán, and a tall slim guy playing a lively melody on a recorder. Davina grins and bops in time with the music. Nola was right—this is good for the soul.

The barman is as energetic as the musicians, running along

the bar taking orders and sprinting back in-between to pour pints. It's great that we got this corner stool to share because now it's standing room only. When the band takes a break, Davina rushes off to the loo. The musicians come up for their free drinks and the recorder player is squashed against me. As he turns with his beer he's bumped from behind and spills it down the sleeve of my shirt. I jump off the stool and bump into him, making it worse.

He puts his beer down on the bar and brushes his other hand down my sleeve, shouting an apology.

"Don't worry about it," I shout back.

But he's already calling to the barman. "Ah, Séamus, look what I've done, will you? Bring us a towel, and another drink for the young lady." Then he slips a hand under my elbow and ushers me backwards onto my stool. "You won't want to be giving up your seat or you'll never get it back."

Séamus hands over a dry handtowel and the recorder player gets to work scrubbing at my sleeve.

"Enough," I shout. "I'm fine."

He smiles a crooked smile and leans in close to make himself heard. "It's the way I meet all the girls, but my aim is usually better. Down the front." He nods towards my cleavage, hidden by my shirt, then puts out his hand. "Finn Cormack."

His flirting is making me uncomfortable and the strangest words come out of my mouth. "Bridie," I say. "Bridie O'Connor."

He frowns for a moment. "An Irish name but an Australian accent. Before the night's over I'll woo you with the ceili version of 'Waltzing Matilda'."

It should feel shocking to call myself after the woman everyone thinks was murdered, even if she was my ancestor.

But it doesn't. Davina isn't back yet, and no-one in the pub knows my real name so Bridie's giving me a cover. But why do I think I need it? There's no harm in talking to this guy. It's clear he's got a lot of charm, and in spite of my wet sleeve his company is making me feel warm.

"Is the recorder your favourite instrument?" I ask, trying to find some charm of my own.

"The recorder?" He pulls out his phone and presses a button. "This is a fecking recorder."

"What's it called then, the thing you play?"

"A penny whistle. Invented in Ireland by "

"A girl called Penny."

We both laugh, and he tells me it was an Irishman who made the whistles, before moving to England and selling them from village to village out of his cart. Perhaps the name 'penny whistle' came from the price he charged for them, but no-one knows.

"It's also called a tin whistle," he says, "made from tin by the tinkers way back."

"Tinker's Cuss," I say as the spectre of Brendon Blake crosses my mind.

He nods. "It seemed like a good name after a few pints."

"It makes your band sound ..." He grins as I avoid words like 'dismissive'. "Relaxed."

"Relaxed will do us just fine, Bridie."

"Does your whistle have a name?" I ask, unable to shake the subject of names.

"How did you guess? And it's not Penny."

"What then?"

He answers in rhyme. "Three guesses I'll grant ye, one, two, three. Then if you're wrong, a drink you'll buy me."

"And if I'm right?"

"You won't be, but I'll buy you one of course."

I say the first name that pops into my head:  "Betty the Bugle." It makes us laugh. I try again, using more associations with whistle: blow, fingers, pipe, smoke. "Smokey."

"N O P E," he spells. "Last chance."

A sudden urge to find the right answer overcomes me. "Can I hold it?"

He pulls the whistle from his back pocket and hands it to me, looking bemused. And as soon as it's in my hand, a word pops into my head.

"You've got something," he says. "Don't ever play poker, Bridie O'Connor."

"Princess," I say.  The name I used earlier in my text to Alister.

Finn looks flabbergasted but recovers quickly. "OK, that's pretty impressive, or a good guess. You'll get your drink, but here's another challenge.  Tell me how she came to be my Princess."

It's a pretty obvious name for a guy to call his favourite possession now that I think about it—akin to Gollum and his 'precious'—but I keep holding the whistle and say whatever pops into my head. "Prince. But your whistle is female."

He throws his head back. "You're good. But you're thinking of Prince the musician."

I'm thinking of Alister.

"It's more cryptic than that," he says.

There's something else there, but I've lost it. I hand Princess back. "You got me. Now get me ..."

"A drink."

We've hit it off and he moves a little closer. He's not good-looking with his round face circled by fair curls, but in a boyish way he's cute. And he knows it. He must be younger than me, late twenties, and I'm flattered by the attention. But at the back of my mind a little bell rings a warning. It must be because I'm a long way from home, a long way from the complications I feel around Alister, and I've borrowed Bridie's name. It's as if my identity has slipped away again and that's where the danger lies.

Davina returns just as Finn's moving off. "A queue in the ladies a mile long," she says. "More proof that God's a man. Isn't that guy from the band?"

"He spilled beer on my sleeve then chatted me up."

"Creative."

During the next bracket, Finn doesn't take his eyes off me as he runs his fingers up and down Princess. It's an open invitation, and I hear Alister's voice speaking his other text: ... *unless you're carousing in a bar with a handsome Irish musician.*

At the end of their gig there's a call for one last song. Finn signals to the others and shouts, "For our friends and lovers from Down Under." They launch into a rollicking version of 'Waltzing Matilda', inspiring people to dance. Afterwards, as Finn is looking for me in the crowd, I grab Davina's hand and drag her out the door and up the stairs. In our room, I burst into tears.

"Did you see that musician watching me the whole time he was running his fingers up and down that bloody whistle? I was flirting with him while you were in the loo. Finn Cormack. I'm supposed to be in love with Alister but I'm terrified to sleep with him, so instead I'm giving any cute guy the impression that I'm up for it. When he was doing that thing with his fingers, I even thought about sex."

Davina pulls me onto the bed beside her. "Sex with Finn?"

"He wanted it."

"Of course *he* wanted it. He's a man. He's in a band. It goes with the territory. His gigs must give him access to lots of willing girls. But you didn't run into his arms, Selkie, you ran out the door."

"I suppose." I blow my nose. "Alister even predicted it." I tell her about his text.

"If he can make jokes about it, that says he trusts you—and you've proved him right. Finn's just reminded you that you can be aroused. Because of him you know that it's not the sex itself that's making you afraid of sleeping with Alister. It's something else."

I think of the invisible cord getting tangled as life throws curve balls like Finn Cormack at us, but never breaking. Alister might be thousands of miles away, but the distance and the offer of a stranger have sharpened my perception about how I feel.

But when I tumble into bed, the dream I have is disturbing. I'm standing in a doorway to a pub, like the one downstairs but the laneway is dark, lit only by a distant streetlamp. I'm observing myself from outside, as if my soul has slipped from my body and is hovering above it. There's strange music coming from the pub and I'm drawn to knock on the door, but when it opens a couple emerges. It's Alister, with a beautiful Chinese princess on his arm. Fleur. They don't see me because they only have eyes for each other. As they walk away, the light spilling from the open doorway splits my face in two. Half is dark, half is light. I'm a hybrid being living on the threshold of two worlds—the lonely lane and the busy pub. I'm on the brink, unsure which choice is safer: to stay hidden by the dark or to step into the glare.

My silent scream wakes me up, and I realise there's something under my mattress. I know it's probably down to Fiona, and the sounds of Davina breathing in the other bed calm me. But after the dream, the thought of the bedside lamp seems more frightening than the dark and I can't stir myself to turn it on. Eventually I drift off, until I'm woken again by the rays of a weak sun seeping around the edges of the curtain.

I get up straight away and check what I've been sleeping on. A knife. A bread and butter knife.

At the sight of it, I reach for the pendant lying on the bedside table. Fashioned from a knife handle. I've been so focused on the chain, I've forgotten about the pendant.

# Chapter 14

"Get Nola to recommend a jeweller," Davina says. "If the pendant belonged to Bridie, it might have been the fashion back then. A local jeweller's likely to have seen something like it, from a deceased estate or an auction."

It's a good idea. I've also got an appointment with an open book at the museum. Davina doesn't want to miss the maid's-eye view of the O'Connors either, but first she wants to search the adoption records online.

"I've been thinking about Peggy," she says. "It's the kind of nickname she might have had as a teenager. And it's not so common."

"But they treated those unmarried mothers like criminals. Surely they'd have recorded her birth name rather than her nickname?"

Her face falls. "I have to give it a try, Selkie."

Of course she does. Waiting for Dervla is killing her so she has to take some action. But we both know she'll come up empty.

When I have a quiet word with Nola outside the break-fast room, she accepts the knife and offers another apology. "You'll be thinking I'm not a fit mother, letting Fiona play with knives."

"It's only a butter knife—it's harmless." But it might have given my nightmare its sharp edge.

* * *

I forgot to ask Nola about a jeweller, so I wander the narrow streets letting my intuition guide me. A shop called Timepieces of Tralee attracts me but I'm taken aback when I step inside and come face to face with Finn Cormack emerging from a backroom in response to the bell on the door.

"Well, if it isn't the girl who gave me the slip last night. But she's so overcome with remorse she's tracked me down to apologise. I accept." He takes a bow.

Part of me wants to turn around and find a jeweller with less cheek, but that feels churlish. And last night I met a jeweller without realising it. He might be the person I need.

"If you're a jeweller," I say, "and not just a charmer, I might be in the right place."

As I take the chain and pendant from my neck, Finn turns professional, spreading a velvet cloth on the counter. He pulls out an eyeglass for a better look.

"Albert chain. Circa late 1800s. Eighteen-carat gold. Been repaired." He looks up. "Worth a bit. If I hadn't been distracted by your eyes last night, I might have noticed it around your neck. Then I would have been *really* charming."

He winks and I relax. He is a charmer, but I won't be falling for it.

He picks up the pendant and lets out a whistle. "Do you know what this is? Is it the real reason you tracked me down?"

"A knife handle, isn't it—bamboo-style, fashioned into a

locket."

He waits for more, but I've finished.

"It might be a locket now," he says, "but it used to be something else. And I mean since it was buttering toast." He picks it up and takes it through to his workshop. "Come on," he calls over his shoulder. "And don't get the willies when you see what I'm up to. It's all reversible."

First he opens the lid of the locket, flipping it right back on its hinge. Then he uses a tool to push out the base of the bamboo tube so it's open at each end. Next he unscrews each of the different-coloured stones that form buttons down the length of the pendant, and puts them on the bench. The segmented tube now has a row of unevenly spaced holes where the gems used to be.

He holds it up. "Have you guessed yet?"

It's the holes that give it away, but something's missing. "It looks like ... a penny whistle. Without the part where you blow."

"The fipple."

He goes to a leather satchel and pulls out an instrument case containing Princess and several fipples. With a flourish he takes one and inserts it into the top of my pendant where the notch cut for the locket catch creates an air-hole. It's perfect.

Finn gives me a wink and begins to play a jig. The workshop is a tiny space but we dance around each other laughing.

"It's much more inspiring than an empty locket," I say when we stop and catch our breath.

"You'll have to learn how to play it," he says. "I happen to know a very good teacher."

"You must be surrounded by girls half my age, so stop coming on to me."

"Sure the Tralee girls won't leave me alone, but your accent is much more *inspiring*. Not to mention your jewellery." But he's got the message. He pulls a couple of stools out from under the workbench and we sit down. "So tell me, Bridie O'Connor, how did you come upon this?"

"I'll tell you the whole story," including my real name, "but first, where do you think it was made? If you don't know anything of its history, you'll be coming to it with an empty mind."

The door of the shop tinkles and he leaves me to deal with a customer collecting a repair. Then he sits down again and picks up his eyeglass, rolling the whistle around in his fingers.

"It's too crude for a craftsman, but the maker had some skill. And he knew his whistles—the length and diameter needed for a working instrument, and where to drill the holes for each note."

"Is that why they're not evenly spaced?"

"Yeah. The position of the gemstones gives away its hidden past. And recycling it from a piece of discarded cutlery—I'm not sure if it was a knife or a fork—says two things. Late nineteenth century, the same age as the fob chain." He pauses. "And the handiwork of a tinker."

Shit. Brendon Blake.

He sees the light dawning behind my eyes. "Your turn, Bridie. How close did I get?"

First I tell him my name.

He's miffed that I misled him, but when I tell him the story of the real Bridie, he remembers her from the exhibition.

"And here I was thinking your accent was fascinating. That's just the tip of the iceberg isn't it, *Selkie*?" He's still getting used to my name so I have to put up with some sea puns.

"This whistle-cum-locket has some provenance—worn by a so-called murdered girl, probably made by her so-called murderer. It'd be of interest to a collector if you're thinking of sending it to auction. I could arrange that for you."

I shake my head. "It's a family heirloom. You've revealed its secret—I could never have discovered that on my own." Nor if I'd stayed in Honolulu. Davina was right—it needed an Irish jeweller. And a whistle player. "But I want to know why my great-grandmother sent it to me."

"Well, I'm not sure I can help you with that but I doubt it was ever a locket. From where I'm sitting, the lids each end, the stones masking the finger holes, it was a penny whistle disguised as a locket."

"But the whipple's missing."

"Fipple," he says. I'm getting my fipples mixed up with my wimples. "And a fipple's small enough to hide somewhere else. But the beautiful part of the instrument could be worn as a piece of jewellery, hidden in plain sight."

I think about how his theory works into the puzzle. "It proves that Brendon Blake was seeing one of the O'Connor twins in secret. He could have given her the pendant fashioned from his own penny whistle. That would be a very special gift."

Finn nods. "A gift of love." The gleam in his eyes says he's moved. "So where does that leave us?"

"It's a good reason for my great-grandmother to send me the locket," I say, thinking aloud. "Perhaps it was always empty, now that we know its true function. But which twin did Brendon Blake give it to behind her father's back?"

"You said the murder happened in Dingle," Finn says, "but you're searching for answers in Tralee."

"The museum is here."

"But not the sights and smells of where it happened."

"Finn, it happened over a century ago."

He throws back his head and laughs. "You might have a Celtic name, Selkie Moon, but you've got a few things to learn about Ireland. All our history is carried in every rock and every field. Whatever happened in 1896, it's all still here, just waiting for you to *feel* it. That's how you guessed the name of my Princess."

And that's when I know where the name came from. Helped by my red heart. Another coincidence? "You play her with your fingers. Fingers, finger*prints*, prince, princess."

His eyes widen. "You really have got the gift." Another customer enters the shop and he stands to go and serve them. "Look, I'm going to Dingle this afternoon to pick up some repair jobs from the crystal shop. I can drop you off wherever you want."

Dingle, where the murder took place. By getting my information from a museum display, I've been able to play detective while keeping the horror at arm's length.

Finn watches the emotions at war behind my eyes. Of course I'm going to Dingle, but I don't want him to think it's his idea.

"Wonderful," I say. "Thank you. It'll be more fun than catching the bus."

* * *

After arranging to meet Finn in a couple of hours, I stop by Nola's to pick up Davina. She's had no luck finding an unmarried mother listed as Peggy or anything else of interest. As we make our way to the museum again I distract her from her disappointment with news of Finn and the pendant.

"It's another reason for meeting him," she says. "He's tied up in your quest somehow."

"I hope not. His flirting is annoying."

But the whistle is another chink in the secret, and now we're about to read the interview with the O'Connors' maid.

Sheila's been good to her word and the book is open at the right double-page spread. Davina blocks the attendant's view while I photograph both pages, then we huddle over it and start reading.

Sibby Dolan worked as a maid for the O'Connor family since their arrival in Dingle, when Thomas took on the management of the Double-D Co-operative. The girls were thirteen at the time and Sibby was twenty, only seven years their senior, so when the murder happened she was twenty-three. By the time the journalist interviewed her in 1937 she was in her mid-sixties—and at the same time my great-grandmother and Patrick Ryan were the parents of my teenage grandfather and living in Melbourne. From the words attributed to her, it seems Sibby was still loyal to the family even after forty years, but some of the facts are telling.

*With his new position at the Dairy Co-operative, Mr Thomas O'Connor wanted a maid around the house to allow his wife and daughters to join the middle class. They couldn't do that with their hands in a laundry tub. The co-op was a new venture so there wasn't a lot of money at the start. I got the job because I could be more than a maid—but you want to be knowing about the twins. I was clever with my hands, and with my help the girls made dresses in a fashionable style, and I showed them tricks such as how to make a basic dress look plain or fancy with a change of collar and cuffs.*

*They were both schooled by the nuns in Dingle. Miss Bridie was the clever one, reading and writing and playing the piano. Miss Ciara was a simple soul after what happened to her as a baby. It was Bridie got the brains, you see, and Ciara who got starved of air when they were born. She was never quite right from the day she took her first breath. But she was blessed with a heart of gold and the voice of a nightingale.*

*They often played tricks on everyone by pretending to be each other. Bridie, being the firstborn, wore a ring from her grandmother, but that didn't help if the girls were wearing gloves. You always knew who was who as soon as they opened their mouths. Ciara was one to giggle at the drop of a hat, but Bridie was becoming a woman.*

*For their sixteenth birthdays, Bridie got the watch chain she'd begged her father for—the very one they say killed her. She was very determined was Miss Bridie. Miss Ciara got a pretty brooch in the shape of a bird. She loved birds. Mrs O'Connor planned a party in the garden, but many of the neighbours sent their apologies. The farmers in the co-op knew it was their duty to come, but their wives were wary of the faerie ring up behind the house. There was an old church there too, but because of the faeries they forbid the children to go near it.*

*I remember the party because it was only a few days later that I was sent away. It was a beautiful day and the girls looked so pretty in the summer frocks we'd made. I made sandwiches and party punch, and the adults did their best to keep an eye on the children while they played Blind Man's Buff. Ciara joined in too, but I was surprised when Bridie did, her being too much of a young lady for childish things. At the end of the game Bridie couldn't be found and everyone was afeared she'd been stolen away by the faeries. One little boy started crying that he'd thought of hiding in the faery ring until he saw two faeries there. Was it Bridie being taken away? The child's mother spanked him for disobeying her. She said he'd probably been stolen too and the faeries had sent a useless changeling in his place, and when they went home she would sit him on a hot shovel to burn the faerie out of him. The other children started crying, but just before the party was spoiled Bridie came back safe and sound with mud on her dress. She wouldn't say where her hiding place was but she must have fallen asleep.*

*You want to know about the night of the murder, but there's nothing I can tell you that wasn't in the newspapers for all to see. Bridie and her father had a row. I can't tell you what they argued about—I'm no earwigger—but she was sent to her room, Ciara too. I never saw either of them again.*

*The next morning Mrs O'Connor came to me. In such a state she was. Something terrible had happened, she said. The constabulary were going to be called and Mr O'Connor wanted me out of the way to protect me. She gave me a reference that said I'd worked as a governess—something I'd only ever dreamed of being—and a letter of introduction to an agency in Dublin. I still have them to this day. I was given only five minutes to pack my things and was bundled onto a trap for the train in Tralee. It was only afterwards that I read about the murder. I was upset and curious, but grateful to be out of it.*

In whispers, Davina and I pick out the interesting facts. Fear of faeries didn't just apply to James Sullivan—it was a superstition that controlled the whole community. Bridie came back with mud on her dress. Ciara was a giggler, a child in a woman's body—something Stella once said about my mother. Bridie fought with her father the night of the murder. And Sibby was bundled out of the way with a glowing reference, making her unable to report on the most important thing—which twin was murdered.

Surely it was Ciara at the well that night, squealing like a child that Brendon's touch tickled. For some reason she'd gone there in Bridie's place, wearing her chain, and was then murdered with it. And afterwards the family lied, saying it was Bridie who'd died. Then they'd labelled her Ciara, locked her away and prevented her from giving evidence. Why?

My first thought is that she was pregnant. She was sixteen, Brendon was twenty—their relationship could have gone that far. Except it doesn't fit with what Sheila said: that she refused to marry James Sullivan. If Bridie was pregnant to Brendon, surely the family would have forced her to marry James to prevent the scandal of an out-of-wedlock birth. The reason for the subterfuge must be something more complicated.

While Davina frowns in thought, I send the photos of Sibby's interview to Derek and ask for his take on the folklore.

* * *

On our way back to Nola's I get an email from Dervla, which is something I wasn't expecting.

"It's an introduction to a retreat centre not far from Tralee," I tell Davina. "They run business programs with a spiritual element and they've been let down by a presenter for a two-day conference at the end of the week. Dervla says they'd like to talk to me about a gig."

I stop walking and look at Davina. "I didn't tell her I run seminars."

Davina comes clean. "I had to tell her, Selkie. She went on and on, wanting to know all about you and what I'd told you about the past. I didn't want to let on how much you know

170

about us swapping places when we were teens, so I told her about your seminar work instead."

"OK, now she knows I'm not a journalist. But why would Dervla want to help me?"

"Because you're my friend." Pause. "You could use the money, couldn't you?"

This gig is Davina's doing, I'm sure of it, asking Dervla if she could find me something. But after checking my bank account this morning, the injection of funds is tempting.

Back at the B&B, Davina goes up to our room to research forced adoptions in the 1970s, hoping to find something useful. I call Abbeymare Retreat Centre, wondering if she oversold Being Sleek to Dervla and if it's a suitable fit for their program.

Sister Kevin has a thin elderly voice, which makes her sound very traditional. She's already looked at my website—information courtesy of Mother Clare—and thinks Being Sleek would be a delightful addition to the Soul Work conference.

"Seal work is soul work," she gushes. "Communion with our aquatic cousins."

A traditional old thing with a spark of imagination.

She tells me the sessions will be ninety minutes long, so I make some serious mental adjustments to my usual two-day program.

"We'll do some group mind-mapping," I say, thinking aloud, "so I'll need poster paper and sticky notes."

"Ooh, that sounds ... quirky. Tell me more."

I haven't got to the quirky part yet. "I'll get them brainstorming the qualities we can learn from seals—for our businesses and personal lives."

She starts brainstorming herself. "Playful. And busy. Their lives are perfectly balanced. And they know their place in God's scheme of things. No hubris. Humans aren't so good at that."

I agree, and add a few more things to the list of materials, then suggest she takes a description of the course from my website.

The centre is hard to reach by bus, she tells me, so she'll send someone to pick me up from Nola's on Thursday afternoon. Mother Clare has insisted that they include my accommodation. It couldn't be more perfect.

# Chapter 15

The drive to Dingle is a rollicking one, if that's the right word for Finn using both sides of the narrow road as he pleases. Focused on watching for oncoming cars, I only get fleeting glimpses of undulating fields and picturesque cottages. It's a hair-raising reminder of the old joke: after joining the EU, Ireland was going to switch to driving on the right, but to give the community time to adjust, for the first six months they'd make it optional.

Meanwhile, Finn is doing all the talking. He's trying to educate me about Irish Travellers, his eyes leaving the road to grin at me way too often. Perhaps it works with the younger girls but it's wearing thin with me.

"They're not gypsies, you know," he says. "They're ethnic Irish."

"It must have been a hard life. And cold." Even in June I'm wearing a sweatshirt. The winters here must be punishing.

Finn turns wistful. "I would have liked that ... the freedom of the road."

"They don't travel any more though," I say, my heart in my mouth as a car crests the hill and misses us. "I read that at the museum."

"Some still do. You see them camping in the old places. Until the work runs out. Then they're gone."

"What kind of work? In Brendon Blake's day there were pots to mend."

And girls to seduce; that hasn't changed.

"And instruments to play." He laughs. "These days they still deal in scrap metal and horses, breed racing dogs. Some do physical work that other people won't. They get by."

The villages we pass through are tiny, just a few huddled-together buildings including at least one pub. And there are few houses clustered around the fringes of the towns; instead they seem to be dotted across the landscape, isolated and lonely.

When the road dips into Dingle, the undulating hills flatten out into a low township wrapped around a bay with two headlands jutting out to sea. Behind the town, twin peaks disappear into mist. I can't get away from twins.

Finn parks in a small open lot and I breathe with relief that we've arrived in one piece. A light drizzle accentuates the brightly coloured shopfronts clinging to the narrow pavements. But in spite of the vibrant paint, there's an outpost quality to the place, as if the hardship of their history is imprinted beneath the warm facades. This is Gaelic territory, as the signs in both languages confirm.

Finn surprises me by suggesting I show the pendant to his crystal lady. "She'll know if the stones mean anything. Back in Victorian times they chose gems for their mystical powers."

It's an angle I haven't thought of. "Did the tinkers believe in magic?"

"Of course, but no more than everyone else around here. Those gems are an odd assortment though, so there's a fine chance they mean something. Pixie will know."

Pixie?

We run across the wet road to a shop called Stepping Stones. As water drips down my neck from an overflowing roof, I catch a glimpse of the window display full of purple satin and dream-catchers.

"It rains here every day," I say as we rush inside, "but none of the buildings have awnings or eaves."

"You haven't made the acquaintance of an Atlantic gale, I see. Awnings make the best flying decapitators. In some places people have to tie their roofs down with rocks."

The woman behind the counter has bright red hair dragged up into a topknot, taking the corners of her eyes with it. To complete the image she's gone heavy on the eyeliner and donned a tie-dyed kaftan over her full figure. Finn introduces us.

When he asks her to look at the stones on the pendant, she's intrigued. "Let's see now. Have you identified any of them, Finn?"

"The precious ones—ruby and emerald and diamond. And this looks like ivory."

Pixie doesn't get out an eyeglass but moves her hand over the gems. "The messages are jumbled. Can I hold them one at a time?"

I nod and Finn unscrews the unidentified ones. She rolls each one around in her palm, closes her eyes and waits. It's not unlike Coral's process, but a little more conventional—using her hands instead of her feet, wearing a kaftan instead of a muumuu. And the bus shelter is missing.

"Iolite," she says about the one that I hoped might be a sapphire. "Deep blue on top, but see how it's almost colourless from the side? And this golden one is ... beryl."

"Like the woman's name?" I ask.

"The same. Gems make good names. Jade, Amber … Coral."

Did she just pick up my thought?

"Do any of these stones mean anything?" I ask as Finn screws them back into the holes with his musician's fingers.

"Well, the pendant's from the late nineteenth century, you said. They were mad about anything oriental back then so that explains the bamboo. And each stone has mystical powers, but the Victorians also invented acrostic jewellery. A collection of different stones like this might be spelling something."

I don't know what she means.

"Are they in the right order?" she asks Finn.

He pulls a face. "As if I'd mix them up."

Pixie takes out a pen and writes the beginning letter of each gemstone: EIDIRB.

I'm strangely relieved that it only spells nonsense—unless it's Irish. But the relief doesn't last.

"Silly me," Pixie says. "I've written it backwards."

She scribes it from top to bottom, as if the whistle was in the playing position.

BRIDIE.

In spite of my theories, it's caught me unawares. I gasp. It's proof, as certain as an engraving. The pendant belonged to Bridie, almost certainly fashioned by her lover, Brendon Blake. And on the flipside is what it *doesn't* spell: CIARA.

I hold it for a moment and sense how precious it was to Bridie. A gift of love. But then tragedy struck. Why?

* * *

Finn collects the week's repairs, and I buy an A–Z of gems and their meanings as a thank you. And it might be useful.

On the way back to the car, we pass a bus stop and I'm struck by something I've totally forgotten: Coral's prediction: *Hokio*. I hear her murmur the word in her deep laconic voice. And Wanda's hands-on-hips translation: 'Whichever way you spin it, Selkie, *hokio* still means whistle.' Coral knew. I remind myself never to doubt the *kahuna*'s strange pronouncements. She's more than an oracle; she's a bloody miracle.

Then I remember that Bridie couldn't blow the whistle, not without a fipple. And until I met Finn, neither could I. Something about that fact feels important, but Coral isn't here to ask.

"Where to now?" Finn asks.

I look at the sky. It's stopped raining. "The cliff at Beenbawn. It's at the mouth –"

"I know where it is."

He drives back the way we came, then turns up a steep road towards the mouth of Dingle Bay. It ends at a treeless headland covered in windswept grass where a few new houses cling. The view is a dream, if waves crashing on rocks don't give you nightmares. After the past few months in Hawaii and my various encounters with the sea, my phobia isn't as severe as it used to be, but I'm still not a fan of cliffs.

Finn stops the car. "It's back to Tralee for me. Unless you want me to wait for you?"

As helpful as he's been, I don't want him knowing any more about my family business. I could also do without the death-defying drive. "Thanks, but I'll be a while absorbing the vibes around here. I'll get the bus back."

We say goodbye, and I walk as far as I dare towards the cliff. The headland slopes away from the road, getting steeper and steeper near the edge. Out of view of the road there's an extensive ledge covered in a stone structure—a circular wall with an arched entrance enclosing interior walls that indicate rooms. A sign says: *Beenbawn Promontory Fort.* Part of the far edge has crumbled into the sea, and there's emergency tape across the entry to prevent access. You wouldn't catch me in there anyway.

There's a stiff wind off the sea. When I turn my back on it for a moment, I'm shocked to see over the rise that Finn is still sitting in his car. Watching me. I have no idea why, unless he's been following my tight jeans. He needs to swap his one-night stands for a steady girlfriend. When he sees me looking, he starts the engine and drives off.

I turn back to the cliff. This is where the police suggested that Brendon brought the body of the murdered twin on the back of a horse and tossed her into the sea. No evidence was mentioned for the theory. With the slope getting steeper it wouldn't be easy to find the edge in the dark—except in my vision there was a moon. And a body wrapped in a blanket and tied with rope could be rolled all the way to a watery grave. There are rocks at the foot of the opposite headland so there must be rocks below this cliff too. Depending on the tide they'd catch a body, and would a rug be heavy enough to ensure she was never washed into the bay? I suspect this wasn't investigated. As Mary at the museum said, they didn't waste time hanging Brendon Blake.

I shiver. The wind is cold and my sweatshirt is too thin. Before it starts raining again, I hurry back down the road to Dingle. It's quite a walk to my next stop: the Double-D Brewing Company in Lismore Lane. It's another lucky discovery. The brewery's got the same name as the old dairy co-op because it's in the same building.

A text from Derek gives me an excuse to perch on someone's front wall for a breather. He's responding to Sibby Dolan's interview. He can't get enough of a Victorian murder, especially if it's dripping with folklore.

*Stay away from this ruined church inside a rath*, he says. *Those parents at Bridie's party kept the kids away for good reason. It's probably still there even if the house isn't. It's a faerie place and dangerous. Especially at night.*

*What's a rath?* I text back. *In case I trip over it by mistake.*

*A megalithic installation built inside a circle. AKA a faerie ring. Even the shape is meaningful.*

A circle. Just like the promontory fort I've just seen at Beenbawn. And the shape made by the giant fingers in my dream. Something about rings. *Even the shape is meaningful.* Like the ring of truth and the napkin ring under my mattress. It's all very symbolic, but what I need is some real evidence to unravel the threads of the mystery, as unrealistic as that may be after all this time.

At the edge of town, two roads merge in a V opposite a complex of modern buildings, including a stonemason and a conference centre, with fields stretching all the way to the foothills of the mountains behind. The Double-D Brewing Company is a box-shaped building with a grey slate roof and little square windows dwarfed by heavy timber frames—like a house drawn by a child.

It's got a storefront on the street and inside I find an old man behind the counter. He's short and wizened and wearing a cloth cap.

"Just minding the shop, lass," he says. "But I know how to sell beer. What's your fancy?"

"Not beer today, thanks. Information."

"Aye?"

"This building used to be the Double-D Dairy Co-op, is that right?"

"Way back. That little display over there is all that's left. It's not much, but the boss likes to boast about the heritage of the place. Thinks it's good for business—brings in the tourists, like you. Don't mind a bit of history meself, but we're not selling cream any more."

I wander over to a bunch of old milk bottles sitting on a table, each one bearing a large handwritten number. The old guy joins me.

"It was the latest thing back then. Each farmer had his own number. He brought them in full and got paid by the bottle." He laughs. "They did regular checks to make sure they weren't watering 'em down, human nature being the same then as it is now."

"Interesting," I say, picking up a bottle. "Do you know any stories about the people involved in the co-op right at the start? I'm … doing some research."

"Research, is it? You're nosier than most. You'll be here about … the murder."

His straight talking makes me come clean. "I'm a descendant."

It's the right thing to say. The Irish like their descendants—especially young females with Australian accents. We introduce ourselves. His name is Vincent.

Before he can probe into my family tree, I get in first. "When you were a boy it was still a celebrated case, I suppose? A tinker hanged for killing a local girl he was known to be seeing on the sly."

He nods. "They call them Travellers now. More respectful. But they'll always be tinkers or pavees. It's not racist, it's just history. My family never had a problem with them, but my grandfather said it didn't take the law long to string up Brendon Blake."

"Your family knew him?"

"Grandpap did. Dingle was a small place back then. Up at Tralee they had the canal and Fenit Harbour to keep them busy with the trade, but down here we had a few families and a lot of cows and sheep. The tinker and his father used to come around mending pots and knackering horses. Brendon Blake showed Grandpap—he was still a boy back then—how to play the penny whistle."

Brendon played the penny whistle. That's why he made one for Bridie. As the pendant nestles against my chest I can almost feel his breath making it sing.

"Grandpap was pretty upset when his hero was done for murder," Vincent is saying. "He never believed it."

"Did your grandfather ever say which twin was seeing Brendon?"

"Common knowledge it was that it was Miss Bridie. The other sister –"

"Ciara."

"Aye. Miss Ciara. Born in Cork they were, before the family moved here, and Ciara's birthday eight days after her sister's. *Eight.*" He shakes his head.

"Eight days? It doesn't seem possible." But if they didn't share a birth date, it explains why I couldn't find them registered as twins.

"So the story goes. Twins born apart like that—one on the breast while the mother's still carrying the other one—it's not natural. Those eight days inside without enough oxygen made her simple, they said. But everyone knew that child was marked by magic."

The superstitions still run deep, it seems, woven into the old stories, all the way up to the present. If people thought Ciara was 'marked by magic', that's what they saw. Just like Davina knew the novice nun at the Swap Meet was the fetch she'd always feared would come back for her.

"What else do you remember hearing about them?" I ask. "Gossip is good."

"Well, gossip is hearsay now, isn't it, since those of us still around heard about it from someone else years after. Like the Bible, isn't it?" He chuckles and looks over his shoulder as if to make sure a priest isn't loitering in the doorway. "And our memories have rubbed the edges off the facts. Like the Atlantic wind shapes the cliffs to its will."

Vincent is a poet. While he waits for my response, I decide to take a risk.

"In the museum in Tralee, they're saying the murdered girl was Bridie. But my great-grandmother was one of the O'Connor twins—and that's what she called herself. Bridie."

He's quiet for a moment, as if I haven't surprised him. "Well, no-one at the museum asked anyone from round here, did they? They dug in their *archives* and they got their newspaper clippings and blew 'em up nice and big, and collected their tinker trinkets. Their display is fancy so it must be true."

"So you're saying it was Ciara who was murdered, but for some reason their identities got ... swapped?"

But Vincent is busy drawing something on a piece of paper. A mud map. "It's still there, the old O'Connor house. You can't go in—Americans own it now. But you can follow the boreen and see the outside, and the path to the well where it happened. Ask me your questions when you get back."

The outside of the house mightn't tell me much, but the rain is holding off and I have to see where it happened. The suburban road that takes me up the hill from the brewery is lined by modern two-storey terraced houses made of stone or brick, with handkerchief gardens and views across Dingle town towards the sea. In some yards peat logs are stacked, and smoke is rising from chimneys on this cool summer day.

As the houses dwindle at the edge of town, I see a farmhouse in the distance, its roof secured with rocks tied at the ends of ropes. So Finn was telling the truth about that. Taking the mud map out of my pocket to see where to go next, I notice Vincent's drawn it on the back of a leaflet.

When I turn it over, elongated white letters scream:

*Ghost Tour!*

*Meet the Dead Denizens of Dingle ... If You Dare!*

*Tuesday, Friday & Saturday nights*

*Small Groups—Bookings Essential*

The image shows a gothic-style haunted house, all soaring gables and dormer windows not quite hiding spectral silhouettes backlit in orange.

Back down the hill I go, and when Vincent sees me his eyes twinkle.

"Why did you draw the map on the back of this leaflet? Has this got anything to do with the twin who was murdered?"

"If it was murder," Vincent says. "Some say the faeries took back their own. Or the family sent her back—Ciara the faerie child—and covered it up by changing her sister's name. You wouldn't want the neighbours knowing you were dabbling in faerie business."

Better to be dabbling in identity theft and murder?

"But don't take my word for it," he says, nodding towards the leaflet in my hand. "Ask her yourself."

"Who?" But the hairs on the back of my neck know.

"She's still there. Up at the old house. Her *ghost*."

"The ghost of ... the murdered girl?"

"So they say."

It's my turn to be quiet. Dumbstruck.

"There's a tour tomorrow tonight," Vincent says. "Tell Josephine I sent you. It's been busier since the murder exhibition. She'll make sure you don't miss out."

I study the leaflet. The ghost tour is expensive and I suspect he's getting a commission. He's very effective with his subtle sell. Just like Bridie and her parcels. The O'Connor house is still here. Along with its resident ghost. My visions about Ciara are true, and her ghost is going to help me solve the riddle. Do I believe that? Or the tour is just a hoax for the tourists. But before I can change my mind, I phone the number and book a ticket. Then breathe out.

"Does she always ... appear?" I ask Vincent.

"If you're meant to meet her, you will," he says.

Then I remember the mannequin. I can only hope meeting her ghost doesn't inspire a rerun of that episode. I want more than reliving the murder. I want answers.

It seems that everyone around here knew which twin was which. Putting the faerie superstitions aside, surely Vincent's comments confirm that Ciara was murdered, not Bridie? So why did the family lie? And why did Bridie enter a Dublin convent bearing her sister's name and wearing her sister's murder weapon at her own throat?

* * *

It's a steady climb up the slope again. As instructed on the map, I *turn right at black cow down boreen*, as far as a locked gate. Vincent said the O'Connor property stretches away behind the house up into the foothills of the mountains to the north, and across a series of fields separated by stone walls to the east, where there's a sheer drop to a road below—the road that the tinkers once used. Their campsite is still visible, he said, but the path down the cliff is overgrown with blackberries and he warned against trying to climb down.

At the gate I get a shock. The house has been renovated. The mortar is so clean and intact that the old stone walls must have been demolished and rebuilt. But if the ghost tour is to be believed, the ghost wasn't demolished with them. Where did she go while her home was under construction?

Peering over the gate, I take in the place where my ancestors lived—and died. What happened here? I feel nothing as I stare at the steep slate roof and the new double-glazed windows. In the daylight it looks like any other charming two-storey cottage with a new extension downstairs, renovated by Americans buying up Irish real estate during the boom times. The house is isolated. Perhaps Thomas wanted to keep a few cows and his connection with rural life. At what cost?

My phone chirps with an email from Sister Kevin. She's put the description of Being Sleek in the conference program and wants my approval. That done, I make my way along the low stone wall that skirts the property. On the hill high above the house is what looks like the remains of the church that James and Sibby mentioned. It must have had a commanding view back across Dingle to the sea, but I'd need to trespass to see it myself. And I remember Derek's warning about the rath, which must be the circle of mounded ground and stones around the ruin.

I keep walking, past a copse of very old trees inside the property, and spy the remains of the stone well, overgrown with fuchsias. If Bridie and Brendon met here as lovers, their trysts would have been screened from the house by what were young trees back then.

Then my way is blocked by blackberries, and I gaze over the edge to the road below and a wide flat area that would once have been alive with wagons and campfires. I'm at the divide of their worlds, Bridie's and Brendon's. It feels symbolic as I turn to look back at the well, trying to pick up any ambiance. In that moment the sun bursts through the clouds and the day suddenly becomes less melancholy. It's a reminder that before the murder and Brendon's execution, the lovers shared moments of joy here.

Back at the front gate, I look up at the dormer windows and wonder which bedroom belonged to the twins. From the gate there's only a glimpse of the sea, but from the second floor the view must be panoramic. Then I notice a sign under the eaves: *Is this your next retreat? Call Josephine.* And a number. I check the leaflet. It's the same number as the ghost tour. Vincent didn't say you could stay here. Standing on my toes I can see through a window that the house is fully furnished—a haunted holiday let.

It's another long walk back to civilisation and I'm starving. While I wait for the bus, I grab some chowder and soda bread in a café and send Derek a text: *Going on a ghost tour to meet my murdered ancestor. Wish you were coming.*

# Chapter 16

"My mother's starting to feel like a ghost," Davina says, "the longer it takes Dervla to find out where she's disappeared to."

She's read a lot today about the abuse of young unmarried mothers at hands of the infamous Magdalene Laundries and it's depressed her to think what her own mother must have gone through.

"Sometimes the nuns let the mother hold her baby and feed it once, before they ripped it from her breast and took it away forever. To get her motherly instincts flowing and inflict the maximum pain. I just want to hug my mam, you know, and say that forty years is a very long time to not know what happened to your precious daughters, but now we're back."

We both tear up, and I envy her. I won't be meeting my mother except in my dreams.

"Now this ghost tour," she says, wiping her eyes. "I'm coming with you. No arguments. How much is it?"

"Great. I'd love your company. But if we can get you a ticket, I'm paying. *No arguments.* You've got me a paying job with Sister Kevin, and you'll be working for nothing detecting my ghost."

"You're the detective, Selkie, the one with the family genes.

But I might be able to make some sense of what you feel. And let's hope she's the talking kind and not the throw-things-around-the-room kind."

Shit.

Davina sees me go pale. "Are you thinking, if she's in charge of what happens was she the one who slipped inside your skin last time, not the other way round?"

I nod. "And could she do it again?"

She thinks for a moment. "If this ghost really is Ciara, she might not be clever enough to do that."

Why doesn't that make me feel better?

* * *

Davina and I sleep in, which suits Nola who regards serving breakfast a minute before nine o'clock as 'the middle of the night'. When I woke briefly during the early hours and removed Fiona's latest gift from under the mattress—a spoon—I could hear the pub still rocking downstairs. While Davina takes a shower, I think of Alister—the bangle he gave me is fashioned from a spoon. It's his only gift; that and his fingerprint inside my locket and the love that goes with it. The further I am away from him the more I feel it. A fingerprint with the power to touch my heart from the other side of the world. Magic.

Over breakfast a line of enquiry pops into my head: old newspapers. Delving into them was part of my initial plan, but I got sidetracked by the museum exhibition and the trip to Dingle. Now I wonder if broadening my search to faeries and the superstitions surrounding them might help me find another chink in the secret.

Nola tells us that *The Kerryman* has an office almost next door to the museum. We've been walking right past it on our way back and forth.

Davina comes with me and a helpful woman collects us from reception. She shows us to neighbouring computers in an unoccupied room. "We've a subscription to the Irish News Archive," she says, "with access to newspapers going back as far as 1735."

"Wow," I say, and Davina grins. We both know I'm a fraud as a historian. But mentioning *The Kerryman* articles in the murder exhibition was enough to get us this far.

The woman shows us how to input keywords.

"The year 1896," I tell her. "Dingle. Faeries."

"The news, the social pages, the classifieds?"

"Everything. I know it's broad, but we want to get a feel for the folklore of rural Dingle at that time."

She leaves us with a long list of resulting links. Sharing the task with Davina makes it less daunting, but I wish Derek was here. Sometimes he's exasperating, but he's got a knack of exploring tangents and uncovering unexpected angles.

I look at the time. "My eyes and my stomach can probably manage two hours," I whisper, and Davina nods.

Speak of the devil, there's a text from Derek: *Sorry to miss the haunted house hop. Hope it's not a gimmick. Remember ghosts can take different forms, like a memory that got imprinted and replays itself to people sensitive enough to detect it.*

It's like Finn said—the past is there, waiting.

*Sounds creepier than a spectre in a sheet*, I text back.

*You can run away from spectres. Or turn on a light. But these ghost memories get under your skin and seep into your soul.*

Shit.

*I'll watch out for seepage. Thanks, DD.*

* * *

Several hours later, Davina and I stop for lunch. After our finds in the archives we're feeling as grey as the office buildings around us, but then we spy an open door with a flight of stone steps leading down to a cellar-like restaurant glowing with orange lamps. It's like a glimpse into the wild faerie world that hovers just beneath the sophisticated face of modern Ireland. Their menu is posted on the street and when we see their 'Soup-o'-stition' made from 'organic vegetables grown inside a faerie ring', we smile at each other and descend into the netherworld.

As we wait for our soup we look at the printouts of what we found. Not all are from Dingle in 1896, but they reflect a serious belief in the power of the faerie folk to interfere with human lives—with devastating results.

*July, 1895: Faerie-Faith on Trial. The trial of Michael Cleary, a cooper in County Tipperary, has heard evidence from the accused that the burned body of a woman found in a shallow grave was not that of his missing wife, twenty-six-year-old dressmaker and milliner Bridget Cleary, but a changeling left in her place. Cleary told the court that his true wife had been abducted by faeries and that he had only set fire to the changeling. When he was arrested he claimed to be keeping vigil with his neighbours for the return of his wife. The men stayed up all night at a faerie ring, believing that a faerie procession would pass by with Bridget Cleary in its midst riding a grey horse. They were armed with black-handled knives, ready to leap forward and cut her bonds, thus releasing her to return to her husband. Addressing the jury,*

*Judge O'Brien, a Roman Catholic, said: "This case demonstrates a degree of darkness in the mind ... a moral darkness, even religious darkness ..."*

"It's like that mother in Sibby Dolan's interview," Davina says, "telling her child that she was going to burn the faerie out of him on a hot shovel."

The story's appalling, but something else is making my skin prickle: the connection between changelings and identity swaps and twins. Is it a clue?

"Thank God the superstitions these days are less ... barbaric," I say.

"But you went back there, Selkie, That mannequin sent you right back to 1896."

"You mean if I have a repeat of the vision ... I might not be safe?"

"I wish I knew," she says, frowning.

We both know we're not going to withdraw from the ghost tour, so we avoid the implications of further time travel and return to the printouts.

*May 1, 1896: Bealtaine Festival News. To celebrate the beginning of the butter season and to protect the butter from the faeries, farmers' wives sprinkled primroses on the doorstep of the Double-D Dairy Co-operative.*

*May 1, 1897: Bealtaine Festival News. Investigations are taking place into last night's bonfire in Chapel Lane which may have been fuelled by furniture taken from the O'Connor house. Mr and Mrs Thomas O'Connor recently returned to Cork, leaving everything behind. Almost a year ago their daughter Bridie was murdered by the tinker Brendon Blake; and it is rumoured that their other daughter, Ciara, betrothed to James Sullivan but confined to the house with hysteria since her twin sister's death, disappeared a few weeks ago. Has Ciara been stolen by the faeries? Readers will recall that her sister's body was never found, but neighbours claim to have seen her ghost prior to the fire.*

Mary at the museum said the tinkers burned Brendon's wagon to drive away his ghost. Is that what the O'Connors' neighbours were up to with their bonfire?

The item reveals some interesting facts beyond the folklore. The twin known as Ciara was betrothed to James Sullivan, corroborating what Sheila at the exhibition said. And her 'disappearance' in April happened almost a year after the murder of her twin and just before the arrival of Ciara O'Connor at St Scholastica's in Dublin. It doesn't resolve the identity issue, but it adds more pieces to the puzzle.

Davina confirms that Bealtaine still happens every first of May, with bonfires and partying. And when I do a quick search on my phone, Wiki says that Bealtaine had a strong association with the earliest stories from Irish mythology, when flames, smoke and ashes were used for their protective powers and to celebrate the change of season between spring and summer.

As we're eating our soup, a text comes from Dervla.

"She's found Peggy," Davina cries, her eyes twinkling with tears. "She's staying in a cottage in the countryside. It's not near any town so Dervla will meet me off the train in Bantry and drive me there, the day after tomorrow."

Bantry. I shiver. Now's not the time to remind Davina, but I'm thinking of Bantry's Bluff, a beach in Hawaii nicknamed by a homesick Irishman. It's where some strange things have happened to me.

I join in the excitement. "Will you call her Mam or Peggy?"

"Haven't I been worrying about that. If I call her Mam I'll collapse in tears, and she's the real one who's suffered. I don't want her thinking that I've been hankering for a mam all these years, that she neglected me by giving me up."

"And if you call her Peggy?"

"It sounds disrespectful and a bit cold. Like I'm her hairdresser or something. I'm wishing now that I hadn't pressed Dervla for her name."

Spurred on by me.

* * *

The bus deposits me in Dingle with time to kill before the ghost tour. Davina will join me later—she's been neglecting her website but now she can stop searching for Peggy and do some catching up. I'm wondering what I can do to further my research when I stroll past Stepping Stones and see it's empty. Pixie is sure to have an opinion about the tour.

She nods at my question. "It's popular," she says, giving nothing away.

"Are there ... any ghosts?"

She looks around as if to make sure we're alone, then drops her voice. "It depends who you ask. There are three stops on the tour. Widow Winsome lives at the old gatehouse—with a very troublesome sheehogue, so she says. Sheehogues are supposed to sap your energy and make you sickly, but the widow's as fit as a fiddle—and the tour supplements her pension." She pauses to let her scepticism sink in. "Then there's the cellar at O'Shaughnessy's pub. An old drunk died down there sheltering from the guards and his ghost is still blaming them for it. You can listen to him rant. The last stop is the old O'Connor house. A young girl was murdered out there over a hundred years ago." She hasn't made the link between the Bridie who owned my pendant and Bridie O'Connor. "That house was built too close to the ring fort so it's always been a thin place."

"Thin?" Like my voice when I say it.

"A place where the faerie world and the real world meet. Asking for trouble."

The O'Connors got that all right.

"What kind of trouble?"

"Faerie trouble. They love to party all night up at the old faerie ring and they don't appreciate humans asking them to shut up. There are lots of stories about stolen babies and other horrors. It's why the house was empty when the O'Connors moved in. The faeries had driven out the previous tenants, but the O'Connors were blow-ins from Cork so they didn't know the Dingle stories. Everyone knew they'd have been better off in town."

It sounds like the O'Connors were 'marked by magic' in more ways than one. First Ciara at her birth, then the house.

"So the ghost tour visits the house where the girl died?" I ask.

"It's been rebuilt."

"So why is it haunted?"

"It was rebuilt in the exact same place using the same stone. By Americans this time, who also wouldn't listen to why the house had been left to fall down. Rathbone their name is—*Rath*bone. It was an omen."

"Why?" It's the first time I've heard their name and I want her to tell me about raths.

"Rath is another name for a faerie ring. In these parts we call them cashels, except for that one. It's been called the rath ever since the Rathbones bought the house. They spent a fortune doing the place up. The stonemasons were out there for months, taking their time if you know what I mean. They didn't mind the steady work with a boss on the other side of the Atlantic. During daylight hours there wasn't much risk of disturbing the faerie folk, although," she drops her voice to a whisper, "they found something up there that made some of them quit—and refuse to talk about it afterwards."

If she's trying to scare me off it's working. I'm remembering Derek's warning to stay away from the faerie ring. Was it just superstition or does it have something to do with the murder? And all the burning that went on might explain why she was never found. Did her family incinerate her body, then cover it up? The thought of reliving that is making me break out in a sweat.

"Finally the Rathbones got fed up," Pixie says, "and sent their own man over to pressure the stonemasons into finishing the job. Then the family came over from New York for a grand unveiling and the teenage daughter freaked out."

"What happened?"

"She said there was a woman at the end of her bed laughing at her."

"Laughing?" Vincent didn't mention that. "Do ghosts … laugh?"

She shrugs. "They're supposed to be vengeful or wanting something. And the O'Connor girl was murdered so why is she laughing? But teenagers are open to messages from the spirit world, so I believe the Rathbone girl. And after all the stories about the faerie ring, everyone else around here believes her too. It's the third stop on the tour—the laughing ghost."

A ghost who laughs doesn't fit with my visions. Maybe I'm wrong to be fearing dark forces. Or is the ghost someone else?

"What happened after the sighting?" I ask.

"The Rathbones left and never came back. They tried to rent the place out for holidays, but no-one around here was prepared to go inside to do the cleaning and all. And anyone who came to stay didn't last more than one night. It got a reputation, and now they're trying to make some of their money back by joining the ghost tour."

Before leaving the shop I browse Pixie's bookshelf looking for something about faerie rings. The non-fiction books are all about the archaeology of ring forts and other megalithic structures—interesting but too scientific. And the mystical ones are dripping with curses and bad behaviour. At last I find a book that covers both, and I take it to O'Shaughnessy's pub to wait for Davina.

# Chapter 17

It doesn't get dark till well after ten, so assembly time for the tour isn't till nine fifteen. Davina's texted me that she'll eat in Tralee and catch a late bus to Dingle, so I order a meal in the pub. The barman recommends the coddle, a combination of the usual thigh-expanding ingredients: bacon, sausages, onions and potato, stewed in layers until they melt in your mouth. I order a hand-poured pint of Guinness too—'a tall blonde in a black dress' as the barman quips in response to my accent. Probably not the best thing to be imbibing before my spectral encounter, but I need to settle my nerves.

I find a table away from the bar and open my new book at the section on ring forts.

*Many people in Early Christian and Early Medieval Ireland lived in enclosed farmsteads called ring forts. Dating between 550 to 900 AD, they were circular areas measuring up to sixty metres in diameter, usually enclosed by one or more earthen bank walls and often topped with a timber palisade. Inside the ring fort, people lived in wooden huts; but in the west of Ireland, ring forts—known as cashels—were enclosed by stone walls with stone huts inside. With up to sixty thousand surviving examples, ring forts are the most common field monument from this period.*

So the ring fort above the O'Connor house was once a

functional enclosure where people lived.  If there are sixty thousand of them, it suggests the whole country is overrun with faeries, but the book doesn't mention the origins of the faerie myths.

Google brings up an article from *The Examiner* just before the Bealtaine festival in 2010 that asks if the Irish are 'still away with the faeries'. An agricultural consultant is quoted: *Even today, younger farmers won't damage a faerie fort. They'll tell you stories about someone who did and died suddenly or suffered some other tragedy.* An expert in folklore states: *People today are reluctant to admit to a belief in faeries, but the superstitions are still there just below the surface.*

As I read, the pub gradually fills with patrons—mostly men, looking like they've just stepped off a fishing boat judging by their jackets and wellies. Some are joking and chivvying each other at the bar and I realise they're talking about me.

"Go on, Rory," someone shouts. "Show her who she's up against."

The group roars as a stocky man in a windcheater and knitted beanie strides towards my table. The skin on his face is almost purple as if he's skirting a heart attack.

He towers over me and doesn't remove his cap. "You've been asking questions about the O'Connors from Chapel Lane." He's hardly able to get the words out for puffing.

Wow. The grapevine is impressive. How many people have I spoken to in Dingle? Only Vincent and Pixie.

"Yes."

"You're an O'Connor."

*Who wants to know?* I want to ask.  But I remember the burning of the O'Connors' furniture by men who might have been this guy's ancestors. And he's strong enough to knock my head off, egged on by the audience.

"Yes," I say, keeping my voice as friendly as my sudden fear allows.

"You're poking around in the feckin' murder."

I swallow. "Yes."

"Don't," he says, his voice taking on an extra edge. "The killer was found—over a hundred feckin' years ago. Go back to where you came from. There be nothing to see here."

It sounds like the longest speech he's ever made. And his message is loud and clear. The audience claps and hoots as he stalks back to the bar. I realise I'm trembling. It never occurred to me that anyone would try to stop my investigation. Like the guy said, it was *over a hundred feckin' years ago.*

The barmaid brings my meal—a steaming bowl that mirrors the steam coming out my ears. "Don't pay Rory no heed," she murmurs.

"He more or less told me to leave town. If that isn't a threat I don't know what is."

"Nah, not Rory. He wouldn't hurt a flea. It took a lot of shoving from them lot for him to talk to you."

"What's his problem?"

She looks over her shoulder at the watching crowd, then says in a low voice, "I go for my break at eight. Meet me out the back." Then louder as she walks away, "Enjoy your meal."

I've got no idea who Rory is, but he's protecting someone's reputation—he has to be. Not Brendon Blake's, that's obvious. Is he a descendant of one of the minor players? Maybe a policeman who arrested Brendon and ignored any other suspects. In a small town such blatant bias might inspire lingering rumours, especially if Thomas O'Connor wasn't well-liked. But I'm putting my money on James Sullivan. Did he kill one sister so he could marry the other one?

Then I remember what Sheila said about Sullivan's descendants: that one of them is in jail for some kind of sexual violence. If Rory's related to him, I need to be careful.

* * *

Just before eight I make my way to the loo, then through a rear door into an empty lane. It's a few minutes before the barmaid joins me.

"I'm Bonnie," she says as she lights up a cigarette. "Don't let on I'm telling you anything."

"Thanks. Why does this guy Rory care so much about an old murder?"

"Rory Flynn. I only know what I've overheard more than once, 'cause he'll tell anyone who'll listen. He's descended from one of them that was caught up in it—the murder. Forget his name."

"James Sullivan?"

"That's him. Well, he was Rory's grandfather—if he can believe what his old gran told him when she was sober."

"Does he know what happened to James after the murder?"

"Nothing, that's what happened. Rory says his grandfather was going to marry one of the O'Connor twins that lived up in Chapel Lane. The Rathbone house these days. This James was going to work his way up to be manager at the old dairy co-op. Where the brewery is now. Double-D—sounds like a bra." She laughs then coughs. "Rory goes on and on about how their father—the girls' father—had given James his word."

"Thomas O'Connor," I say.

"Yeah. It was all looking grand for James, then one of the

twins gets herself murdered, and the tinker gets blamed, then hanged. Rory's grandpa got caught up in it. He was hiding down by the well and practically saw the tinker throttle the girl. His testimony did it for the tinker. But afterwards James couldn't shake the rumours. Why was he near the well that night? His story didn't add up."

"So James married Rory's gran instead?"

"Not *married*." She rolls her eyes. "He knocked her up, then knocked her around. That's why his gran was so pissed off and Rory still is. James never stopped telling her she wasn't as good as the twin who jilted him. Bridget O'Connor—Bridie—that's her name. His gran got mighty sick of her man going on and on about the one that got away."

"But that doesn't explain why Rory wants me to stop digging into the murder."

"For a start you're a blow-in with a funny accent. None of your business, is it?"

She must have overheard that I'm a descendant too, but I let it go.

She exhales smoke and thinks a bit more about my question. "This James was a drunk and a rapist. Being descended from him is bad enough for Rory, but at least he didn't go killing anyone. It wouldn't be easy living round here if your grandpa turned out to be a murderer."

"What evidence could I possibly find after more than a century?"

It's the question I keep asking myself.

She shrugs, stubs out her cigarette and turns to go, then stops. "They never found her body."

It's my quest in a nutshell: the body holds the answer. Bridie was on the other side of the world so she couldn't solve the mystery. But she knew that if I found Ciara's body, there was a chance the murder would be solved. That means she knew the killer wasn't Brendon Blake.

* * *

Back inside, Rory and most of the fishermen have gone. I walk up to the bar and order a soft drink. Bonnie thinks Rory's harmless but his threat has made me wary. What would he do to protect himself from being descended from a murderer?

There are still a few fishermen knocking back last drinks, but I don't dare ask them the question that's popped into my head: *If you threw a body off Beenbawn where would it go? Out to sea?*

Bonnie moves past me at the bar, wiping up spills with a cloth. "You might want to talk to Dermot Donnelly," she whispers, flicking her eyes towards a guy in overalls who's wedged on a stool in the corner. He's covered from head to toe in powder like a French baker and his eyes are glazed with drink. "He was the stonemason up at the Rathbone house. Hasn't stopped drinking since."

The stonemason. Shit. Pixie said they made a discovery up there that made some of them quit. Like finding Ciara's skeleton under the floor—and covering it up again?

"C'mon," Bonnie says, breezing along the bar, "I'll get him talking."

Rory's absence makes me brave. But as I pick up my drink and move towards Dermot, I see that he's watching my approach with the hooded eyes of the seriously intoxicated.

Bonnie raises her voice. "Doesn't look like you've had much luck stopping that ghost tour, Dermot."

He grunts as if he's just woken up.

"There's another one tonight," she continues. "They'll be up at the Rathbone place, trying to get that ghost to tell them where her body's buried."

As I wonder if Dermot's going to take the bait, a roaring sound like the rumble of thunder rises from his chest, then pours out of his mouth, filling the room with a stream of invective.

"That feckin' tour. If there was a ghost, wouldn't I be the one to know about it? But will they listen to the man who rebuilt the place? Not while there's money to be made. The eejits'll swarm all over that house, stirring up they don't know what."

"If you mean the old O'Connor house," I say, getting as close as I dare, "I walked past there yesterday. The stonework is beautiful."

He eyes me warily. "What's your accent? Are you related to them Americans?"

"I'm related to the O'Connors." As I say my name I put out my hand, but he shrinks away. "I'm Australian," I add, "here to research my family roots."

If I thought that would smooth the way it has the opposite effect.

"An O'C-c-connor," he stammers, crossing himself. "From … down … there?"

He's pointing to the ground between his feet, and when I laugh and nod it makes things worse. He lurches forward off the stool and looms over me. He's a big man, and as I shrink away, he leans against the bar, lifts one foot, wobbles, then pulls off one of his boots.

"Be gone with you," he roars, waving the boot above his

head. "We want no faerie trouble here."

Faerie trouble? I'm so mesmerised that I stop backing away and when he throws the boot, it gets me full in the chest, striking the pendant and sending a searing pain through my sternum. The force of it knocks me over.

As I go down, Dermot falls to his knees. "Jaysus," he hisses, "haven't I prayed every night to be spared."

Then we both start to cry.

Suddenly Bonnie is helping me to my feet and guiding me into a room behind the bar. She opens my shirt, pulls the pendant aside and puts an icepack against my chest.

"That's a steel-capped boot he hurled at you and it's got you right on the breastbone. It didn't break the skin or your pendant but it's made a nasty mark. You're going to have a bruise the colour and shape of a Guinness. Otherwise ... you're OK, aren't you?"

I don't know.

"Dermot hasn't been the same since he worked on that house," she adds. "But who would've thought he'd be dangerous. He's curled up out there sobbing like a baby. The boss called his wife to come and get him. He's hoping you won't ... press charges."

Of course. I've been assaulted—with bruises to prove it, imprinting the pendant against my chest. The injury is already throbbing as the shock subsides, and the pain brings on a surge of anger. Leave town. Stop investigating. Don't press charges. It's only making me more determined to find out what everyone's hiding.

Bonnie brings me a cup of tea, and as it calms me I think about what Dermot yelled just before he launched his missile: *We want no faerie trouble here.* Right after I mentioned my connection to the O'Connors, then Australia made him point to the floor. It's as if he just stepped out of the pages of *The Kerryman: Stonemason in fear of faeries after rebuilding house in shadow of rath.* But it's no longer 1896. It makes me wonder just what happened at the house that's made him fear faerie reprisals with every bone in his body. Enough to hurl a boot at a woman half his size.

Bonnie returns to the bar, and I send a text to Derek: *Just met the stonemason who rebuilt Bridie's house. When I said I'm an O'Connor from Australia he freaked out, pointed to the floor and started gibbering about faerie trouble. Any ideas?*

# Chapter 18

As I stand with Davina and a handful of others beside a minibus, I'm still feeling jumpy and sore. After the violence in the pub, my determination to meet Ciara's ghost—if she's the laughing ghost—seems insane. And if it is Ciara, what's the chance that she'll recognise a descendant, keep her distance and tell me all about the murder? Information I now can't reveal without exposing myself to further attack.

Davina's excitement is palpable and I decide not to mention the assault for now.

The others on the tour are couples and singles out for an adventure. I can hear American and Irish accents. Our guide is Josephine herself, a slim woman of about my age with short brown hair and no makeup. Her ghost hunting gear is unmistakeable: black jeans and a sweatshirt matching the tour leaflet. We make an odd number, until a car screams into the parking lot and Finn Cormack falls out.

"Wasn't I sure I was going to be late," he says.

I don't hide my annoyance. "How did you know I was on the tour?"

He laughs. "If you've got a secret don't go sharing it with Aunty Nola."

He gives me a wink and bounds onto the bus, so I'm saved from introducing him to Davina.

The first stop is an old gatehouse at the entrance to a ruined mansion. Widow Winsome is a hunched old thing with sharp eyes. She greets our group at the door, and as soon as we step inside Davina stiffens beside me.

The widow moves us out of the entry hall and into her kitchen, where she starts a well-rehearsed tale about the sheehogue that lives there. To demonstrate its presence, the cups rattle on their hooks on the old dresser and I wonder how she manages it.

"Don't be leaving your doors or windows open of an evening," she warns. "That's how they get in. This one arrived the night my Donal died and I thought it was him coming home so I called out that I was in the kitchen stirring the soup and in came this ... creature. As if it knew Donal was gone."

The tension goes up a notch. Someone asks what the thing looks like.

"It's been in the bed with me more than once. Made me jump out of my skin the first time, I can tell ye. I screamed and screamed, and the thing threw back the covers and in the moonlight coming through the window I saw it. Arms so long its hands were brushing the floor. And its head ... well, it was on sideways so I couldn't see its face."

Horror tinged with disbelief ripples through the group. Finn who's standing opposite winks at me and I ignore him.

The widow drops her voice like a true storyteller. "Then it cackled. And ... spoke." She pauses to make sure she's got us. "'My name, my name, my name,' it jabbered. 'Guess my name and I'll leave you be. Get it wrong and you're stuck with me.'

Then it cackled again and disappeared."

The rhyme sounds vaguely familiar, but now Widow Winsome is regaling us with her failed guesses and the sheehogue's antics: stealing tea towels and making them dance, sending potatoes flying across the room, making voices call from the bucket in the corner.

As she invites us to write down our guesses of its name and post them in a slotted box, Davina slips back into the hall and I follow her.

"Something violent happened here," she whispers, sniffing the air.

That's when I get something. An oppressiveness. A deep despair. My blood runs cold, but it gives me confidence that I might be psychic enough to tune in to my ancestor's ghost.

The next stop isn't the pub cellar, which has been flooded by a broken water pipe. At the last minute Josephine has substituted something else: an unmarked graveyard for unbaptised babies. We huddle together at the side of a field as she explains that we won't be going any closer due to the vengeance that babies robbed of life and a consecrated grave can exact on the living. She shares a story about a local boy who got lost one night and accidentally took a short cut across this field. "He didn't know that he just had to turn his coat inside out to find his way home." In the morning he was stiff to the touch, with a mask of horror instead of a face.

Then she hands out binoculars and urges us to report any shadows or strange phenomena. Someone says they see a wisp of smoke, but Davina is walking back to the minibus and I don't blame her. I'm sure she'll be thinking of herself and Dervla, innocent babies taken from their mother and each other—and the abuse they suffered as a consequence.

We get back on the bus for the last stop: the laughing ghost. As we take the route I walked yesterday up the hill to Chapel Lane, my anticipation mounts. Once we've turned at the black cow into the boreen, Josephine asks us not to speak from now on.

She ushers us out of the bus, unlocks the gate, then the front door. Opposite the short entry hall, stairs lead to an upper-storey landing with doors to what I assume are two bedrooms. To the right downstairs there's a modern kitchen and sunroom with big windows facing the hill.

Leading us left into the downstairs sitting room, Josephine explains in subdued tones that the laughing ghost can be encountered in the bedroom directly above us. Everyone looks up at the ceiling and there's a ripple of apprehension, but I feel nothing else.

"You'll go upstairs in ones or twos, without speaking," Josephine murmurs. "When you get inside, stand still and wait. You might hear her laughing. Some do, some don't. When you've been up there five minutes I'll ring a little bell for you to come down again."

As she asks for volunteers, Davina and I move around the downstairs rooms doing what we did at the gatehouse. Davina stops here and there and sniffs, but shakes her head. My efforts to sense a presence reveal nothing either. It seems that all traces of the former inhabitants have been expunged by new plaster and gleaming appliances. There's nothing of the O'Connors left; even the exterior stone dates back to before their time.

When we return to the sitting room, a couple goes upstairs, followed by a guy on his own because his wife has changed her mind. This is the one room we haven't explored and I gaze around, not wanting to be too obvious. This must be where the family photo was taken, but there's no piano now and the sharpness of the new plasterwork screams 'modern'—except for one thing. Next to the new fireplace there's a rectangular iron grille screwed to the wall over what looks like a ventilation hole. Something about it attracts me—but now it's Davina's turn upstairs and people are getting restless. It seems that the ghost isn't co-operating. Josephine puts her finger to her lips.

When Davina comes back I'm not sure what her expression means. Then I move to the foot of the stairs, and Finn is suddenly beside me. What? I frown and shake my head. He's not sharing this.

I climb to the landing, trying to breathe through my expectation and my fear. The others are here for fun. But I'm *family*. The word that usually drips with baggage has morphed into a deep connection with my twin ancestors. It's crept up on me with each clue, and after the warnings to leave the past alone I'm determined to find out the truth—for Bridie's sake and my own.

The room is lit only by the dusk and a porch light downstairs. Opposite the door are two dormer windows, under each a single iron bedstead painted white. Between them, the mirror on a reproduction dressing table gives me glimpses of myself and the fireplace beside the door. The Rathbones' daughter sensed a woman laughing at the end of the bed, but which bed?

I move to the head of one bed, turn and start with fright. But it's only the light through the window throwing my shadow against a wall. Calming myself with some deep breaths, I remain standing and wait.

After several minutes nothing's happened. Perhaps it's not dark enough. Or I'm looking in the wrong place. Or maybe I'm expecting a cookie-cutter ghost, something filmy and white, but she's taking another form? As I try to remember what's been said about memories imprinting themselves, my eyes scan the walls for some kind of sign. Then I hear the tinkle of Josephine's bell.

I curse under my breath and touch the iron bedpost—and that's when it happens.

A trill of laughter. Right up my spine.

I don't move.

The woman laughs again and I realise I'm not hearing it, I'm feeling it. Through the bedpost. My whole body is quivering with it.

The bell tinkles. I ignore it. When Josephine appears in the doorway ringing the bell again, I've felt the burst of laughter three times. And something else. Echoed words?

But they're drowned out by the bell.

Josephine's expression flips from anxious to annoyed. With a sharp flick of her head she signals for me to leave.

I'm furious about missing that phrase. I let go of the bedpost, walk to the doorway and hiss in her ear, "I'm a descendant of the O'Connors."

She makes a moue with her mouth as if I've tricked her. She conducts ghost tours for tourists, not channelling sessions for inquisitive offspring. She must be the only person in Dingle who doesn't know who I am. Vincent mustn't have told her in case she wouldn't sell me a ticket and he lost his commission.

"Talk to me afterwards," she snarls.

You bet. We're not done here yet, because my sixth sense didn't let me down. I'm sure it's Ciara I heard—the girl James Sullivan heard giggling by the well—but why is she laughing if she was murdered? And did she say something to me or did my heightened state imagine it?

* * *

We join the others downstairs. Davina squeezes my hand and I'm glad she's with me. Finn raises his eyebrows, but I don't respond. When he doesn't take a turn upstairs, I wonder why he's here.

We all fall into line behind Josephine—through the kitchen extension to the back of the house and out through the rear door, which she unlocks. There's a hold-up ahead and we stop in a mudroom full of boots and coats. Davina's in front of me and without warning she turns and grabs my arm, and I'm drenched by a sudden chill. More than that. A cold moment of dread. Davina closes her eyes and beads of sweat pop up on her forehead, before her eyes fly open again.

Then we're stepping into the back garden, where Josephine is pointing to the ruined church.

"It's built on the same spot as an old pagan ring fort known as a cashel or rath. It's always been a spiritual place—a thin place—so it was an obvious site for a church. But it turned into a battleground."

"What happened?" someone asks.

"It's a faerie place and the faeries never give a place up. As much as the priest exorcised the building night and day, they kept coming back and mocking him. Like that sheehogue at Widow Winsome's but much worse. The faeries taunted that poor priest until he was so exhausted he collapsed and fell into a deep sleep. He was never the same afterwards, and it was the last time anyone set foot in that church." There's a hushed silence as we wait for the punchline. "The faeries demolished the walls around him while he slept."

"O-overnight?" a woman stammers.

"Overnight."

Everyone is looking up at the crumbling remains and I'm blown away by the power of folklore to wrap us in its spell.

"We won't be going any closer," Josephine says. "Don't ever visit a faerie ring after dark. You might not come back."

As our silent group turns down the side path to head back to the bus, we're stopped by the call of a bird. It's singing its heart out just above the ruin, piercing and beautiful.

"A nightingale," says an American guy in the group.

"No nightingales in Ireland," says an Irish guy.

"Only when there's magic in Berkeley Square," says Finn, singing a bar of the melody.

The others laugh. But I'm still affected by the call of the bird and the trill of laughter I heard upstairs.

And something else. I'd almost forgotten my injury from Dermot's boot, but now it's started to throb. And when I look across at Davina, I remember the sudden chill in the mudroom and the beads of sweat on her brow.

* * *

The tour ends at O'Shaughnessy's pub for refreshments, and there's a band in the other room if we want to join the audience there. Sitting around a large table with the others, Davina and I listen to the manager's tale of the ghost we might have met if the cellar hadn't flooded.

Afterwards, Josephine takes me aside. "You should have told me you were family," she says.

"I didn't think it mattered."

"Of course it matters." She notices my accent. "You're American."

"Australian. My great-grandmother was an O'Connor. She emigrated there in 1917."

"What did you hear up there tonight?"

"When I touched the bedpost, I felt it. The laughing."

She nods. "Like the Rathbone girl. I haven't felt it myself, and with the house being rebuilt I've wondered how it could be true. But that explains it. Laughter vibrating up through the ground, being replayed by the earth."

It's a powerful image and we both fall silent.

"I've heard that the Rathbones didn't come back," I say. "Their daughter was seriously spooked."

She laughs. "Who told you that? It was her parents that were spooked. They rushed her back to the States in double-quick time but she still insisted on changing her name."

Now I'm spooked.

"The spelling, I mean," Josephine adds. "Her name's Keira with a K. After she met the laughing ghost, she changed it to the Irish spelling."

She's just confirmed the identity of the ghost.

"You sensed something else up there," Josephine says. "I saw it on your face."

"I'm not sure." But I need her help so I don't mention that it was her bloody bell that got in the way. She waits, and what I say next doesn't surprise her. "I want to stay there. Tonight."

She agrees on the spot and asks for a sizable amount in cash, which we both know she's going to pocket. The Rathbones will never know.

I've got nothing much in my tote bag except a lipstick and two phones—my idea of emergency supplies—so she suggests

I enjoy the pub refreshments included in the tour while she organises a toothbrush, changes the sheets and turns on the hot water at the house, then puts together a breakfast basket. Otherwise the place is fully equipped, just as the Rathbones left it.

Davina doesn't try to talk me out of it. We've found a table away from the group and we share our experiences of the upstairs bedroom.

"There's a lot of emotion in that room," she says. "The air is thick with it."

Something I missed—because I was so focused on hearing the laughter? Davina didn't feel the laughter herself, but after the incident with the mannequin she's not surprised that I got a strong connection.

"This time we were separate," I say. "Thank God."

"That was different. The mannequin pressed some kind of psychic button in you—with its missing finger, I suspect—but this was a ghost. If you want to hear the words you missed, you'll need to repeat what you did tonight as exactly as you can remember. If you change the sequence you might get nothing."

"Do ghosts have a routine?"

She nods. "It's what defines them. They're stuck in a series of moments—of joy or pain or some other emotion. And they repeat them over and over."

"This was joy. So it doesn't fit with being murdered."

But I won't believe that my visions are wrong.

"The sequence might start with laughter," she says, "then shift into pain in a flash. Be ready for the shift. Their emotions are powerful—that's what makes them stick—so whatever's coming, it'll knock you over if you're not prepared."

As spooked as I am, I have to do this alone. I still haven't told Davina what happened in the pub earlier in case she insists on coming with me. I've been worried that Bonnie might come over to our table and ask me about my bruises, but she's too busy behind the bar.

But Davina has another warning. "Stay away from that flagstone, Selkie." It's what she was standing on inside the back door.

"When you touched me I felt … as cold as ice," I say. "What was it? Your eyes flew open." And I haven't forgotten the beads of sweat.

"It was like a doorway," she says. "A dark opening. I was standing on the edge and in a flash it was calling me … down, down, down."

"What was calling you? Did you hear a voice?"

But Davina's still back there, remembering it. "Down into the loneliest place in the world."

As lonely as the grave, I think. Does the flagstone mark the spot where Ciara's body's been buried, lonely and forgotten for over a hundred years?

When I tell Davina my theory, she tilts her head and thinks. "A grave feels too literal. And that stone isn't under the upstairs bedroom so I don't think it's linked to the ghost. Anyway, if she was buried there, the builders would have found her when they dug the footings for the extension."

She doesn't know about Dermot so I don't mention my theory that the crew might have found Ciara's remains and been ordered to cover them up to avoid more delays. It seems like the only explanation for men leaving the job and Dermot being so terrified. As head stonemason, he might be charged with an offence if it turns out he didn't report the find to the guards.

"Don't go standing on that stone tonight," Davina warns. "That doorway might swallow you up and you'll disappear like Ciara."

# Chapter 19

The supper is good, and Davina's company and the noisy pub dilute any second thoughts. I'm about to spend the night alone in a house where the ghost of my murdered great-great-aunt whispered something to me.

A couple from the tour offer to take Davina back to Tralee. She'll let Nola know that I won't be there for breakfast. After we hug and she leaves, I realise that Finn is nowhere to be seen. I've been expecting him to sidle up and offer me a lift; if he's left early it couldn't suit me better. But when Josephine returns and we cross the parking lot to the minibus, Finn's car is still parked at the same angle as his earlier arrival. Where is he? Then I remember the band at the pub and the soaring notes of a penny whistle.

We drive in silence to Chapel Lane, then Josephine waves goodbye as she backs the minibus down the lane.

After checking the locks on the doors, I go round the house and turn on all the lights. Suddenly I'm in a fishbowl so I douse most of them again. So much for my false courage. Now that I'm here and totally alone, I'm spooked.

This house is isolated. Up on the hill below the ring fort in haunted territory, with only the faeries—and the black cow—for company. If anyone sees the lights, I hope they put it down to ghosts and decide not to investigate. If there's a knock on the door I'll scream my head off.

A text from Derek reminds me that he's with me in spirit. The phrase makes me smile.

*Found a folk tale about the faerie realm. It's beneath our feet. A guy tries to stop the faeries from partying all night in the faerie ring behind his house and they lure him down, down, down to the netherworld. Just a guess, but from Ireland that could look like Australia.*

It's ridiculous, but I already know this is a superstitious place. Derek's theory might explain Dermot's meltdown, especially with his sanity diluted by alcohol.

I text back my thanks and feel glad that Dermot's home with his wife. But Derek's used the same words that Davina used about the flagstone. Down, down, down. What she experienced wasn't a folk tale.

It's time to go upstairs and get it over with, but the hole in the wall I noticed during the tour pops into my mind. I go into the living room and look at it. It's bigger than a brick, and the grille is decorative with art nouveau curls. But it's in an odd place—next to the fireplace and not close to the ceiling—so it can't be for ventilation. Intrigued, I get a stool from the kitchen and climb up, but the overhead light throws a shadow and I can't see what's behind the grille.

When I return the stool, I notice that Josephine's included a block of chocolate in the supplies. Putting off the trip upstairs, I sit at the kitchen counter and consume the whole lot while I read more about ring forts.

*The many ring forts in Ireland are known locally as faerie rings: magical places protected by spells. Even today, although people might hide their superstitions, no-one disturbs a faerie ring for fear of retribution. The person might never have a good night's sleep again; or worse, over time he might dissolve and gradually fall apart.*

It's a good description of what's happening to Dermot: falling apart and dissolving himself in whiskey. But is any of this relevant to my quest? Both Sibby Dolan and Josephine had stories about the faerie ring above the house. The tales of faerie trouble date back to long before the O'Connors moved in, then Ciara's intellectual insufficiencies added to the belief in magic. Might all the superstition explain why her body was never found? I've been worrying about the role that fire might have played, but there may never have been a proper search. While the police were making a public show of convicting Brendon Blake for murder, the belief that the body of the missing twin was stolen by the faeries might have prevented any real investigation.

As I'm thinking about this, I hear something. The nightingale. Even through the double-glazing its vibrant call, strong and poignant, is unmistakable. The bruise on my chest starts to throb.

I get off the stool and go to the sunroom window. It's dark now, but the birdsong seems to be coming from high above the ruined church, hidden in the mist shrouding the mountain. But there are no nightingales in Ireland. Only magic ones.

Closing the shutters, I turn from the window, race through the kitchen and up the stairs. As I enter the room with the twin beds, I'm suddenly calm. When I touch the bedpost, the laughter is there instantly, like a recording running on constant replay. It's a delightful sound, childlike and playful. Trilling notes of joy like water bouncing over pebbles. Or a penny whistle in full flight. Or the song of a nightingale.

I listen for a while, until I want more than the laughter. The message I came for.

Trying to remember what triggered the words last time, I stare at the walls of this room that the twins shared. After what seems like an age nothing else happens.

I'm exhausted but the laughter has dispelled my fear. Returning to the kitchen for the toothbrush, I turn off all the lights. Back upstairs I take a shower in the new ensuite. Then feeling calm about my role as channel, I slip under the covers of the laughing bed.

Even though I try to stay alert, my eyes won't stay open, and when I wake later it's from a deep sleep. Something woke me up.

I lie very still until I hear it again.

*No, Bridie, no!*

Even though Davina warned me to be ready, my whole body stiffens with the shock.

*No, Bridie, no!*

This has nothing to do with the laughter, but it's the voice I heard under the ringing of Josephine's bell. A childlike voice. Ciara's voice.

As it echoes around the room, the emotions are so strong I almost burst into tears.

*No, Bridie, no!*

The implications spin past. Bridie is doing something Ciara doesn't like and her sister is begging her to stop. My fingers fumble for the chain on the bedside table. After Ciara met Brendon down by the well, did she come back and boast to Bridie that she'd stolen a kiss from her lover? Perhaps more than a kiss from the red-blooded tinker. In spite of my visions, I'm now terrified that Bridie, in a jealous rage, strangled her sister in this very room while Ciara begged her to stop.

The words of the song are tattooed on my memory:

*The very first time that the fiddle did play,*
  *It sang of the murder that happened that day.*

*'My sister killed me,' is the song that it sang.*
  *'She is the one who surely should hang.'*

*But the song came too late, the miller was dead.*
  *The sister never lay in his wedding bed.*

*The rings in his pocket pointed the blame*
  *And the murderous sister lived with the shame.*

In the heat of the moment, did Bridie take off her necklace and strangle her sister? Then it hits me. It wasn't a necklace for Bridie.

The photo of the twins at the piano is in my bag. I reach for it and there it is, the glimpse of the chain peeping from Bridie's pocket. As a watch chain, it would have been within easy reach.

But even if I deny that I stepped into Ciara's shoes and saw the man who choked her, how could Bridie have hidden her sister's body, then masqueraded as Ciara? The answer to that is in plain sight. Bridie's parents had lost one daughter that night; they wouldn't have wanted to lose the other one. They said it was Bridie who'd been murdered—because as Ciara, a child in a woman's body, she couldn't be charged with murder?

Then a darker reason fills me with dread. If the O'Connors said it was Bridie who'd been killed, they could pin the murder on Brendon Blake and save their other daughter. Thomas could have grabbed the bloody chain from Bridie's hands and tossed it into the rubbish heap to implicate the tinker.

But why hide Ciara's body where it could never be found?

*No, Bridie, no!*

The words intrude again and I notice what I've missed. The realisation knocks the wind out of me. Ciara isn't pleading for her life; she's throwing a tantrum. And her emotions were so strong that they imprinted her words in this room forever—because she never came back to erase them.

The landscape is breathing its history. And as I inhale it, I'm suddenly inside Bridie's skin.

*I don't care.*

*Pa shouted at me and sent me to our room. 'You're too strong-willed to be my daughter. If you want to be away with the faeries, a changeling you must be.'*

*But I have a secret. When they're all asleep I'm going to meet Brendon. I'm so excited I can hardly breathe. He's waiting for me down by the well, and he's going to take me away from here, all the way to China.*

*Ciara is crying. She can't tear her eyes away from the bag I've packed. She might be a simple thing but she knows what I plan to do. She doesn't want to lose me, her precious twin sister.*

*"No, Bridie, no!"*

*"Shhh, darling."*

*I take her in my arms, but she grabs my new fob chain and pushes me away. My button pops off, and I hear her feet thump down the stairs. I know where she's going. But I can't follow her. If Pa catches me defying him, he'll lock me in. Hasn't he threatened to do it more than once.*

*Ciara wants to make Brendon go away. She will give him the chain because everyone knows that tinkers love gold more than anything. She doesn't understand that Brendon doesn't care about the chain; he wants me.*

*I'm in agony but I can only wait till he sends her back. She'll be tired from her crying, poor sweet thing, and fall asleep. Then, as hard as it is to leave her behind, I'll go.*

As Bridie's anguish turns to confidence in her man, I find myself back in my own skin.  The truth of what I've just witnessed settles in my heart and I'm crying with relief. There was no murder here.

But other things happened in this room. The sorrow of them is seeping from the stone walls in spite of the new plaster. Emotions deep and raw wash over me. Not murder. Something worse. Darkness.

The darkness is suffocating and I look around for a light. And through the dormer window, that's what I see. Lights. Moving lights.

Has it happened? Are the faeries partying up on the hill?

I pull on my jeans and sweatshirt, before feeling my way across the room and down the stairs. At the sunroom window I peep through the shutters and find the outline of the ruined church, fully expecting to see an explosion of lights. But the ruin is in darkness.  The lights are coming from a different direction.

The well.

There's a small torch in a kitchen drawer, but I hope I won't have to use it and draw attention to myself. At the back door, I remember to sidestep the flagstone. The slight chill as I hurry past might just be my memory.

On the path, the copse of trees screens me from the lights, but before I get there I'm slapped in the face by an invisible wall. As I fall back, sticky tentacles entrap me and all hope is sucked from me. It's the darkness again—a cocktail of anger and misery and horror ensnaring me in an unseen web. As I flail my arms, desperate to escape, I feel something else. Evil. It's sticking to my skin and seeping into my soul.

At last my thrashing catapults me out the other side. I double over, breathing hard and feeling … violated. It's the site of the murder, I'm sure of it. This is where I came in my vision, but this was the flipside of being Ciara fighting for her life. I've just seen the mind of her killer.

Trying not to cry, I focus on the path ahead. The lights are further on, rising up from the valley below. I creep forward, using their brightness to see by, ignoring the blackberries. At the edge, I crouch down and peep over.

Below me people are moving about in a kind of systematic chaos. Caravans are being set up. There are folding chairs around campfires in braziers, laughter and chatter. Women of all shapes and ages are stringing up clothes lines or stirring cooking pots. Their garments are an odd assortment, like hand-me-downs. Men and boys are carrying buckets and moving barrels. Children are being told to go to bed and are doing the opposite. I watch in amazement until I understand. If these were wagons drawn by horses I'd be reimagining the past again, but these caravans are pulled by cars. The tinkers have arrived.

I watch them for a while, wondering about the timing. Vincent gave the impression that Travellers no longer use this site. Why are they here?

Then, just as I'm shrinking back from my viewing spot, something odd happens. A man with a craggy unshaven face stops dead still and looks up. I know I'm invisible, camouflaged by shadows, but at the same time I'm quite sure he's staring at me. He doesn't avert his gaze until I slither back from the edge, catching some thorns in my jeans.

Feeling unnerved, I make a run for the house.

On the way back I bypass the site of my encounter with the killer's mind, pushing the horror away. I'll need to think about those dark emotions, but not now.

I slip through the back door, relieved to lock myself in. Stepping over the flagstone, I shrug off its chilly vibes. The trip to the well has been a minefield, and in a rack in the kitchen I spy some wine and feel tempted. Then I remember it's 3 am. The tinkers distracted me from my listening post upstairs, but the evil vision on the path might bring the answers closer.

The stairs creak as I climb but I'm too overwhelmed to be spooked. Until I'm under the covers again—and I hear a sound downstairs. The unmistakable sound of wine being poured into a glass.

I left the door unlocked when I went down to the well.

# Chapter 20

I slow my breathing and will myself to think. Rory wants me out of town and I've defied him. Then there's Dermot. What violence might he perform to purge his life of faerie trouble? I remember the man who burned his wife because he believed she was a changeling and start to sweat. Can I smell smoke?

Then there's the ghost I just aroused on the path. After more than a century in limbo could the murderer be primed for another victim?

Maybe it's just someone who's seen the lights on. Or Josephine's told someone I'm staying here. But why sneak in and hide, then make yourself at home?

Widow Winsome told us it's what sheehogues do. And once they're in, you've got to order them out with all your heart or they'll make the place uninhabitable with their tricks. The last thing I need is a supernatural creature spoiling my research. But a real person could be worse.

I have no idea what to do. There's no chance that the intruder's popped in to drink some wine and leave. They must know I'm here. For several long minutes I strain to listen. Bumps are followed by thuds—things are being thrown around. Small things. Cutlery rattles to the floor. Like a sheehogue on the loose. Bloody hell.

The stairs are the only exit. If I have to make a run for it, I'm wearing a T-shirt and knickers and my shoes are on the mat inside the back door. My jeans are on the other bed. I slither from under the covers and creep across the floor to put them on.

As I tiptoe towards the door, the fireplace catches my eye, with its fire tools hanging on a stand. But I don't need a poker. The widow said fury and confidence will do.

When I'm on the stairs, the creature starts to cackle. But before I can prepare my banishment cry, the cackle turns into a laugh. A laugh I know. Finn Cormack. He's playing the sheehogue to frighten me. The bastard.

Fuelled by an explosion of outrage, I race down the stairs yelling like a banshee. He's sitting at the kitchen counter holding up a glass of wine.

"Get out!" I scream, throwing open the front door and pointing.

"Guess who I am, I'll leave you be. Get it wrong, you're stuck with me."

"Get out now!"

"I don't think so," his voice is low with menace, "great-granddaughter of Bridie O-*fecking*-Connor."

"I'll call the police."

"Do that. The guards always come running when a cousin pops in for a drink."

What? He's doing my head in. And his manner is making my skin prickle.

"I want you to *go*."

He gets off the stool and walks towards me. I'm willing him to leave, but when he stops and towers over me, I feel the sweat trickling down my spine. Then he grabs the pendant at my neck and pulls.

The next thing I know, he's pushed me backwards onto the floor and landed on top of me. He's breathing hard and his wild eyes are inches from mine. For a long terrifying moment I know I'm going to be strangled just like Ciara—using the same weapon.

These thoughts fly by while I'm writhing and hitting him with my fists, and he's twisting the chain tighter, making me gag.

Then he's off me.

"You bloody eejit!" a man snarls, punching Finn hard in the face so he falls backwards.

"Wearing it like a trophy, she is," Finn says, getting up and wiping his bloody nose on his sleeve. "And it's not hers to own. And don't you ever call me an eejit."

"I'll deal with you later," my rescuer says. "Now do what the lady said. Get out." He frogmarches Finn to the door and shoves him through it. "And sober the feck up. You eejit."

Then he locks the door.

I've rolled into a ball, coughing and sobbing. Adrenaline is coursing through me and I can feel the burn marks on my neck. And now I'm locked inside with a stranger, a man bigger than Finn.

He goes to the counter and pours more wine, his slow deliberate movements calming me. Then he walks to where I'm hunched on the floor and offers me the glass.

"You've had a shock." His voice is gentle. "Get some of this into you."

The tears keep flowing, but I take the wine and swallow.

He sits in an armchair with his own glass. "Michael Cormack.

Call me Mikey."

"Cormack," I whisper.

"Finn's father."

My hackles rise. "Your *son* was going to strangle me. He's got some stupid idea that this chain isn't mine. He's wrong."

"He's hot-headed. And plastered on poteen. I feared he might do something stupid when he told me you'd turned up."

My head is spinning. "He should be behind bars."

He nods. "Call the guards if you must, it's your right. But before you do, get some wine into you and let me tell you a story."

He watches me with an expression that's strong but kind and I realise where I've seen his craggy face. Looking up at me from the caravans.

"Finn's a tinker," I say.

Mikey nods. "And an O'Connor."

Shit.

After the silence that follows this revelation, Mikey begins his story.

"She was pregnant, Bridie was. I don't think she knew it that night because Brendon didn't know. But she knew soon enough. And by then he'd swung for her murder."

I shiver and pull a rug off the sofa. I'm remembering Bridie's words upstairs, how excited she was. How in love.

"What happened to the baby?"

"I'll tell you everything I know, everything my grandpap told me, but I'm getting ahead of myself.

"They'd agreed to run away as soon as Bridie turned sixteen. Travellers marry young even today so it was the natural thing to do. But according to Brendon, they didn't make love until her birthday."

It ties in with what the maid, Sibby, remembered—when Bridie disappeared from the party and came back with mud on her dress. No wonder she didn't know she was pregnant until many weeks later. And by then her lover was dead. Waves of emotion flow through me as I picture her alone, pregnant, renamed Ciara for reasons I fear were about her family's revenge on the tinker, her sister and her lover dead, and her future in tatters. Perhaps Finn's attack has heightened my awareness, because my tears won't stop.

"They were going to meet by the well that night," Mikey continues. "Brendon had a horse and wagon ready, gifted to him by the clan. He had a yearning to see the Far East so they were going to travel to the coast, take a boat to England, then to Europe and the Silk Road."

It explains the bamboo. He gave Bridie her half of the whistle—for her birthday? When she combined it with his fipple, it would be a symbol of their union. The grand adventure was before them: a life on the road, free of the strictures of Bridie's middle-class upbringing. Together they were going to make music.

"But Ciara turned up in Bridie's place," I say, "and waved the gold chain in his face."

"Brendon sent her home. *With* the chain."

"So how did it turn up in the rubbish heap near your camp with blood all over it?"

"You've been doing your homework. Finn said you were digging and wouldn't stop. I told him to leave it till I got here, but ever since that exhibition he's been a hen on a hot griddle. That's why he got legless on poteen, then went for you tonight. He's in a fury that you've ended up with Brendon's whistle, thinks it should be his." He lowers his eyes, then looks up.

"And he's ashamed."

"Of what?"

He looks me straight in the eye. "That the world thinks he's descended from a murderer."

Shit. We're back to the baby. My great-grandmother's first child.

Mikey resumes his story. "About the chain, we don't know. Brendon swore black and blue that he didn't witness the murder. He was thrown into a spin when he realised it was Ciara he was kissing and saw the chain in her hand. He knew it was Bridie's birthday present from her parents. Had Bridie sent Ciara with a message that she'd changed her mind? He ran home in a panic, but his father sent him back and told him not to be a fool, that he must wait for Bridie as planned."

Even though I sense what's coming, dread is seeping through me.

"And Bridie did turn up. Frantic and crying." He pauses for the revelation. "Because she'd tripped over Ciara's body on the path."

With his words I'm back inside Bridie's skin.

*Something's wrong. I can't wait for Ciara any longer. The house is quiet so I creep through the kitchen and out the back door, then I run. It's what I've dreamed of doing for so long, running into Brendon's arms and away forever.*

*On the path, I miss my footing and fall but my scream sticks in my throat. My sister's face stares back at me, red and bloated, with my fob chain cutting into her neck.*

*I brush my fingers along her still warm cheek, sobbing. What monster has done this? There must be thieves and murderers about, but why didn't they take the chain?*

*I say a prayer for my darling sister's blameless soul, then run to the well, falling again and again, this time blinded by my tears.*

*Brendon is waiting and he takes me in his arms. Then he sees my face.*

*I grab his hand and take him back to Ciara. He falls to his knees in prayer, but there's nothing we can do to save my baby sister.*

*Our plans are ruined. When they find Ciara they'll point the finger at Brendon, a tinker and no good. If we run away now it will only confirm his guilt.*

"They hid her body," Mikey says, bringing me back. "Nothing could save Ciara, but if she disappeared, they figured that Brendon couldn't be accused of her murder."

"Until the police found the bloody chain."

"It was missing when they ran back to Ciara. They knew the chain could still point the blame at Brendon, but they couldn't find it and had to give up."

I can feel the damning evidence encircling my neck. The burn marks from Finn's attack and the bruises on my chest throb. My mind latches onto my encounter with evil on the path—and the other person who was there that night, by his own admission. James Sullivan. Obsessed with Bridie, stalking both girls at every chance. Overhearing the kiss with Brendon, then finding his chance to have Ciara—and choking her in the process. It seems he'd have been ruthless enough to then point the finger at the tinker.

"How could they have hidden her body in a place so secret that she's never been discovered?"

"My great-grandfather wouldn't say. Then no-one could be forced to tell."

"Your great-grandfather?"

"Brendon Blake."

After slipping into Bridie's skin, I can guess what he's going to tell me but I have to hear it from his lips. He pours us both another glass.

"You'll have to fill in the gaps yourself," he says. "You've got the gift or you wouldn't be here."

Finn must have told him my story, but I'm not going to think about Finn right now.

"About eight months after Brendon was hanged, a woman arrived in the camp. Mrs Thomas O'Connor herself. Not that anyone would know her wrapped up as she was in a pauper's shawl with a bundle in her arms that she refused to look at. She spoke to the Blakes, told them she and her husband wouldn't be keeping a tinker brat, not after the shame and tragedy we'd brought on her daughters. She'd gladly kill the child but not at the risk of damning her own soul."

Mikey's eyes smoulder and I remember the field of unbaptised babies forever damned in spite of their innocence.

"She was saving her own soul," he says. "Her own grandchild counted for nothing because he was half tinker. Brendon's sister had just married a Cormack so she took the boy and gave him the Cormack name."

I'm crying. Unbearable wouldn't begin to describe Bridie's anguish. For nine months she had to endure the agony of her murdered sister and her executed lover. She must have wondered every day if the nightmare would ever end. Then her mother ripped Bridie's newborn child from her breast and handed him over to the tinkers. Bridie not only lost her man, she lost the most precious thing she had to remember him by.

That's when I remember Finn's comment when he broke in. "Finn was going to murder his own cousin," I murmur.

"He can't think straight. I grew up with the shame of being the descendant of a convicted murderer, and so did Finn. It flows through all of us like the blood in our veins. Even though Finn's got Brendon's gift for music and jewellery, and I've given him a better future than the road, he can't shake off the injustice. And then you turn up, untouched by our tragedy, calling yourself Bridie and flaunting Brendon's whistle like a good luck charm. Finn called me straight away and I told him to wait till I got here. But the eejit got into the poteen."

Drink doesn't turn gentle guys into stranglers, but I don't put the thought into words.

"He cried down the phone that he'd played Brendon's whistle," Mikey says. "That's what he was ripping off your neck—the whistle not the chain."

"One murder doesn't solve another," I say. Finn could have taken the whistle from me several times. He didn't have to kill me for it. "Why did you want to speak to me?"

"We've been waiting for over a century for someone with the gift to uncover the truth, to clear Brendon's name."

"Really? Finn made it very clear he doesn't want any more O'Connors meddling in tinker business. Even though it's my story as much as his."

"You're both O'Connors, but he's a Blake too and that makes the world of difference. And when the clan hears what happened here tonight there'll be members who agree with him. An O'Connor repeating history in the very same place."

Repeating history. It feels like a curse.

"How can it possibly be my fault?"

"Brendon was strung up as a murderer because of Bridie. And if you go to the guards with your bruises, our Finn will be labelled one too."

"It wasn't Bridie's fault." Or mine.

"Wasn't it? She could have saved him, but she didn't say a

word. He was charged with murdering her and she was *alive*. She didn't kill him with her own hands, but make no mistake, it was Bridie O'Connor let him go to the gallows."

"She was only sixteen," I protest. "How can you be sure she had a choice? She was locked away, unable to speak on his behalf. That bedroom upstairs, there's agony seeping from the walls. She blamed herself for Ciara's death, and because she was trapped she let Brendon hang. Her guilt was the air she breathed right up to her death."

When she could pass the responsibility for finding the truth on to me.

"Some say it was Bridie herself killed Ciara," Mikey tells me. "That's why I wanted to meet you. We've been waiting for the truth for over a century but what will you do if you discover that?"

It's a good question. I'm confident now that Bridie wasn't Ciara's murderer, but not at all confident that my visions will clear anyone's name.

"You'll just have to trust me," I say. "What will you do if the clues point to Brendon after all?"

Mikey's eyes show confidence too. And a determination that reminds me there's a lot at stake for him and his family and I should watch my step.

"I'll deal with that if it happens," he says.

* * *

Mikey assures me that Finn won't bother me again, but when he sees the fear in my eyes he offers to sleep on the sofa.

Back upstairs, I get under the shower and wash off Finn's violation, blessing Josephine for the hot water, letting the tears flow.

But I can't wash off my connection with the twins. I've already relived the trauma of Ciara's last moments, but now I'm back inside Bridie's skin.

*They're keeping me indoors and calling me Ciara. They sent Sibby away so there's no-one to say which twin is living upstairs and suffering from 'hysteria'. My mother calls me Ciara whenever she speaks to me. It's an extra punishment—reminding me that it's my fault my sister is dead.*

*But I don't need reminding. If I hadn't loved Brendon she'd still be alive. Don't I blame myself every day for being so selfish. And what of Brendon? I'm afeared the man I love will soon be dead too.*

I know the consequences Bridie lived with—consequences so traumatic that they drove her into a convent in Dublin and a new life in Australia.

She lived the secret of what happened here every day of her life. I owe it to her to unravel the mystery if I can.

# Chapter 21

The sounds and smells of breakfast greet me at the top of the stairs—eggs and bacon and coffee. Having just checked my bruises in the mirror, the memory of Finn's intrusion makes me tense up, but when I enter the kitchen Mikey is alone.

He gestures towards the table and places the plate in front of me. "Feeding the Irish in you. Psychic work is hungry work."

"Just don't expect the impossible," I tell him. "After more than a hundred years my psychic discoveries are hardly likely to lead to Brendon's exoneration."

He grins. "I've got more confidence in you than you have. You went somewhere last night. I saw it in your eyes."

But that was between me and Bridie. "If I discover any evidence," I say, "you'll be the first to know."

There's an understanding between us: he'll keep Finn away while I do my best to uncover the truth. Even if the outcome isn't what either of us expects.

We exchange mobile numbers, and he leaves.

My courage fortified by food, I borrow a light jacket from a hook inside the back door. As I jump over the flagstone the rush of ice does its thing. Even though it's part of the new extension, there's something I need to investigate right here in this mudroom. But after Davina's warning I'm afraid to linger on my own.

The day is overcast but dry. I follow a low stone wall that snakes up the hill, separating two fields. The ruin of the church looms above me, solemn and majestic in its crumbled state. It's a hike, and when I stop for breath I turn and take in the view as it gradually emerges from the green folds below—the blue horizon, then the bay, then the hobbit houses of Dingle. This property is some real estate, marred only by superstition.

Before I reach the ruin I take a photo. I don't really know what I'm doing here, but I've been drawn to it and the magic of the place is palpable. The circular earth-and-stone wall of the old ring fort is easy to find, and the ditch around it that provided the soil. A megalithic treasure sitting in a farmer's field with only the sheep for company. I circumnavigate the wall, taking more photos.

The church was constructed within. I planned to explore the whole ruin, but now that I'm just outside the circle my reluctance is strong. If I hadn't read so much about the mythology, I'd put it down to the altitude, but now I'm not so sure. Something in me doesn't want to violate the faerie ring.

Violate. My mind stumbles on the word at the same moment as my feet stumble on some stones. There's an ugly scar in the side of the fort where stones have been excavated, not all that long ago. Did they need extra stones for the extension of the house? If so, it could explain poor Dermot Donnelly's state. If he supervised the violation of the faerie ring, he might have lived in fear of their reprisals ever since.

* * *

Josephine picks me up at the house to drive me back into Dingle. On the way she quizzes me about the ghost, but my answers are so vague she stops asking. I hope she hasn't noticed the marks on my neck. I'll keep Finn's attack to myself for now, but I took some photos of the bruises.

On the bus to Tralee, it's a welcome distraction to turn my thoughts to the Soul Work conference. I've run one- and two-day programs several times, but sessions of ninety minutes will be more intense. My brainstorming outline to Sister Kevin still feels like the best way to trigger my creativity on the run. I've learnt that the workshop goes best if I start with the right activity and let it flow from there.

Before my lift to the conference arrives, I want to debrief with Davina about last night. But when I get off the bus I'm drawn to the murder exhibition, as if there's something there I've missed.

One of the glass cases now includes the family photo they copied from mine. I glance at it and see Bridie's ring, just visible on her right hand as it rests on the piano keys. Strange that I haven't noticed it before. It's the one that Sibby said was used to tell the twins apart when they weren't wearing gloves. It makes me think of the missing finger on the mannequin and all the strange clues about fingers and rings. The words 'ring of truth' pop into my mind. But a ring still seems trivial compared to the history that the chain and the whistle pendant are carrying.

Nothing else catches my attention until I'm on my way out again and the room full of archaeology draws me in. The dioramas of megalithic monuments show ring forts and portal tombs and underground tunnels called souterrains. Portals into what, I wonder. The superstitious types around here have got a pretty good idea.

Back at the B&B, I manage to avoid Nola who I now know is a spy for the tinkers. She might not be related to the Blakes but I don't want her knowing my business. In our room, Davina gives me a welcome hug and sees the marks on my neck.

"They're not telepathic bruises," I say. "They're real." I tell her everything that happened at the house.

"So it's not a coincidence that you met Finn," she says.

"I know, but he frightens me. And he's getting in the way."

"You're not in control of the clues, Selkie. They'll keep coming at you from all directions and your job is to ride them like a bucking seal and not fall off."

That makes me smile. Selkie Moon astride a seal is one of the images a newspaper used when I turned up like a stranded mermaid. The press went crazy over the selkie myth that inspired my name.

"Now tell me exactly what happened in the upstairs bedroom," she says.

She listens to how my encounter with Ciara's ghost suddenly flipped and I was inside Bridie's skin. "It was just like the mannequin, only this time I was Bridie."

"It's always been about you and Bridie," she says. "The mannequin was a one-off—maybe to do with that missing finger, maybe not. You'll discover why when you find Ciara. But the psychic seed that Bridie planted when you were just born, that's blossomed. She wants you to solve Ciara's murder for sure, but if you're slipping inside her skin she's got a message for you too. You're likely to keep getting the visions until you get the message."

"If I last long enough. I'm in overwhelm."

"You just need to catch up on some sleep."

Davina bundles me into bed with a promise to wake me in time to pack for the seminar. Then later she comes down to the street with me to wait for the nun who's collecting me.

While I've been meeting ghosts, she's been reading up on Dervla.

"Anything interesting?" I ask.

"Nothing. It's the same biography everywhere: unconfirmed rumours that she was stolen from her mother and adopted, abused by her stepfather, went into the convent straight out of school and rose up the ladder in the church."

"Any mention of her twin sister?"

"No, but she didn't find out about me until she started digging in the adoption archives for her doctorate."

Something's bothering me—and I sense Davina's bothered too or she wouldn't be googling Dervla's history. What are the chances that both babies would end up with abusive stepfathers? But now's not the moment to question Dervla's sincerity.

When a car pulls up, we hug each other goodbye. While I'm away she'll be off to meet her mother.

Feeling lost for the right words, I say, "Fill your phone with photos."

"Haven't I got two phones," she says through her tears.

"Yes, but you have to actually press the shutter. So don't forget to do it. I want to see this amazing woman who's survived losing her babies. She'll be so proud of who you are."

* * *

Abbeymare Retreat Centre is located on the coast north of Tralee, and after the events of last night in Dingle I'm pleased to be travelling in the opposite direction. Two days of presenting Being Sleek to a receptive audience will ground me again; not to mention the boost to my bank account. It also means I can claim part of my travel costs against my earnings.

My driver is Sister Bernadette and she chats away while navigating the roads almost as wildly as Finn. It must be something in the Irish gene pool, so I've probably got it too. That makes me smile.

There's a no-phone policy at the centre, which surprises me at first, then makes sense. As I'm firing off texts to Alister and Davina and Gretel to let them know, one comes in from Derek.

*Waikiki hotel has cancellation in September. Two days. Should I book it and update your website? DD xx*

What would I do without him? Agreeing and thanking him, I tell him I'm off the air then lock both phones into the tiny locker provided.

Before dinner, I wander into the garden and let the perfume of the blooms work its magic on my soul. Then I go indoors and find that the seminar room I'll be using tomorrow overlooks the sea. After checking that all my materials are ready, I look out the window and am startled to see seals basking on the beach right outside. Because of my phobia I've never been this close to my namesakes, but their presence confirms that this interlude is just what I need to make sense of everything; some distance to reflect on what my family history means for me.

After dinner I get the urge to do something I've never done—stroll along the path above the shore and watch the seals. It's low tide so there are no waves to bother me. A seal pup and its mother are lying on the beach, just being there. There's something very intimate about being almost close enough to touch them.  With their sandy coats they look anything but sleek, off-duty in their clever camouflage. Neither of them has peeled off its pelt and started dancing, so they're not the same species as me. That thought makes me laugh. But then the moon isn't full yet.

Suddenly I realise the summer solstice is only two nights away. For the first time in my life I'll be wrapped in my Celtic roots on this very special date. I've never really wondered how the myth of the selkies evolved, but it seems auspicious that I'm here right now. It would be magical to see what happens. I decide to ask Sister Kevin if I can stay an extra night.

Back in my private cell, my encounter with the seals reminds me of when I met Alister. He gatecrashed my first seminar in Honolulu and witnessed the way Being Sleek popped up in my goals seminar and took over. The magical links between the wisdom of seals and the world of business blew everyone away, and afterwards he invited me to become one of his presenters. For a whole lot of reasons I've stayed independent, and that decision has given us space to discover that we're destined to be lovers—when I get my act together—connected by an invisible red thread.

* * *

On the first day of the conference I'm presenting one session before and one after lunch, then the same again tomorrow. Delegates can select the sessions they attend and Being Sleek, the most 'quirky' thing on offer, proves popular. People fill the room to bulging.

The seals are still frequenting the beach below our window, so on a whim I take the participants outside. It's more difficult to use the poster paper, but the centre's so close to the beach that I get two guys to tape the blank posters up on an outside wall.

"OK," I say, after breaking them into groups, "each group is an office team informing each other of the tasks for the day. Think 'task', then look at the seals and think 'value'. Write both on the paper. Then later we'll make a map."

"Task:  loyalty email to customers," one woman begins. "Value: make them feel part of the pod."

Everyone laughs and they're away.

"Task: review our vision statement." The guy looks at the seals. "Value: lose the jargon and focus on authentic."

Everyone is so energised by the proximity of our mentors that the lists in each group grow quickly.

Then I get them to link similar tasks and values with coloured lines to make maps of Being Sleek. It's rewarding for me too, and afterwards it still has the power to amaze me how the 'soul work' created itself in the company of our 'aquatic cousins'.

* * *

It's in the middle of my second night at the centre, that I'm disturbed by a dream.  Rocks are falling into the sea like confetti, each one wrapped in white paper.  I know they're letters that I have to read.  My arms are as long as a sheehogue's, but as hard as I try to catch one of the stones, I can't quite reach it. One after the other they go under the water, taking their messages with them.

I wake in a sweat knowing that I have to check my phone. But it's more complicated than just opening my locker. The locker room is locked and I have to wander along endless corridors before I find someone to open it. It's 1 am and the nun who's summoned, keys hanging from her chatelaine, isn't impressed. Not by the timing or my intuition. She stands at the door of the locker room like a jailer, her arms folded and her jaw set, while I check what she believes to be trivial messages on my phone.

The one from Davina isn't trivial. *Hiding underground. Dervla thinks I'm dead.*

Bloody hell. I flop onto a chair and read the rest.

*Don't phone. Saving battery. Get guards. Near river with ravine one hour south of Bantry, I think.*

She's attached several photos that she must have taken en route. In a panic I scroll through them. A hand-painted sign on a gatepost: *Witching Rods 2 Euros.* A roadside shrine cut into a hedge with a pure-white Virgin standing in it. A tree hung with rags. Not a single bloody clue to indicate her location.

My head is spinning. *Hiding underground. Dervla thinks I'm dead*—what does that mean? Is she hiding from Dervla? But they were going to meet their mother.

The message is an hour old. Do I risk texting back so she knows I've got it? But if Dervla's *hunting* for her—the word pops into my head—and hears the phone ...

I walk along the corridor a little, out of earshot of the nun. The guard who picks up my call is bemused. No doubt my accent screams 'tourist'.

His tone is patronising. "Well, she's not dead if she's sending texts, is she, darlin'?"

"Someone's trying to kill her," I whisper.

"That's not what she says, is it?" Shit. I shouldn't have read him the message. "You take yourself back to the land of nod, and if your friend hasn't come out of her hiding place by the mornin', give us another tinkle."

I'm pacing, wondering what else I can do, when the nun emerges from the locker room and glares at my phone.

"It's an emergency," I say. "My friend's in danger. I have to keep making calls."

Who to? Not Dervla. But who else do I know who can help?

As the nun shows me into a seminar room, my chest is gripped by the old fear—I'm adrift in a foreign place, power-less and alone. I'm the only person who can help Davina and I'm clueless about what to do.

I look out the window. The building's exterior lights illumi-nate the beach. And the seals. And then I'm running, driven by something primal—out the door in my pyjamas, down the steps and onto the shore. Seals are lazing on the beach and bobbing in the water. Their expressions seem to be asking what I'm doing here as I fall to my knees on the sand.

A Canadian man in one of my seminars once told me about the Native American shamans who used to go down to the shore to draw wisdom from the orcas. He called me a seal whisperer, which seemed crazy given my water phobia. I talk *about* seals; I don't communicate *with* them. Until now.

"Help me," I hear myself whisper. "My sister's in trouble." My soul sister.

What I'm expecting I have no idea. A message? But one of the prone seals turns its head and makes eye contact with me. Behind its long lashes it blinks three times. 'Hello, cousin,' it seems to say. And in a flash I know what to do.

As I run back to my room, I'm already texting my own cousin—Mikey Cormack.

*Urgent. Friend in trouble. Do you know these places? Near*

*Bantry. A river with a ravine.*

Within minutes he's phoned me and heard the whole story, and the photos are being circulated around the Traveller network.

"Sit tight," Mikey says. "We know every landmark in the country. I'll pick you up and we'll drive to Bantry. By the time we get there, we'll have a good idea where she is."

After getting dressed I wait at the Abbeymare entrance, wondering what else I can do besides endless pacing. I send the images to Derek. He'll have software that might match the photos to their locations. I tell him it's urgent, that Davina's in trouble.

*On it*, he replies, for once not asking for more details.

That's when I notice another text. Not from Davina or Derek. Not from anyone I know.

*Kill a cat and hide a shoe. A charm against faeries, that means YOU.*

I shiver. It's like a playground chant, but it's clearly a threat and I feel threatened.

Then I see headlights and Mikey's pulling up.

# Chapter 22

With texts chirping as different clans argue about the locations of the photos, the journey through the night would be the grandest of adventures if I wasn't so worried about Davina. As I google 'rivers' and 'ravines' in Ireland's south-west, I'm wondering if her birth mother even exists. My imagination is spinning tales of deception and betrayal, with Davina the innocent victim of a monster.

The roadside shrine could be anywhere, but there's a positive ID on the rag tree—near a holy well for Saint Gobnait. *I tied a rag there only last week for my sick mam*, texts a woman called Rylee. *I recognise the floral pattern.*

Mikey's using a radio to chat to other Travellers and no-one knows of a river with a ravine an hour south of Bantry.

"It must be Lough Hyne," he says after much discussion. "A lake that's open to the sea, with rapids and high cliffs on one side."

"Rapids?" I squeak. "Cliffs?"

"As long as she sits tight in her souterrain she'll be safe," Mikey says.

As I ask him what a souterrain is, I remember the diorama at the museum. A kind of megalithic tunnel, lined with rocks and used for storage or refuge, from two French words: '*sous*' meaning 'under' and '*terre*' meaning 'earth'.

"There's one at Beenbawn," Mikey says, "but it's crumbled away and you can't crawl along it any more."

I remember the emergency tape at the promontory fort on the cliff, and imagine Davina cringing in a tunnel that's teetering above raging rapids, only to be discovered by Dervla. And then what? Into the arms of her sister—or over the edge? For the first time I realise just how much Dervla's got to lose if Davina spills what she knows about her past.

"Is there a souterrain at Lough Hyne?" I ask.

"I don't know," Mikey says, "but they're all over the place. They're often buried until earthmoving for a road or something finds them."

His phone buzzes. Another Traveller woman knows the witching rod sign. *An old woman bends coathangers, swears they find ley lines and buried treasure. On the back road to Lough Hyne.*

Lough Hyne again. And the back road—that would be Dervla's style. Contort Davina's sense of direction and avoid the CCTV on the highways. Was she always planning to kill her?

Then Derek comes through with a match for the roadside shrine. *Found it on a website for religious pilgrims on a budget,* he texts, giving the location. *Let me know when you find her, if she's safe. And if there's anyone I can kill. I've been boning up on voodoo.*

Mikey alters his GPS in response to each clue. Plotted on a map, the references stretch from Bantry to Lough Hyne. We head for the eastern side of the lake where a forest borders the high cliffs. According to the Travellers, it's the only place that could be mistaken for a ravine.

When we finally reach a lonely rural road dotted with a few farmhouses, dawn is breaking. We don't have the technology to pinpoint Davina's phone, but the GPS shows that the road ends at the lake. If this is her 'ravine' then her hiding place is close.

Where the fields and hedgerows give way to forest, the road ends abruptly. The cliffs must be hidden by the trees and I swallow at the thought of falling. Why did Dervla bring Davina to this place? There can only be one reason.

Mikey turns off the engine, and when we get out he takes my hand which is wet with sweat.

"No sense either of us going over," he says, and I tear up.

The forest swallows us. Filtered early light throws shadows into the abyss on my left that must be the lake below. Squeezing Mikey's hand I push forward step by slow step, trying to focus on why we're here. It's hours since I heard from Davina. What if Dervla found her first?

The ground cover is thick making the going slow. We can't help crunching sticks underfoot, so if Dervla's still around she'll hear us.

Then we stop and I send Davina a text, then dial her number and strain my ears. I can hear it! A soft ringtone. But is she still with her phone?

Forgetting to take hold of Mikey's hand again, I move towards the sound. The edge of the cliff looms and as I pull back, I fall and he grabs me. Then twigs are breaking and we turn to see a woman rushing through the trees and into the clearing behind a house. Her red hair is flying and she's covered in dirt and twigs.

"It's Davina," I scream. I race after her, and reach her just as she collapses.

"Selkie," she moans, falling into my arms.

I look around, fearing she's running from Dervla, but there's only an old woman standing nearby, moaning and wild-eyed.

"Came up out of the ground, she did. And wasn't I just going for the eggs."

Mikey carries Davina back to the car and we wrap her in a blanket. It's several long minutes before she opens her eyes. She seems to have lost the power of speech, but she sits up and sips hot chocolate from a thermos—Mikey thought of everything—while I inspect her cuts and bruises and the tears in her clothes. When I touch her shoulder she winces.

"You're hurt," I say, but she doesn't answer.

"I know a place nearby," Mikey says. "Let her sleep till we get there."

* * *

After another journey along back roads, we reach the outskirts of a small town and pull up beside a cluster of caravans nestled between two rows of identical houses.

"We'll be looked after here," Mikey says.

He gets out and speaks to a guy who looks to be in charge, and soon we're being ushered into a caravan that was vacated moments earlier.

Mikey leaves me to shower Davina and dress her in the clothes our hosts have provided, including a pair of shoes because she's lost one of hers. Then a woman with waist-length hair and a lined face comes in to look at her shoulder.

"Broken collarbone, I'd say." She opens a cupboard and pulls out a roll of fabric strips like the rags on the tree in the photo. "The doctor will be putting your arm in a sling," she says as she peels off a strip and ties it around Davina's wrist and neck, "but this will do the same thing for now."

I ask her if she was the person who recognised the rag tree and she nods. Her name is Rylee. I thank her and she leaves.

The Travellers bring us breakfast and a tisane of herbs for Davina's pain. She looks for all the world like a changeling: the light in her eyes that says she's Davina has departed. But she eats. And drinks several mugs of tea.

She needs to rest, and I'm just wondering how she'll sleep with her arm in a sling when she speaks for the first time.

"There never was a Peggy," she murmurs. "But for a while I thought she was a murderer."

"Your mam? What about Dervla?"

"Now I know it was Dervla. She thinks I went into the water, so I hid all night to make sure she was gone. And when I came out, my phone started ringing and that old woman started screaming."

"You did look like a faerie."

She manages a smile. "That place must be an old faerie fort because it was the faeries that saved me last night."

Then she tells me quite a story.

"I caught the train to Bantry and Dervla was there to pick me up. She drove us to a cottage near the forest where you found me."

"Lough Hyne," I say.

"She didn't tell me where we were, but the cottage was already cosy when we got there. A turf fire was burning in the grate and there was hot soup on the stove. On the table we found a note: *Picking mushrooms. Back soon.* That felt odd. Didn't our mam know I was coming soon? But we waited and waited. After a while I told Dervla I was worried, but she said our mother had probably lost track of time filling her basket with mushrooms, that she was a little absent-minded these days. She chatted as if everything was fine, the way she'd done in the car. She asked me lots of questions about my design work. It was late and I was hungry, but I didn't want to start on the soup and have my mam catch her first glimpse of me eating without her.

"When it started to get dark I couldn't wait any longer. But I was focused on finding Peggy, not on the prickling of my skin. I left Dervla, who was still telling me to wait, and headed off into the forest. In the twilight I knew I was in danger of getting lost, but I didn't know about the ravine. Next thing, someone gave me an almighty shove in the back and I was falling into blackness, screaming. I hit a ledge and my collarbone cracked so I kept screaming, and all the while rocks were bouncing around me down the cliff and splashing into water way below."

"My God," I say. "It's a miracle you didn't follow them into the lake."

The rocks in my dream pop into my mind and I fight back tears. I came very close to losing my friend last night.

"There was a silhouette peeping over the edge above me, and I was crying, thinking it must be my mam who'd pushed me over, because Dervla was still in the cottage. There was no time to think why she'd want to kill me. I shrank against the cliff into a hollow, but like magic it opened into a tunnel lined with stones."

"A souterrain."

She nods. "I rolled inside and nearly cried out with the pain, but kept quiet. When I could think straight, I went over what had happened and it didn't make sense. Then something made me look at Dervla's business card, the one she gave you. It was in my pocket. That's how I knew she'd concocted the whole story. Remember my dream way back—the one with the letters DK and everything else was smudged out?"

I nod. "Smudged out in red. We thought it meant someone with the initials DK was going to die." Shit.

"Red stains and a number eight," she says. "But it wasn't an eight, Selkie. I saw it on the back of her business card—the letter 'g'. She writes it like a printed 'g', shaped like an eight. It was in the message she wrote: *Ring me*. I remembered it was the same 'g' in the note in the cottage: *picking mushrooms*. It's the reason the note seemed odd—I'd noticed the 'g' without realising it." She stifles a sob. "My dream was warning me about Dervla. That's when I sent you that text. Thank God for the second phone. My other one was in my bag in the cottage."

"You poor thing," I say, imagining the horror of thinking it was her mother who'd pushed her over the cliff. "Injured and alone, wondering if you'd ever be found. Wondering if bloody Dervla was still there waiting to finish you off."

"My shoulder was screaming fit to wake the dead, but the souterrain felt like a refuge. I was pretty sure Dervla thought those falling rocks were me."

It's a moment before I ask, "Did you ever suspect the whole story was a lie?"

She nods and starts to cry. "It's why Peggy didn't seem real, but ... I wanted to meet my mam with all my heart."

I hold her hand and we sit in silence. The question of Dervla's motive is hanging between us, but first Davina needs to finish her story.

"You said the faeries saved you?" I ask.

She nods. "Souterrains are closed at one end, but the end

of this one must have crumbled away over the cliff, so when it started to get light I could see there was another way out. The pain nearly killed me, but I crawled on one hand up to the opening. It was blocked by fallen branches and moss, but I pushed through."

Just as Mikey and I arrived. "What about the cottage and the soup?" I ask.

"I've had all night to think about that. She must have hired the place furnished, and made the fire and the soup and written the note herself. Before she picked me up at the station."

"Why? It's a hell of an elaborate way to ... kill your sister."

*As the sister leaned over the river rim*

*The envious one pushed her in.*

"Remember our switcheroo when we were teens?" Davina's saying. "Dervla's a woman who covers her tracks. She set me up to go willingly into the forest, and then all she had to do was give me a shove and I'd disappear. She's probably ditched my handbag. Thank God I had that extra phone. It was your idea to buy them."

"Yeah. And it was my idea to visit Saint Scholastica's, which brought you two back together." I'll deal with the guilt later. "OK, I get the planning. But Dervla tried to kill you, Davina, and the big question is: why? Just so you can't squeal to the press about her past?"

I remember her extreme reaction at the convent when she assumed I was a journalist and Davina was after something. That just doesn't seem like a strong enough motive for murder.

There's a knock on the door and Mikey comes in with the clan leader, Johnny. We tell them Davina's story, and Johnny explains how Lough Hyne might have disposed of her body if she'd followed the falling rocks into the water.

"At low tide the lough rushes out to sea through a narrow channel. The rapids aren't deep but they're fast, and if you were injured or dazed or worse you'd find yourself in the ocean soon enough."

"Dervla's been waiting for the tides to be perfect," I realise. "A low tide after midnight so there'd be no-one to see a body floating by."

It explains my gig at the conference too: get me out of the way with my phone stashed in a locker. If I hadn't had that dream and checked my messages, Davina would be wandering around dazed and confused, maybe being mistaken for a faerie with who knows what consequences.

"How did this Dervla think she'd get away with making you disappear?" Mikey asks.

"Selkie's the only person in Ireland who knows me," Davina says.

"And if I didn't hear from you again," I say, "and I asked Dervla about it, she'd have some story ready about how you were spending private time with your mother. I wouldn't want to butt in on that."

Seamless planning from a master. No wonder her career has been meteoric.

Johnny moves to the door. "Stay as long as you need. Rylee's moved in with someone else. She says you can have this van to yourself."

I'm blown away by the generosity of these people who have very little and share it anyway.

"Thank you," Davina says. "I feel safe here. If I lie low, Dervla will keep thinking she's won."

"The guards need to be told," Mikey says. "It's attempted murder, if the evidence doesn't go cold."

The irony of getting the police involved isn't lost on me after Finn's attack.

Johnny nods that it's OK, but Davina cries, "She's my sister! I've only had her for a week—and you want to arrest her."

I'm floored. "Davina, you can't be serious."

Mikey makes eye contact with me. We're both thinking post-traumatic stress.

"After you've had a rest," he tells Davina carefully, "let's go back to the cottage. At least you can take some photos of your ordeal."

We arrange to meet up with Mikey in an hour and the men leave.

"So you still think she's your twin?" I say, keeping my tone casual.

"Why else would she try to kill me? A twin who looks just like her, the mother superior who's only a few votes away from being the most powerful woman in the Holy See. She doesn't want me popping up and crowding her limelight. The press would love it. And they'd have more access to me than to her. Suddenly I'm all over the front pages being pressured by journalists, and I've got dirt on her, lots of it."

I'm not sure about any of this. Why claim your twin and then bump her off? And there must be a mother somewhere, even if she's in the cemetery.

# Chapter 23

I need to tell Sister Kevin that I won't be returning to the conference, but I don't want anything to get back to Dervla. It means I have to bend the truth a little.

"I'm so sorry," I say on the phone, "but I'm in Ireland to investigate a family matter and something urgent came up last night."

"And aren't all the delegates asking for Being Sleek. You'll have to come back and run it another time, you know. So I can tell them they haven't missed out."

I agree, then grab an hour of sleep. When I wake, it's to find that a local doctor the Travellers trust has made Davina a proper sling and given her strong painkillers.

As Mikey drives us to the cottage, Davina remembers something strange. "I dropped off to sleep in the *souterrain*—not for long, but I had that dream again. The one where you lose a trinket in the rubbish heap and find a finger instead."

"Oh. That's odd." I mean it's odd that Davina was dreaming about me in the middle of her own trauma. But now I'm remembering the rubbish heap where the chain was found after Ciara was murdered.

"Along with the mannequin and its missing finger," she says, "I thought it was symbolic of someone pointing the finger at Brendon Blake. But now I'm sure there's more to it—I just don't know what."

Mikey says nothing. I suspect he's giving us space to work through these psychic clues ourselves.

The road to the cottage is lined with hedgerows. Along a ridge several farmhouses come into view—two-storey boxes in earthy tones with a chimney at each end and tiny dormer windows in the roof. They remind me of the Rathbone house.

The cottage Dervla rented is a similar style, isolated and all locked up. But if there was any doubt about Davina's story, the trace of smoke from the chimney confirms it. While Mikey photographs the chimney, then tries to get some photos through the windows, I walk back along the road a little way to the old woman's cottage. In the front yard there's a sheep with a black face. As I knock I notice a horseshoe nailed over the doorway.

"Sorry to bother you," I say as the woman peers through the crack in the door. "I was here earlier today. I'm wondering how to rent the empty cottage. It's such a beautiful place for a holiday."

They probably don't get many strangers around here so she must remember me from rescuing Davina, but she doesn't slam the door.

"What's your accent?" she asks.

"Welsh." I want to avoid any association with the nether side of the planet.

"She was here yesterday," the woman says. "Haven't seen any of them for donkey's years."

"Any of them?"

"Kelly, that's the name. Didn't they come down from Dublin every summer and ignore their neighbours. Too high and mighty for the likes of us, until they needed something. Used to send the girl over for eggs. She's not a girl now. Never liked her eyes."

So it's Dervla's family cottage, unused for years. It makes me wonder what happened to her parents. I ask her for the Kellys' phone number, but she shakes her head.

"Not surprising to see a faerie," she says, "it being Midsummer Eve."

She's talking about Davina and her fey-like sprinkling of twigs. They must have masked her resemblance to Dervla.

"But this house is protected," the woman adds.

She looks up at the horseshoe and I see it's adorned with a fresh bunch of foliage. It reminds me of the item from the press archive: the women back in Bridie's day sprinkling primroses around the dairy co-op to protect the butter from the faeries.

The woman mutters something and closes the door. She might be a superstitious old thing, but if the guards call by she'll remember the incident, the Kelly name and the date. All facts to corroborate Davina's story.

With painkillers making her more comfortable, Davina's able to retrace her steps from this morning. The forest area isn't large and we have to keep our eyes out for the edge, but the daylight makes it easier than last time. We find her lost shoe and photograph it. And a basket full of mushrooms. No wonder Davina thought her mother was the one who'd pushed her. Dervla's attention to detail screams 'psychopath'.

Under all the leaf litter there's no visible evidence of a ring fort, but the dark hole that leads to the souterrain is marked by some fabric torn from Davina's shirt. Mikey volunteers to climb into the tunnel and take photos of the ledge, but we decide he'll disturb any evidence. I'm still hoping Davina will report the incident so we tie the rag that was Rylee's sling to a tree to guide the guards to the opening.

* * *

Back in the van at the Travellers' camp, Davina sleeps. But as Mikey and I are getting ready to drive back to Dingle, she's up again and sitting at the table surrounded by photos printed by Rylee from all our phones. Mikey even snapped the moment when Davina collapsed into my arms.

"I wonder why Dervla let you take those photos as you drove to the cottage," I say. "She must have worried you were leaving crumbs."

"Shrines and rag trees are everywhere," Davina says, "so they'd not be easy to trace. And she planned to destroy my phone, not knowing I was snapping them on a second one. I wondered why she was so interested in my design work. She must have been keeping me talking so I wouldn't try to send the photos to anyone."

In the car, I text Derek that Davina's safe and ask him to do some serious digging into Dervla's background. With his superior research skills maybe he can unearth the missing motive.

*Attempted murder?* he texts back. It's all the inspiration he needs.

"I wonder what Dervla's done since last night," I say to Mikey. "Did she push Davina off the cliff, return to the cottage to wash her hands and eat the soup, then go straight back to Saint Scholastica's cool as an ice queen?" If so, her nerve is chilling.

"That sounds like her style." He pauses. "If Davina doesn't report her, I know people who can ... deal with her. She'll be trouble if she gets that promotion to Rome."

Shit. It reminds me that Travellers have a strong religious ethic and their own rough justice.

When Mikey stops for petrol, I use the loo. A newspaper on a stand is full of the summer solstice. That's when I notice the date: June 20. The same day Ciara was murdered. I've been so distracted by collecting clues I missed the most obvious one. Today is the anniversary. Surely that means that tonight must be the night. That all the clues will collide to solve Ciara's murder.

But the timing of Davina's ordeal also feels like a clue. Two sisters. It can't be a coincidence that Bridie led me to Dervla, and Dervla almost fulfilled the prophecy of Bridie's song. And the souterrain sounds just like the drain where my mother nearly died as a toddler. It could be the other link—a case of one sister trying to murder another.

With that thought, I call Stella. She picks up after a couple of rings and I hope I've caught her off-guard.

"I'm in Ireland investigating the death of Bridie's sister," I say.

She snorts. "What sister?"

"Ciara O'Connor was murdered, Stella. And that article Bridie sent me about Prunella being trapped in a drain for three days was followed by a song about how one sister murdered the other one."

I hear her intake of breath. "Your mother fell into that drain and couldn't get out. I was the one who found her."

"You might not have pushed her in, but I know you left her there. For three days. Then you got punished with boarding school after you played the hero. What I don't understand is why."

"Bloody Bridie." Stella never swears. "Until Prunella came along I was Bridie's golden girl. In the holidays she was always trying to see if I had psychic gifts."

"And did you?" She's shown some scary prescience lately.

Stella doesn't reply. "Ireland," she says at last. "You're serious. And you think Bridie had a sister who was murdered?"

"On the twentieth of June 1896."

"That's today. So what have you discovered over a hundred years after it happened?" Her tone is derisive but I can tell she's intrigued.

"She was strangled by a fob chain," I say. "Bridie sent me the chain."

Stella must know I've had visions because she says, "I stopped having visions after the incident with your mother. If they were visions and not just me trying to please Bridie. But suddenly Bridie didn't want me to be psychic any more."

Because she thought history was repeating itself?

Stella continues, sharing the story at last. "Prunella was a magical child and she adored Celtic faerie tales. The selkie story was her favourite but that came later. When she was a toddler she became fixated on one story—about the faeries stealing a human baby. She used to get me to read it to her over and over."

I shiver. "Sounds obsessive."

"Tell me about it. She was too young for a story like that but she'd throw a tantrum if anyone tried to read her anything else. And there was something dark behind her eyes as she listened. Then she started play-acting the story with her dolls. She was always the faerie and I had to play the mother with the baby. The whole thing gave me the creeps. And each time she stole my baby in the game she'd say, 'I'm going to steal your baby one day.' I knew she meant it."

I wonder if Bridie, having lost her own first child, ever heard my mother say that.

"So when Prunella fell in a drain," I say, "you left her there to die."

"Judge me if you want. She was one scary child, your mother. And in the end I couldn't go through with it."

And Prunella eventually had me.

"The prophecy came true," I murmur. It's what I discovered when I first went to Hawaii—the best-kept secret about my mother.

"She stole my first child in the cruellest way possible," Stella says and hangs up.

*  *  *

Josephine agrees to meet me at the Rathbone house this afternoon when she'll swap the key for more cash, but I won't be able to take up residence until after tonight's ghost tour. It gives me time to go back to the retreat centre to get my things. I never got around to asking if I could stay an extra night for the solstice and now the anniversary of Ciara's murder means I've got to return to the house, not loiter on the beach hoping something magical happens with my namesakes.

While Mikey waits in the car, I collect my bag from Sister Bernadette at reception and notice the jailer nun lurking at the end of the hall. She just seemed super prickly and officious last night, but now her presence as I'm leaving seems deliberate. I realise how hard she worked to keep me away from my phone—taking her time to emerge in her dressing gown, making a fuss about being woken up, trying endless keys on her chatelaine before she found the right one, then hovering too close while I read Davina's text.

I try to remember what I said to her. She didn't overhear me call the guards, but I did call it an emergency and tell her my friend was in danger. Shit. If she's a spy for Mother Clare, then Dervla might already suspect that Davina isn't dead. That puts Davina back in danger, and she can't stay with the Travellers forever.

But Dervla doesn't know about the second phone. I can make her believe that Davina's text to me came from the cottage, not after she fell.

When Sister Bernadette hands over my bag, I say a little louder than normal, "I'm so sorry about missing today's seminars. I've spent all night trying to find out where my friend's gone. She sent a text saying that her mother might have wandered off, but she didn't say where she was and now she's not answering my calls. But the guards said to sit tight, she'll turn up, so I'm going back to Tralee to wait for her. I hope she's just turned off her phone and I'm worrying about nothing."

The mention of Tralee shows I'm nowhere near Lough Hyne. Done.

When I get back to the car, Mikey's fallen asleep and on a whim I race down to the beach. It's empty. No seals. Although I think I catch sight of one just offshore, its shiny domed head bobbing like a jewel in the ocean. Are they getting ready to return tonight? Or maybe they've gone and if I was here for the full moon there'd be nothing to see. It's a reminder that I'm not here to re-enact the selkie story. If it wasn't for Bridie and Ciara, I wouldn't be in Ireland at all. Then an odd thought pops into my head and it takes my breath away. Is that seal working his magic from a distance?

I race back to the car to find Mikey awake.

"I need Finn's help," I say as he starts the engine. "He's the only one who can do it. But I won't speak to him myself."

"I'll make sure he does it," he says. "Whatever it is."

"Make new buttons for Brendon's whistle pendant using gems to spell Ciara."

The whistle is the key and I've missed it.

Mikey passes me his phone and I write the text as if it's from him. Finn's reply is quick. Since he doesn't know it's me, he's reverted from strangler to jeweller, a definite improvement.

*All new letters? Or can we poach some from Bridie?*

We. It was his jealousy about the whistle that tipped him over the edge. Now that he's got a part to play maybe he'll co-operate.

*Poaching OK. Good in fact. It'll link the two sisters, taking me right back to that bloody song. Which gems will you use?*

*Citrine, amethyst & aquamarine. I've got some stones. Get Pixie to say whether to use the ivory or the iolite.*

It's still early afternoon. Finn confirms that he can deliver the gems before ten tonight.

* * *

When Josephine meets me at the locked gate, she frowns and fingers a bunch of foliage tied to it. "What's this doing here?" She looks across to the front door. There's another bunch there.

"What is it?" I ask.

She unlocks the gate and walks towards the back of the house. I hurry to catch up and arrive in time to hear her gasp. She's looking up at the lintel above the back door.

"Jesus, Mary and Joseph," she says, crossing herself.

I follow her gaze. Something tan and shrivelled is nailed there, something that used to be an animal. Its face is contorted in pain like a victim of Mount Vesuvius.

"Protection," Josephine says, "against faeries.

I feel sick. Even though the thing is very dead, the malevolence behind the act is coming off it in waves. Then I remember the text message, anonymous and threatening: *Kill a cat and hide a shoe. A charm against faeries, that means YOU.*

"Is it a ... cat?" I ask.

"A dried cat. Wring its neck and put it in the chimney to keep the faeries away."

I shudder. It smacks of witchcraft. "Do people do the same thing with ... shoes?" I can't keep the tremble from my voice.

"It's an old custom," Josephine says. "A cat or a shoe. A lock of hair. Faeries might slip into your house like the widow's sheehogue. They're always looking for a way in. Under the door, through a crack, down the chimney. But an old shoe has all the qualities of the human who wore it, so the faeries can't get past it and invade the house."

"A shoe I can handle." Almost. "A dead cat feels like a threat."

"From an eejit who doesn't know that Ciara's ghost is already *in* this house."

"Not Ciara," I say. "Me."

Josephine looks at me but says nothing. She unlocks the back door and gets a stepladder from a cupboard under the stairs, then some rubber gloves from the kitchen.

"I'd rather not … touch it," she says, looking less businesslike for a moment. "And it's better not to remove it completely and cause more harm."

Whatever more harm might look like. Shit. I keep telling myself that Ciara's death is a simple case of murder by a human predator, but it looks like the locals have other ideas.

Josephine won't let me touch the posies so I just watch as she carries them around the back. Climbing up to the dead cat, she wrinkles her nose and hooks the twigs over it until it's mostly hidden. Now it looks like a Christmas wreath planned by a committee, and I remember the foliage hooked over the old woman's horseshoe, freshly picked after her encounter with Davina.

"It'll concentrate the protection over the back door," Josephine says, "and hide the cat until the next gale. I'll get my Sean to nail a board over it tomorrow."

She's not worried about me. She's looking after the sensibilities of the guests in tonight's ghost tour.

When the ladder is back under the stairs I make a cup of tea, but my hands won't stop shaking.

"Who did this?" I ask.

"Who wants you out of town?"

I shake my head but there's a list. Finn. He tried to scare me last time. What's he been up to while Mikey and I were rescuing Davina? Then there's Rory. He must know I'm still digging. And Dermot. If his boot was shoe magic, is the cat also his handiwork? But why do I think it's a woman? A very frightened woman.

* * *

When Josephine goes, I stash my things out of sight and look up the hill to the ruin. It seems to be waiting for me, but that's for later. If I can hold my nerve. A call from Derek adds an extra layer to the tension that's gathering in my belly. He's just realised that it's Midsummer Eve—a non-event in Hawaii but of high significance in the Celtic calendar. He wants to warn me about what he's just found in the folk tales.

"What happened to Ciara's body?" he asks.

"I don't know. Bridie knows and I hope to find out tonight. Find her ... skeleton."

But after the shrivelled cat, I'm hoping I can still go through with it.

Derek is silent for a long moment. "This folk tale is macabre and shocking so I'll spare you the details –"

"Thank you."

"But the theme is about the dead's desire to come back and fulfil ... earthly needs."

"If you mention zombies I'll hang up."

"What if Ciara's looking for her sister? It sounds like it's because of Bridie that she was killed. You're channelling Bridie to fulfil her mission, so you're appearing in Bridie's place—and after more than a century Ciara might be desperate for some kind of ... reunion."

Bloody hell. I remember Ciara's desperate call in the bedroom—*No, Bridie, no!*—and her attempt to rid them of Brendon so the sisters could stay together. Her ghost is trapped in that mindset.

Then there's Davina's experience on the flagstone; the sensation that something was calling her, down, down, down.

"It depends what the dead person wants," Derek says. "But if they present a compelling pretext and talk you into going with them, you ... won't come back."

Macabre is right, and Derek's doing what he always does—burdening something simple with layers of folklore.

I thank him for the warning and hang up, reminding myself that Ciara was strangled and her body was hidden in a very secret place. More than one person might be trying to stop me, but my job is to follow the signs and find it.

# Chapter 24

In between worrying about Davina, driving up and down the countryside, and receiving curses against faeries, that cavity behind the grille has been bothering me. Mikey's lent me a screwdriver and I get myself a stool to stand on. The screws have been painted over by a sloppy painter—Dermot himself, after all the other tradesmen ran away?—and when I've removed them, the grille needs a bit of levering where the paint has stuck.

I rest it on the mantelpiece and stare into the hole. It contains a shoe. An old-fashioned woman's shoe. Black leather with buttons up the side.

*Kill a cat and hide a shoe. A charm against faeries, that means YOU.*

But this shoe has been around longer than the cat. Over a hundred years longer.

* * *

Dermot Donnelly is working on a headstone. Or I think the wizened creature in the overalls is the same man. He reminds me of the cat. When he sees me, he disappears further into the baggy garment, his eyes hollow in his shrunken cheeks.

"It's OK, Dermot," I say, keeping my distance after our last encounter. "I just want to know what happened at the Rathbone house. Then I'll never bother you again."

"Not my firstborn child," he wails.

Bloody hell. Is he channelling Prunella? He should stop reading faerie tales before he goes to bed.

"Nothing like that," I say. "I just want the facts. I want to know what happened at the rath. I know you took some stones for the extension."

"I didn't want to," he cries, "but that builder from America made us do it, made us cut right into the rath and steal the stones from inside. Scared the fecking shite out of us. We knew what we were disturbing."

"You were following orders. I just need to know exactly what you did with the stone."

"Like you said. The conservatory."

"There's a very big flagstone just inside the back door."

"That's the portal stone," he mumbles.

"The portal into what?"

"The ... otherworld." Then suddenly he's shouting like he did in the pub. "We begged him not to use it, said it would bring bad luck to the house for eternity. That's the shape of the walls inside the rath—eternity. You never touch the stones. But would he listen. Some of the men refused, quit. But my wife was ailing and I needed the work."

"So the portal stone from the rath is the big stone just inside the back door." Calling Davina down to the otherworld. Shit.

He hangs his head. "He said it made a grand flagstone. The fecking eejit."

"Is that why you nailed the cat over the back door?"

"Jaysus," he wails. "I told her you'd know who did it."

"How is your wife now?" I ask. "You said she'd been sick."

He eyes me nervously. I hope he doesn't cry again. "She's grand. She's ... pregnant."

So she's the one who sent me the text, then sent Dermot to neutralise me and the portal stone with a cat. But not a freshly dried one. If they've left their own home exposed to faerie invasion they must be desperate. But how did she get my number?

"Tell her I hope to be gone from here very soon," I say.

He looks relieved, but when I ask my next question, "And what about the shoe?" his eyes widen as if we've arrived at the most dangerous thing of all.

Silence. I'm not sure he'll get through his story without help.

"Dermot, I'm only after the truth about the shoe. Shall I tell you what I think happened and you can nod if I'm right?"

He nods, and I feel encouraged enough to sit down on a block of stone. He actually does the same.

"When you started work on the Rathbone house," I say, "it was in a bad state."

He nods.

"And you found the old shoe when you were demolishing the interior."

"Under the floorboards in the bedroom it was. The boards were rotten and we had a bonfire going. The others told me to burn it—faeries don't like fire."

"You thought it was a faerie shoe?" Not a shoe against faeries.

"It belonged to the O'Connor girl who disappeared. Some say she was a changeling."

"But you preserved it. Why?"

"Look in the tin. It was inside the shoe. The others didn't see it."

I keep the excitement from my voice. "This tin, where is it now?"

"Behind the shoe."

* * *

On the way back to the house I can barely contain myself. The stool is where I left it under the niche in the wall.

I didn't touch the shoe when I found it, but went straight to Dermot. Now I remove it and reach to the back of the hole where my fingers hit on metal. The tin's still here and I almost burst into tears. It seems I'm the only person who's ever been curious about the niche.

I take the tin and the shoe into the kitchen where the windows let in a lot of light. The tin is square and a little bigger than a deck of cards, just small enough to slip into the shoe. It's been decorated with decoupage cut from cards and newspapers. It looks like something the twins might have done of an evening and probably dates back to before the tragedy.

It's a little bit rusty and I don't want to damage it, so it's a few minutes before my fingers prise it open. I spread the contents across the counter.

A key, large and rusted. It looks like a door key for an old mortice lock and my thoughts go to the room upstairs.

A small tube-shaped bottle with a tarnished silver lid and a loop for hanging on a chain. It contains a murky brown liquid that looks like tea and is tinged with mould.

A card with a dark narrow border and a photograph of one of

the twins. The label reads: *Bridget Mary O'Connor 1880–1896.*
Under that a verse printed in Latin. It's a funeral card. From a
funeral for the wrong girl. A funeral without a body.

Sibby Dolan talked about the superstitious neighbours. No
wonder there was talk of faerie intervention with no body to
bury. And Bridie wouldn't have gone to her own funeral. Her
parents brought this card home for 'Ciara' and Bridie kept it, a
card chronicling her own death. The murder obliterated Ciara,
but everything the O'Connors did to Bridie obliterated her too.

Then I see the faint lines of a pencil. The first two names
under the photograph are crossed out and *Ciara Fey* is written
above. The real Ciara even had a faerie middle name. Was that
because she spent another eight days in the womb?

A gold ring has been tied to the bottom of the card with a
ribbon pushed through a hole. When I turn the card over, I
see the words 'faerie ring' handwritten beside it. If they're
a play on words, there's humour behind them. My great-
grandmother was a woman of many parts.

But I stop smiling when I see the other words, almost too
faint to read. When I decipher them I know something I've
probably known from the start: Bridie was a seer.

I stare at them for a long time: *rathbones*, *spell*, *Ciara* and
*faerie ring*. Bridie foresaw the coming of the Rathbones to this
house over a century before it happened. And the spell must be
what she kept talking about until her last breath. Something
to do with Ciara and the ring?

My mind isn't making any sense of it so I turn to the next
item in the tin. It's a folded piece of sheet music torn from a
book. I know what it is before I read the title: 'Two Sisters'.
The printed words of the song are almost the same as the
changes Bridie made to the sheet music she sent me. This is

the song from her song book, but she couldn't take it with her when she was sent to the convent so she bought a copy of the sheet music—not quite the same version—and changed it.

The last thing in the tin is folded and wrapped in tissue paper. I open it with trembling fingers. It's a piece of white cotton fabric, stained with age, decorated with cut-work lace. The work is very fine and I realise how many hours Bridie had to sit alone in the room upstairs and work on something precious. A bib for her baby. And when I see the letters embroidered across the front I know it was one of two.

I call Mikey. "Bridie and Brendon's baby. What was his name?"

He misses a beat, then says, "Orla O'Connor handed him over nameless, so Brendon's sister was going to choose one. Then she saw the bib. It was so beautifully made and with such love that her heart went out to Bridie. She decided to keep his name."

"Ciaran," I say.

"Yes, Ciaran Cormack was my grandfather. I'm sure my mam's still got the bib. What have you found?"

"Bridie made another one. In case the baby was a girl."

This one says *Ciara*. She made two bibs, one for each gender, when she could have made one that said *Ciara*, then added the 'n' afterwards if the child was a boy. There can only be one reason she did this. She knew they'd take her baby. She knew she wouldn't have time to embroider the extra letter. She only just had time to slip the bib into the bundle Orla wrapped him in.

Then another thought chills me. Did she make the bib for him to be buried in? A baby that no-one knew about could so easily have been disposed of—saved only by Orla's fear for her own soul. I'm sure that as Bridie's final punishment they never told her what happened to her child.

Dermot knew I would understand and I do. The tin is a shrine and a time capsule. He recognised that and honoured it; a man with hidden layers of compassion even though preserving it added to his fears of retribution.

I run through the story the time capsule confirms. Bridie was trapped in her bedroom for hours at a time. To protect her—or someone else? Or to punish her? Because they thought she killed Ciara? Or because her forbidden romance caused someone else to kill her?

Losing her identity was a severe price to pay—a kind of living death—and she had hours alone with her grief and her remorse. But she had baby clothes to make. And a shrine to Ciara. She must have removed a piece of the loose floorboard and created the secret space. Then she collected these things and put them in the shoe.

Why a shoe? It must be Ciara's. But if it wasn't to protect against faeries, why keep it? It's not very worn and I wonder if it was part of their birthday outfits. The family photo in my bag doesn't help. The twins' feet are hidden under their long skirts. Then I notice the ring on Bridie's finger again. It must be the one from the tin. She took off her ring and tied it to this mourning card that had her own name on it, calling it a faerie ring as if she herself had been stolen away.

The wall niche feels like the safest place to keep everything until after tonight's tour. I pick up the shoe and notice its weight. There's something inside.

A knife.

That puts me back on the stool. It's a short knife with a stumpy wooden handle and a broad curved blade. Perfect for working up a floorboard. The edge feels blunt, but the sharp point makes me think of another use for it. A weapon. Who did she need to protect herself from?

I think about sharing a house with James Sullivan after the tragedy. Once he knew Bridie was a 'fallen woman' did he regard her as fair game, especially if she was promised to him? Perhaps Bridie kept a knife and locked herself in her room for her own safety. His eyes in the photo make me shiver. Will I ever know if he was the killer?

* * *

I need to talk to Pixie about the gemstones so I walk down the hill to Dingle, but outside her shop I sit on a bench and check my A–Z for insights into the gems that will spell Ciara: citrine, iolite or ivory, amethyst, ruby and aquamarine. Each stone has many 'powers' attributed to it, so I choose the one quality that seems to be what I'll need:

Citrine—dissipates negative energy.

Iolite—fosters clairvoyance.

Ivory—prized in the East but otherwise not mystical.

Amethyst—enhances intuition.

Ruby—fosters the connection with spirit guides.

Aquamarine—overcomes fear of the unknown.

It's a lot of work for six gems—to protect me from anything the netherworld throws at me.

Pixie has a customer so I browse until she's alone. Then she looks at my list of gems and agrees that iolite is the choice for the letter 'i'. "Very uplifting and calming. It assists your inner knowing and brings confidence and wisdom."

"Thanks." I'll need all of that.

"So you're going back there tonight," she says.

The grapevine shouldn't surprise me. Dermot's wife got my phone number somehow, and Pixie's caught up with my link to the O'Connor twins. But what are the other locals saying about my quest? I ask her.

A moment's hesitation. "They think that house has always held secrets, and ... a blow-in from Australia might be out of her depth."

"OK. Anything else?"

"Be careful."

"Careful of what?"

"Thin places. You want answers about the past, but you're naive about the faerie ring. It's the summer solstice, the time when the veil between this world and the next is at its thinnest and the faeries are at their most powerful. Did you know it's the anniversary of Ciara's disappearance?"

Last time she called it murder.

"Yes," I say.

"Some say that's why she was never found," Pixie continues. "She was always a faerie twin, only lent to her sister, and at the summer solstice following her sixteenth birthday she was spirited back to the realm of the Fey."

Ciara's middle name.

"You think I'll need more than a few crystals?" I ask.

"Crystals are powerful. But you'll also need ... trust."

I thought she was going to say 'courage', but 'trust' is a bigger word. It's full of spiritual connotations—from folklore or religion or a blend of the two.

I wait for her to elaborate, but instead she says, "Watch your breath. Between the breathing out and the breathing in ... is the opening."

The opening. The portal. Midsummer Eve, the anniversary of Ciara's disappearance. Was she spirited away to the faerie realm because she was marked by magic? And the O'Connors saw their chance to implicate the tinker?

But the chain around my neck tells a different story.

"Remember the opening," Pixie says again. "You may need it … on your way back."

# Chapter 25

Josephine has rearranged the ghost tour so the pub cellar visit is last. It gives me access to the house well before dark.

Finn breezes in with Mikey as if he didn't try to strangle me the last time we met, but if the poteen has fogged his memory he can look at the marks on my neck. It was his intrusion last time that interrupted my visions of the night Ciara disappeared. It's why I've had to come back. But the delay has brought me to the summer solstice and the anniversary—and in the intervening days, the clues have gathered at the thin place.

I undo the chain and place the whistle pendant and my own red heart on the kitchen counter—I'll wear it tonight so Alister is with me.

Finn ignores it as he removes the gems that spell Bridie and lines up the new and old gems to spell Ciara. It's when the whistle is without its line of buttons that I realise what it resembles and gasp. The three segments of bamboo look for all the world like bones. Finger bones. Like the finger missing from the mannequin and the finger lying in the rubbish heap in Davina's dream. She dreamt that long before she ever saw the pendant.

Finn screws the stones in place and there's one hole leftover at the bottom. Because Ciara has one less letter than Bridie. Shit. I didn't think of that.

"Where do you want the hole?" Finn asks, his tone sharp.

"What do you mean?"

"This is a musical instrument. Each hole is a note. This bottom one is E, but you can move the stones for a different note. Which note do you want to play?" At the frown on my face he snorts and looks at his father. "Didn't I say this was bollocks. The blow-in gets the whistle but she doesn't know a tinker's cuss about blowing."

Mikey throws him a warning look.

Finn might have agreed to make the gems but he can't get past the injustice. And 'blow-in' is the word Pixie used about me. Of course she's been getting her gossip from Finn. It makes her advice feel partial.

"You win for wit," I say. "And you can play for the ghosts if you like. But then you won't hear what *they're* playing."

Maybe I sound like I know what I'm doing, but I'm not here to impress Finn. He shrugs, throws a fipple on the counter and stalks out.

Mikey asks for a key to the house. We agree that he'll wait at the Travellers' camp—out of the way but close.

Then he makes me draft a text on my phone. "So you only need to hit send if you're in trouble," he says.

What kind of trouble he doesn't say. He's never told me whether he believes in faeries.

When he gives me a hug, I realise how much he reminds me of Alister. He's got the same strong centre inside a soft shell. They're probably about the same age, mid forties, although Mikey's face shows the lines of the road. Then he's gone and

I'm alone.

I text Alister. We haven't caught up for a while and I want to give our invisible cord a tug without telling him what I'm risking tonight. I keep it light.

*Spreading faerie dust wherever I go. Sending some to you. S xx*

His reply is almost immediate. What time is it in San Francisco? *Now I know the secret of your sparkle.* It's a private joke. He's always said that the best seminar presenters have one magic quality: spark. Now the word reminds me of fire—a way to deal with faeries—but I'm not going to think about that.

I remove Ciara's gems from the pendant and replace them with Bridie's because she's where it all begins. She's the one who knows where the body is buried. If her letter to me hadn't been ruined I'm sure I'd have known where to look—unless this journey through the labyrinth is as much about me as it is about Ciara. It would explain my commitment to the search.

Working blind has made the mystery seem mystical, but even though superstition might be flowing through the veins of every rural Irish person, I remind myself that it only points the way. After more than one hundred years, anything less than hard evidence of a crime won't impress the guards. Tonight is about finding Ciara's resting place and any clues it reveals about her murder.

I review the qualities of Bridie's gems, hoping they get me started in the right direction:

Beryl—promotes creativity and makes the wearer invincible.

Ruby—connects with spirit guides.

Iolite—fosters clairvoyance.

Diamond—stone of innocence and invulnerability, brings

clarity.

Ivory—prized in the East so a psychic link to Brendon.

Emerald—stone of prophecy, symbol of hope and patience.

Then I get the shoe and the tin from their niche and a torch from the kitchen drawer. It's not dark yet, but I climb the stairs to the bedroom, where the same bed as last time beckons. I unfold Bridie's stained letter and place it under the pillow. Then I make a little shrine of the objects from the tin, spreading them across the pillow within easy reach. With all these talismans in place, I lie flat on the bed with the whistle on my chest, wrapping my fingers around it as if I'm playing.

It's going to take me on a journey. Such journeys have revealed the truth to me in the past: once with the help of hypnosis; and then alone when I didn't expect it. From these experiences I know that I'm never in control of where we're going. Or how long the journey will last.

It's important to relax, but the pressure of time tightens my limbs. In a few hours the collision of clues created by the solstice will pass and Ciara's body will remain hidden. I breathe through it and focus on the rise and fall of my chest, on leaving my own skin behind and descending into deep truth.

It begins slowly at first, then without warning I'm plunged into a dark place. The sadness in this room is as bottomless as a well and I'm drowning—my worst nightmare—as Bridie's emotions wash over me in waves. The shaking and the sobbing racks my body, then the lonely hours staring at the ceiling, the desolation and emptiness stretching to the end of eternity.

By instinct I reach for the key and I'm inside Bridie's skin.

*My eyes are puffy from crying and I can hardly see to make sure the door is still locked, that he hasn't found another key. I've got the poker ready and I'll use it. After causing Ciara's murder, I don't care what I do to James.*

*This morning when my mother was in the garden, he waited till I was bending over the washing basket and tried to slip his hand under my skirt. When I jumped back, he shoved me against the wall so his horrible fingers could squeeze my breast until it hurt, and his other hand could do the same between my legs. And all the while he was sticking his tongue in my ear or my mouth whichever way I thrashed. 'It's not long before you're mine,' he said. 'While the tinker hangs for your murder.' I vomited all over the freshly boiled sheets making him laugh his evil laugh. I'm afeared he won't wait until he's pushed a ring onto my finger to take me. Not if he can get into this room, put his hand over my mouth and claim me as his. But while there's breath in my body I won't ever let him steal that from Brendon.*

*Here I am thinking only of my own troubles. Selfish, selfish, selfish girl. Selfish for loving Brendon after being warned against him, and losing Ciara because of it. Selfish about protecting my virtue when I've already lost it, while Brendon awaits the gallows.*

*My mother is just as cruel when I beg her to let me save Brendon. 'You'd see a member of your own family hang instead of that worthless tinker, would you? Is this the daughter I laboured to bring into this world after I lost so many before you? Or have the faeries swapped you for one of their own while you've been up at the faerie ring? You're no daughter of mine if you love that murderous tinker more than your own flesh and blood.'*

*I know why she's protecting James. He has fooled her ever since we took him in, an orphan. Dressing in my father's hand-me-downs and following him around like a devoted calf. But it wasn't long before he picked Ciara as an easy target and made her cry every time he tried to touch her. On Midsummer Eve he was full of drink and it was my fault that she met him on the path with my fob chain in her hand.*

But blaming myself is selfish. Admitting what I did gives me a reason to be forgiven. Even after a hundred years on my knees in prayer I won't deserve that.

I let go of the key and breathe deeply. Bridie's punishment at the hand of James is making me gag too. She was already queasy from the pregnancy but she didn't know that yet. It's a blow that she doesn't know who killed Ciara, but James was her prime suspect.

I reach for the phial next, and as soon as I touch it I know what it contains.

*When Pa forced me to wear the chain, I knew that it wasn't evidence any more. Brendon was dead. Pa made me stand in front of my mother and James. He said that since it was my tinker who killed Ciara, I must wear the murder weapon around my own neck. I tried not to cry but I couldn't help it.*

*Sometimes when she's sure no-one's going to visit, my mother sends me into the garden to pick beans. I may not go to the well, where I could cry for Brendon's soul until I filled it with my tears. The purple foxgloves are growing wild along the wall. Ciara loved putting their flowers onto her fingers like faerie gloves. I miss her all the time, but especially when the sun is on my face and I remember what it was like to hear her laugh.*

*I hid the foxgloves in my apron pocket and made soup with them. I thought about killing us all with their poison, but when I'm gone the killing can stop. It's a sin but with two deaths on my conscience how could mine matter? I dipped my little perfume bottle into the liquid and burned my hand. As I screamed, I spilled the whole pot onto the fire. My mother yelled at me like she always does: 'Not only selfish, useless too. Poor James getting a wife like you. Don't I wish Sibby was still here and isn't that your fault too.'*

*Every day I lift the floorboard in my room and open the tin to look at the little bottle. But I won't drink it, not now, because I'm with child. Brendon's child. It's the most precious gift he's left for me. A new life.*

When I return the phial to the pillow, my fingers touch the tiny bib.

*My mother can't hide her fury. Only the family will know my shame, so they'll keep me locked away till I give birth.*

*A miscarriage could kill me so James is careful not to hurt me now, but his taunts are always waiting for me when he catches me on my own.*

*The baby growing inside me is my greatest joy and my deepest pain. Sometimes I think Brendon is looking down on us as I make the tiny clothes that I must keep hidden. Every day I think of new ways to escape, because how can I bear what they'll do to my child?*

When Bridie gives birth I'm screaming, and we're both covered in blood and sweat until it's over. When Orla places the baby in my arms, the love is so searing, and so fleeting, I want to die.

Back in my own skin, my fingers touch the murder song and I'm pitched back into the bottomless well. Guilt, guilt, guilt, guilt—it rolls over me like wheels of knives. Guilt for loving Brendon without thought to Ciara; for loving Brendon and letting him die. Then the greatest guilt of all hits me: for murdering Ciara's soul—by denying her a Christian grave.

With urgency now and in floods of tears, I find the mourning card. The funeral was for Bridie not Ciara. Ciara has been left out in the cold. As Bridie's ring slips onto my finger, I read the words she wrote: *rathbones, spell, Ciara, faerie ring.* In a flash I understand.

*Spell Ciara.*

Racing down the stairs, I almost fall. I can't undo Bridie's gems fast enough and I have to slow down to spell Ciara's name. When the gems are in place in the whistle, I'm released from Bridie's pain and for a moment I'm laughing, until I stare at the hole at the bottom.

What about the bloody hole? Finn was right, and Pixie. I'm a blow-in and I'm out of my depth.

That's when the nightingale returns, cutting through with its poignant call. It echoes around the foothills, enfolding all in rapture. Ciara is back. The mind of a child—and the voice of a nightingale.

I run towards the back door.

* * *

On the flagstone, the icy updraft makes me stand very still. When the door is open, there's an uninterrupted view of the ruin, silent and still under the silver light of a solstice moon. The flagstone is the portal stone ripped from the old faerie fort, forever viewing its rightful home from afar.

I can't carry the stone back, but under my feet my understanding turns the chill into warmth. A portal is a doorway. But not this doorway, protected from magic by a dead cat. Instinct makes me reach for the whistle between my breasts. Brendon's whistle. Bridie's whistle. Now Ciara's whistle. *Hokio*, a noun and a verb. A whistle with a hole that creates a special note.

The fipple is in my pocket. I fix it to the whistle, hold it to my lips and blow. The tooting sound makes me jump. It's harmonising with the nightingale.

What now? The ruin is bathed in stillness. The flagstone is

warm. The nightingale is calling. The whistle is my mystical object, with all the powers of its gems: intuition, clairvoyance, fearlessness. It's my only means of communication. I toot it again. Nothing happens.

*Between the breathing out and the breathing in is the opening,* Pixie said.

I take a deep breath, then holding the whistle to my lips ... I breathe out. The third note is a thin note. A thin sound for the thin place. And the thin night, Midsummer Eve.

In the space that follows the third note, an explosion of light blows the lid off the rath.

With my next breath I'm racing up the hill, the whistle banging against its imprint on my chest. I have no idea what I'm running towards. Have the faeries opened a stairway to the underworld? Is that where I'm going to meet Ciara?

The nightingale's song is echoing above the circle of luminescence. A hole has opened up in the earth, invisible until now. I run through the gap in the outer wall of the ring fort, the gap that Dermot made, and stumble towards what's left of the centre rooms. It's where the stonemasons poached the stones: two linked circular walls, razed to the ground but still visible, forming a figure eight. Everything adds up to eight. Eternity or infinity embodied in the shape of an eight.

In the smaller circle, a hole is glowing through the long grass. I drop to my knees and look inside. It's a passage lined with stones. A souterrain. And the walls are glimmering with faerie dust. Pinpricks of light dazzle me—the same lights I've seen in my visions. It's a faerie place opening itself at the summer solstice, lighting the way to the netherworld.

The space is narrow and Derek's warning is in my ears: *It depends what the dead person wants. If they talk you into going with them, you ... won't come back.* I remember Davina's ordeal. But her souterrain was a refuge.

The nightingale's song gets louder, urging me on with her song. Ciara's spirit guide is singing her heart out, saying I'm in the right place at the right time.

Then I understand. I've seen sparks like this before. Not mythology. Glow-worms. With my heart pounding, I stoop through the opening and enter the faerie realm.

Glow-worms cover the ceiling and the walls. As I move along the tunnel, their numbers multiply, drawing me onwards and into a chamber bathed in radiance. A circular room is domed by stones, and in the centre, lying in state, is a skeleton. A human skeleton.

Over the years, the insects have undressed her. Right down to her bones. Rathbones. Her clothes were once a leather belt, a corset, a garment that's dropped its metal buttons, a hair comb and a brooch of a bird. She also wore shoes with little buttons up the side—one of them is missing. Her hands are by her sides. And in the place where her missing finger would be, a cluster of glow-worms form a ring, a faerie ring.

The scene should be ghoulish but it's magical. Just like the local folklore believes, Ciara really was whisked away to the realm of the fey. Or have I conjured her to satisfy Bridie? Because surely someone would have found her before now.

I sit with her for many minutes, paying my respects, as a century of emotion hits me; emotion from a life stunted just out of childhood, then unlived with nowhere to go until now. It begins with Ciara's laughter, her playful games and her blind adoration of Bridie. Her mother's disappointment that confused her; and her awe, even fear, of her father.

When they moved to Dingle she was afraid that the new nuns

would smack her for not being clever, that she wouldn't make friends. But she always felt safe with Bridie, her twin always there to look after her. Then came the shock and the pain of watching Bridie grow away from her, knowing that Brendon Blake was to blame.

Uncorked at last, the emotions rise through me in a rush to escape, then dissolve in puffs of invisible smoke up through the entrance of the souterrain and into the night air.

# Chapter 26

Exhausted from my role as a channel, I take a photo and return to the surface. There's a call to make straight away—the great-grandson of Brendon and Bridie must be the first to know.

"I've found her," I tell Mikey. "There's a souterrain in the rath. Call the guards and meet me at the house."

"Is there ... any other evidence?"

"Her bird brooch shows it's Ciara. Then there's only what's left of her clothes."

But as Mikey hangs up, the whistle gets hot, then starts to vibrate—and its note becomes a song. As I listen in wonder, it cries out the truth of her murder.

*In tune with the fates, the nightingale sings*
*On Midsummer Eve in the faerie ring.*

*In the shape of my finger, the whistle will play*
*And describe how my life was stolen away.*

*'My father choked me,' is the tale it must tell.*
*'For meeting the tinker down by the well.'*

*He thought I was Bridie and rage made him kill,*
*    Then he saw my brooch, but too late, I was still.*

*James slipped from the shadows, said he'd save Father's life,*
*    'If you make me your heir and Bridie my wife.'*

*My father, now powerless, warned Bridie was bold.*
*    'We'll say she was murdered, then she'll do what she's told.'*

*If the tinker killed Bridie, her ring he would take,*
*    So James cut off my finger, a false trail to make.*

*Then James disappeared and planted the chain,*
*    While the lovers carried me to the souterrain.*

*My body was gone, had the fey stolen me?*
*    But the tinker, they said, threw me into the sea.*

*Then James threatened Bridie, 'It's the fey made you bold.*
*    I'll tame you with fire until you're controlled.'*

*Her sister was murdered, her lover soon dead,*
*    And not far away, a cruel wedding bed.*

*But the child in her belly kept the worst threats at bay,*
*    Then after they stole him, she ran away.*

*A nun she would be, with her guilt and her hate,*
*    Till a fireman revealed it's never too late.*

*Bridie lived a long life in the land of the sun,*

*But how could she right the wrong that was done?*

*Her granddaughters scared her, she began to despair,*
 *Was there nobody gifted, the past to repair?*

*Then on her deathbed, the new baby cried,*
 *And their spirits connected before Bridie died.*

*The spell is my name, spelled in buttons of stone,*
 *The whistle has sung, the truth it is known.*

I can't believe what I'm hearing. Thomas killed his own daughter in a fit of blind rage that she was defying him, but he killed the wrong daughter. Then James blackmailed him to cover it up by pointing the finger at Brendon. Now Ciara's missing 'finger' has pointed to the truth.

As I was taking my first baby breaths, Bridie's spirit planted the seed for me to solve the mystery. My visions have held the answers, but they didn't form the truth until now: the chain that caused me to relive Ciara's last breaths; the mugger in Honolulu with a moustache and a waistcoat; the mannequin flipping me into Ciara's skin at the exact moment Thomas thought she was Bridie; the wall of evil that hit me on the path where it happened—Thomas's blind rage mixed with James's evil opportunism.

My words to Finn come back: *You can play for the ghosts if you like, but then you won't hear what they're playing.* Not defensive as it turns out, but prescient; my innocence and my patience rewarded with the song.

Pixie was prescient too. She told me to have trust. And I did: in myself; in Bridie's spirit; in the clues to collide in just the right place at just the right moment; in the truth to reveal itself like a fossil trapped in time.

Ciara's shoe must have fallen off as Bridie and Brendon stumbled up the hill that night, frantic and crying, her body heavy and her finger missing. Bridie must have found the shoe on the way back and kept it. Her secret memento of her sister. What did Josephine say? *A shoe represents the person who wore it.* A charm against the faeries with an ironic twist, because all the time the shoe pointed to the faerie ring where its own twin lay.

The ring on the funeral card was an ironic clue too. James cut off Ciara's finger to add extra horror to his plot to frame Brendon. He couldn't know her body would disappear while he was planting the murder weapon. Maybe he remembered the bird brooch and went back for it, but Ciara was gone.

The faerie ring has done its job. In the souterrain, under the figure of eight, it's preserved Ciara's bones for over a hundred years. Now it's time to show the proof to the guards.

All the way back to the house, the song plays over and over. What it says may not be enough to rewrite the history books, but it will bring some comfort to the Travellers. I get out my phone and record it, even though I don't know if anyone else will be able to hear it. Maybe it's just for me, the guardian of the whistle, so I memorise the words in case they're for my ears alone.

I'm so immersed in my own emotions, and channelling Bridie's relief through every pore, that I enter the house without a thought to anything else. Certainly not my own safety.

Did I leave the lights off? I don't remember. Then I see her silhouette against the shutters. She's sitting in an armchair in the sunroom and until she opens her mouth I almost think she's Davina.

"Put the phone down where I can see it," Dervla says.

I'm suddenly back in my body, drenched by a rush of adrenaline. Very slowly I place my phone on the elevated ledge of the breakfast bar, all the time keeping my lower body out of her line of sight.

"Hello, Dervla." My voice is shaking. "What are you doing here?"

She laughs. It's not a pretty sound. "That Nola at the B&B likes a good chat, doesn't she? She would have given me your date of birth."

My hands are still hidden, and while I keep my eyes on Dervla I slip my hand into my pocket and send Mikey's emergency text on the other phone. But I don't know if he had to drive to Tralee to find a guard who'd take him seriously about Ciara. On Midsummer Eve with their hands full with revellers in druid robes, a skeleton may not seem urgent.

Dervla thinks the buzz is an incoming text on the first phone. "Don't touch it," she says. "And step away from those kitchen drawers in case you were thinking about a knife."

When I move to where she can see me, I can also see her. And her gloves. And her baseball bat.

"I heard you're worried about Davina," she says. "That's a pity."

My speech at the retreat centre was designed to protect Davina. I forgot that it might expose me.

"I assume she's spending time with her mother," I lie, knowing we've gone way beyond fooling each other. "Why the baseball bat?"

The recorder on my phone is still running. Whatever happens, she may incriminate herself.

"We're going to take a little walk," she says. "Down to the well. It's such a beautiful evening."

"The well?" The perfect place for a murder.

"It's amazing what you can find online these days. Ordnance survey maps even show the locations of wells. And old wells are great places to hide things."

"Why kill me? I've done nothing to you."

She sighs. "I won't be spilling my guts like the end of a bad detective novel."

My legs have gone wobbly so I sit down. She won't want to bash me over the head in the house. Too hard to drag my body down to the well.

"I tried to dig up some dirt on you," I say, "but I couldn't find anything."

The psychopath in her can't resist. "That's because there's nothing to find. It's watertight."

She thinks her murder of Davina is watertight too.

"If you hadn't told Davina you were twins, she would have gone back to Hawaii and left you to your career."

"She wanted to make amends for the past. So honourable. But the press can't get enough of me at the moment, and she wasn't going to slip away quietly so I had to ... give her a nudge."

Just like the song.

Dervla's eyes belie her composure. They're dancing. Only last night she pushed Davina off a cliff. Tonight is an unexpected encore.

Possible weapons run through my mind. Bridie's knife, but it's upstairs in Ciara's shoe. The fire poker, but I'd hear the crack of her baseball bat on my skull before I got to it. My god, the chain around my neck ... and I know what choking involves. Strength. Desperation. Madness.

"Let's get this over with," I say, standing up.

"Sit down," she says. She won't have me calling the shots.

That's when I know what my weapon is: time. It was Bridie's weapon too—I'm still channelling her. And something from my patience in finding Ciara tells me I can win. Because Dervla really does want to crow about how clever she is.

"I've been listening to the nightingale," I hear myself say. "It showed me where my great-great-aunt is buried. She was murdered but never found." Just like Dervla plans for me. "When I was up at the ruin just now, I called the guards."

She laughs. She doesn't believe me.

"Davina never got to know why she had to die," she says. Her tone is almost wistful. "She was always so easy to manipulate."

"Until she pretended to be you. While you devoted yourself to a life of ... chastity."

I'm running on adrenaline. And intuition. Ciara's gems are still working their magic.

"She didn't last five minutes as Dervla Kelly," she says. "One look at me in that French market and she took off. But I'd been practising since my teens, she didn't know that. I even did a shift at McDonald's just to prove I could be her. So in the convent I *became* Davina Kennedy—an adopted runaway with an abusive father. The press—and the Church—adore a survivor."

"With your brains and background why not climb the corporate ladder? Or become secretary-general of the United Nations, or head of the IMF?"

She snorts. "As Daddy Kelly's little rich girl? Not when I can be ..." She pauses for the announcement. "The first female Pope."

What? I manage not to guffaw. Hubris like this is seriously delusional and I'm struck by just how much is at stake. If her fake history is ever revealed, this crazy ambition to rule the Catholic Church will be demolished in a heartbeat. It's why she had to kill Davina. And I'm next to be silenced. I look at the baseball bat resting on her lap. She'll use it without a qualm.

But there's something behind her choice of the church. A sadness behind the madness. Not just the power trip and the little rich girl thumbing her nose at her parents. She's a charismatic single woman who demands the highest esteem, with no questions asked about why she has no husband and no children.

I take a stab in the dark. "No more sex for you after that botched abortion."

She jerks forward. "I never told Davina that."

"A wild teen, she said. I just joined the dots."

A moment ago she was boasting, now she's exploding with fury.

"I was packing for a finishing school in Zurich," she hisses, "when my mother found out I was bleeding. But the doctor didn't tell *me* what was wrong, he told *her*. She disowned me on the spot. I was good for nothing but the convent."

She's still leaning towards me, her eyes blazing, when Mikey appears at the back door. Dervla starts in her chair, but Mikey's unruffled.

"Hi, Selkie. Why are you sitting in the dark?"

Dervla's slipped the gloves and the bat out of sight on the floor. Will she hurt Mikey? But a word returns: *trust*.

"Just chatting," I say. "The moonlight is amazing. Mikey,

this is ... Mother Clare."

He strides across the room and puts out his hand. "Michael Cormack."

Dervla goes to shake it, but he grabs her hand, yanks her out of the chair, flips her arm behind her back and hooks the other one. As Finn rushes through the front door, she's on the floor screaming, with Mikey sitting on top of her. While Dervla thrashes and spits, I turn on the lights and they get cable ties around her ankles and wrists. In spite of the commotion, the operation is over in less than a minute.

The trussing complete they pull her back onto the chair, but she jerks forward and sinks her teeth into Finn's arm, drawing blood. He curses and leaps back, slashing his leg open on the edge of the coffee table.

I can hear Derek crowing all the way from Hawaii: 'Cosmic payback.'

* * *

It's a long night. The superintendent of the Dingle Garda office finally arrives, his pyjamas peeping out from under his uniform. He's Nola's brother-in-law, and she finally got him out of bed after the guards on duty told Mikey that a skeleton could wait until a more convenient time. Like another hundred years.

When the superintendent enters the sunroom, Dervla picks him as a Catholic who'll be shocked by her mistreatment and impressed by her credentials: Abbess of St Scholastica's, shortlisted to head up the Pope's special committee on child abuse, PhD in clinical psychology. The list goes on—without her final aspirations to rule the world—and I'm surprised she hasn't been nominated for beatification.

"First she threatened me with a baseball bat," she tells him, nodding towards me. "Then these two thugs tied me up. Release me at once and charge them with assault. The Church's lawyers will file my official complaint."

Her voice has the power of authority, but the superintendent knows Mikey and Finn. He's looking at them for a response, but I've already found the recording. The sunroom fills with Dervla's sarcastic tones as she threatens me with a one-way trip to the well.

The superintendent doesn't wait to hear it all. As Dervla sits sullen and mute, he calls for extra men to take her away to the cells. If she hadn't boasted about who she is she might have kept her identity quiet for a while, but now it will be a sensation.

At last I can show the superintendent the photo I took of Ciara's remains. Leaving Mikey and Finn to keep an eye on Dervla until reinforcements arrive, he follows me up the hill to the ring fort, now in darkness.

# Chapter 27

While Ciara's skeleton is removed, I wait to be interviewed at the Dingle Garda station. When they get to me, I tell the superintendent and his female colleague everything I know and everything I believe about the murder.

The bird brooch is strong evidence that the skeleton is Ciara since she's wearing it in the family photo. Then there's the shoe. But the other objects in the tin point to Bridie, not Ciara. And the song 'Two Sisters' implicates Bridie in her sister's murder, even though I explain the real reasons for her guilt.

There's nothing to prove that Thomas killed his daughter except for the murder ballad. When I tell them about it, about the missing finger and the whistle pendant, they're bemused and more patient than I expected.

They agree to listen to the recording of the whistle's song, but when I play it there's nothing there. I write down as much as I can remember, and they let me make a statement about my psychic visions, even though none of it is evidence.

"Thomas O'Connor argued with Bridie that night," I say. "She'd begged for the watch chain for her birthday, but he gave it to her on condition that she stopped her trysts with Brendon. He may even have guessed how far their relationship had progressed, that she was planning to run away with him."

I fill them in on Ciara's movements. "When Thomas caught Ciara on the path waving Bridie's chain, he thought she was Bridie defying him. It was late and he'd probably been drinking. He must have lost his head."

I explain how James Sullivan implicated Brendon in exchange for Thomas's agreement that he marry Bridie and become his heir. "Bridie was a strong-willed girl so they controlled her by renaming her Ciara. Once Bridie was 'dead' there could be no hint of the identity swap. They kept her indoors with 'hysteria' so she couldn't give evidence that might save Brendon Blake. She wasn't allowed to play her precious piano either. If anyone heard her they'd know she was Bridie not Ciara." I haven't checked with Stella but I suspect Bridie punished herself by never playing the piano again.

"How did the lovers know about the souterrain?" the superintendent asks. "That rath has always been known as a thin place. Everyone keeps well away."

"I think it was their secret place. At the twins' birthday party a child started crying because he'd seen two faeries—I think he came upon Bridie and Brendon making love in the souterrain. They were star-crossed lovers so superstition wasn't going to get in their way. And it was the perfect place to hide Ciara. Although the rumours about a faerie abduction didn't save Brendon from being hanged for murder."

And before they left their special place—now Ciara's gravesite—Brendon gave Bridie the pendant. I'm sure it was to be his going-away gift to her, but when their future was in tatters he gave it to her anyway—as a symbol of what might have been. I cry all over again when I think that they knew in their hearts it would be the last time they saw each other. I'll never know when the whistle was turned into the cross Bridie wore at the convent, but she kept it, as Finn said, 'hidden in plain sight' until she could pass it on to me, a finger-shaped chronicler waiting to sing the horrors of that night.

The female guard asks, "Did Bridie know the murderer was her father? Is that why she sent you the clues?"

"No. Only that it wasn't Brendon. And she blamed herself for loving him. If she hadn't followed her heart, Brendon and Ciara would both have lived. Everyone else blamed her too, especially Orla; and Thomas himself probably blamed her for turning him into a murderer. He even forced her to wear the murder weapon around her own neck as punishment."

"I notice you're wearing it," the female guard says. "It's still the murder weapon, isn't it?"

I tell them about the mugging and my visions. "The chain was carrying the memory of the murder. But now I've uncovered the truth, I expect the visions to stop. It's a family heirloom, a keepsake from my great-grandmother, and I treasure it."

But I'm not sure what to do with the whistle. Finn was prepared to kill me for it. Now that it's done its job, does it belong to me?

* * *

The days that follow are a blur. The discovery of Ciara's skeleton hijacks the front pages of *The Kerryman*. As we wait for a date for the inquest, the paper covers every detail of the 'electrifying find' in the souterrain. It goes into the history of the faerie ring and the Rathbone house, and provides eye-witness encounters with the faeries going back to the 1890s.

One headline screams *House of Rathbone: Bones in Rath*. And after interviews with me and Mikey by a reporter who hung on every detail of my visions: *Firstborn Stolen by Mother, Not Faeries*. News items from the time of Ciara's murder are republished, along with the testimony from the court case convicting Brendon, all to be trounced by the revelations about which twin was killed and possible reasons for the name swap.

The newspapers dig deeper. Superstitions about faerie abductions are explored by experts in folklore and used to explain why the police never entered the rath or looked in the souterrain for Ciara's body. Superstition was a powerful deterrent in 1896.

Experts are interviewed to evaluate the veracity of my visions. An ornithologist confirms that there are no nightingales in Ireland and suggests that the bird I heard might have been a sedge warbler mimicking a nightingale. Then an expert on phosphorescence in insects attests that there are no glow-worms in Ireland either. But there are fireflies in the sea caves of Lough Hyne—fireflies that Davina luckily didn't get to see—and the expert conducts kayak tours to view them. Judging by the letters to the newspaper, their expertise only confirms that what I witnessed was magic.

Historians dig into what happened to Bridie, Thomas and Orla O'Connor and James Sullivan. They track Bridie's flight to St Scholastica's and sensationalise her desire to punish herself with a life of service and to honour her dead sister by continuing to call herself Ciara, then the fire that released her and the romance that took her to Australia.

Meanwhile back in Dingle, with Brendon executed and Bridie gone, Thomas must have felt safe to dishonour his promise to make James his heir. Within a year of Ciara's death, Thomas and Orla returned to a dairy co-op in Cork. Orla tried to bear Thomas a son but died in childbirth, and Thomas became paralysed after being thrown from a horse.

James Sullivan turned to drink and died young, but not before fathering several out-of-wedlock children with women who accused him of rape. His descendants are traced to the present and Rory Flynn gives a brief interview about his great-grandfather. *My ancestor wasn't a murderer* states the caption under his beaming photo.

Mikey and Finn can boast the same thing.

Only Selkie Moon and her family find themselves with that unfortunate distinction.

"Better to live with an uncomfortable truth," Gretel says with her usual wisdom, "than a comfortable lie."

Not for the first time, I'm glad that Gretel and I are two sisters.

A phone call from Stella is a surprise.

"Don't ever quote me on this," she says, "but Bridie couldn't have trusted me or Prunella to investigate this for her."

Is that a compliment?

"I think I know what Bridie was saying about spells," I tell her. "She was saying 'spell Ciara'. That was the 'spell' that solved the mystery."

But Stella isn't listening. She's got a question. "What on earth is a souterrain?"

"An underground tunnel lined with stones." Pause. "A bit like a drain under a road."

She gasps.

"Bridie hid her sister in a souterrain, Stella. And seventy years later you hid your sister in a drain just like it. No wonder she stopped encouraging your psychic skills. She thought it was her fault; that you'd picked up on the events from the past and copied them."

"Her fault," Stella says, sounding both astounded and relieved.

Not Stella's fault. Not completely. Just like Bridie, Stella's blamed herself for a very long time.

* * *

Davina decides to make a statement to the guards.

We don't go to the press, but someone does and I suspect Nola. Her outrage is unstoppable after Dervla got her details from Sister Bernadette and then tricked her into revealing my location.

Journalists in Dublin smell a story and Mother Clare is outed as a liar and a fake. They unearth a photo of Davina from her design award and publish it beside a photograph of Dervla under the headline: *Will the Real Mother Clare Please Stand Up!* Dervla's parents are traced to France, where they died in mysterious circumstances almost twenty years ago after eating mushroom soup. Their vineyard in the Bourgogne wasn't far from the Benedictine convent where they washed their hands of their daughter. In the wake of the media storm, Dervla is charged with attempted murder. There's also speculation that the Church will make an example of her after their appalling record of covering up the crimes of their clergy in the past. And there are whispers about the French police reopening the case on her parents' death. The Garda Síochána found traces of something poisonous—possibly digitalis from foxgloves—in the hastily washed cooking pot Dervla used to make soup in the cottage. It doesn't surprise me that she'd prepared an alternative way to despatch Davina, in case something prevented her from pushing Davina over the cliff.

Meanwhile, Derek's research unearths a tiny item in the French convent's archive. "A fire destroyed their records," he says. "It meant that when Dervla saw her chance to champion child abuse and returned to Ireland, she could assume Davina's history."

I tell Davina. "I don't know if she called herself Davina or just borrowed your life story."

"I've been thinking about that," Davina says. "How she could pass herself off as me. When we were swapping clothes, my adoption papers got lost. I stole them from the tin in my stepmam's kitchen, but when I got to Dublin there was nowhere safe at the boarding house, so I carried them around in my coat. Dervla lost them one night and I was so frantic about it that she helped me apply for new ones. She must have stolen them herself thinking they might be useful one day. I was the orphan with nothing, but she wanted to be me."

"Being suddenly infertile," I say, "and only good for the nunnery pushed her over the edge. Her whole career was based on payback." Then I remember what she told me at the house. "Dervla was the person you saw in the Paris market."

"Oh my god, you think the fetch was her?" Davina can't quite believe it.

"In her novice veil she would have looked like an angel. Or a mirage. Not like wild and wanton Dervla. And she must have hated you for making a success of your life while she'd become invisible. The fetch and its intent got stuck in your mind."

"But I saw it in Honolulu too. That wasn't Dervla."

"That was after you won the design award. If Dervla saw that in the press, she'd have been hating you all over again and you picked it up. Enough to think a novice nun at the Swap Meet was the fetch." And I've remembered something. "But your premonition ... was right."

She's silent while the penny drops. "Dervla as the fetch foretold my death ... then almost made it come true."

The next thought takes my breath away. "But if you hadn't gone into the souterrain—and told me the faeries saved you—I would never have had the courage to follow those glow-worms into the underworld. Derek had warned me against it, and your experience with the flagstone and the superstitions around Midsummer Eve were weighing on me."

"You mean if Dervla hadn't tried to kill me," she whispers, "you wouldn't have found Ciara?"

If we think about this too much—about how tangled the symbols from our pasts and presents have become—we'll go crazy.

Davina's staying on in Ireland until her shoulder heals. And she's found a friend in Rylee. They're already creating a range of fashion designs inspired by tinker traditions. Lots of funky patchwork. Davina will feature them in her next collection and give Rylee her own label: TinkTank. She's also applied to the Church for information about her birth mother. It's possible Dervla befriended her using Davina's name. All part of the smokescreen. If she's still alive, Davina hopes to meet her.

# Chapter 28

The Garda Síochána inform me that, due to a backlog of cases, the inquest won't take place for several months, and my statement will be enough anyway. I'm desperate to get back to Hawaii and Alister. Bridie lost her man; I don't want to lose mine.

Throughout the aftermath of the mystery, Bridie is with me all the way. Her tragedy keeps reminding me to seize the day. The phrase *carpe diem* has become a cliché, but that doesn't diminish its potency. I've lived Bridie's pain through the pores of my own skin. She loved a man from a different world and she lost him in a collision of circumstances beyond her control. But even when everything was against her, she allowed herself to be loved.

I've been holding my man at arm's length for no other reason than fear. Fear that we come from different worlds? I remember the dream where I was caught in the doorway between the dark alley and the lighted bar, and watched him walk away with Fleur, his star-crossed first love, not having the courage to claim him.

On the long flight home, I dream the scene that will play out when I turn up unannounced at Alister's penthouse. His face will light up and I'll smile back and he'll know. He'll say something witty as he wraps me in his arms and my reply will make him laugh. Taking my hand, he'll walk me through the living room to his bedroom, all in slow motion because we've been waiting for this moment for so long.

But when the plane touches down in Honolulu, I'm exhausted. And the dreams about making love haven't calmed my fear. They've re-activated the old issue: expectation.

*Carpe diem*, Bridie reminds me as I go into a restroom and change into my little black dress.

Then in the cab on the way to Alister's, Wanda calls.

"Where are you?" she asks.

"Honolulu. Just touched down."

I don't mention that I'm almost outside Alister's apartment. What I don't need right now is a pep talk about sex.

"Well, get straight over to Alister's," she says.

"Why?" I'm suddenly panicked. "Is he OK?"

"Keep your shirt on, he's fine. I was just down at the bus shelter showing Coral your photo in the Irish press and she pointed to you and said one word: *Hokeo*."

"Yeah. It means whistle. I already know Coral's amazing. She sensed there was a whistle before anyone else."

"That's *hokio*," Wanda says, stressing the vowel sound. "It's a different word. I don't know if Coral said *hokio* or *hokeo* the first time—you sent me a text, remember, so I didn't hear it—but today I heard it myself and it's *hokeo*."

"Wanda, you're doing my head in. And what's any of this got to do with Alister?"

"*Hokio* means 'whistle', but *hokeo*," she pauses for effect, "means 'to cherish in secrecy'."

Bloody hell. It's the hidden emotion behind the whistle pendant. Bridie's secret love for Brendon still there for Coral to feel after more than a hundred years.

"It's you," Wanda says, flipping my theory on its head. "She was pointing at you. That's what you're doing to Alister—loving him in secret. And it's *lolo*." Crazy.

Wanda's words are in my head as I get out of the cab, then ring the bell to Alister's private lift.

It's Sunday and he answers himself.

"Special delivery for Alister Sloane," I say into the intercom. "One exhausted woman, high on jetlag."

"*Selkie.*"

He says my name with such fire that an avalanche of understanding hits me.

By changing Bridie's name, her parents 'killed' her. And after losing the people she loved, she considered herself a dead person. No wonder she took Ciara's name to the convent; Bridie was as gone as her sister was. Until a fire and a fireman brought her back to life. When I was sixteen, the same age as Bridie, my family renamed me Elkie. For almost twenty years Selkie didn't exist. When Alister says my name like this, he ignites me.

The lift deposits me in his foyer, and when he greets me I'm not sure what to look at first—his beaming smile or his bare chest above draw-string pants. It's the first time I've seen him in the raw, and desire and shyness overcome me.

"You're looking a little wild and fey-like," he says, ruffling my hair.

I laugh. "One guy over there was sure my accent was Netherworld."

"He was right. It's got a new lilt."

"That's just Bridie. I've been channelling her for weeks."

As I stand awkwardly in his entrance hall, he puts down my

bag and plants a deep kiss on my lips. "Would Bridie mind if you left her here for a while?"

"She thought you'd never ask."

We don't make it to the bedroom. In a spray of faerie dust we're laughing and disrobing right where we are.

"Have your staff gone home?" I gasp.

"Why?" Alister says. "Do you want a cup of tea?"

He laughs and we can't stop. Not with hysteria. Joy. Not because this is perfect—that was the fantasy that tied me in knots—but because it's not. We're getting to know each other at a whole new level and it's shy and experimental. And reverent. We're finding out what we like—things we didn't know until this moment—together. I've been so focused on how magic it had to be, I missed the magic right in front of me. My feelings for Alister. I knew they were there but they were *hokeo*. Now they've burst through.

Much later I wake in an enormous bed decked with crisp white sheets and, as the afterglow of pleasure washes over me, I watch the past slip by. I never really wanted to be with Andrew, but my ex-husband manipulated and confused me. When I escaped him, I repeated the same pattern. Then I met Alister—the most unlikely of lovers, I thought. We're from different worlds, but that's never been a barrier for him. He doesn't tell me how to dress or how to cut my hair. He doesn't tell me how to *be*, but he tells me the truth as he sees it. We can be on opposite sides of the globe and in the same room because an invisible red cord connects our little fingers. That's magic.

There's a robe draped on the bedpost. I put it on and go to find him. He's making Aussie toast fingers with squashed avocado, crumbled fetta and cracked pepper.

"It's the latest thing stateside," he says. "Little cafés are springing up serving Toby's Estate espresso and a laidback style."

We take the food and a bottle of wine up onto the roof. From the outdoor sofas, the lights of Honolulu spread before us as we share the details of our quests.

"I paid Su Yin what we'd agreed," Alister says. "Then she told me the truth. She's Deshi's cousin, but she's never met him and she's got no idea where he is."

I'm appalled. "So she just wanted to get as much money from you as she could before she told you?"

"She's a student so she's got college fees. But she's agreed to help me find him."

I take his hand. It's such a blow. "Do you believe her after she tricked you?"

"I believe her."

I sense he's got something else to say, but it's not what I'm expecting. He looks me in the eye.

"I have a confession to make, Selkie. About Su Yin. We arranged to meet in a bar, and when I saw this beautiful Chinese girl walking towards me, it was as if I'd opened a time capsule. There was Fleur, just as she was the morning she kissed me goodbye and never came back."

He should be fighting back tears but instead it's me. He told me Su Yin looked just like Fleur, but only my dream knew the implications. It wasn't Fleur I saw him with in my dream, it was Su Yin. They left that bar together, without even noticing me standing alone in the doorway.

I can't bear to wait for his confession, but the crack in my voice betrays my pain. "You ... slept with her."

"No, I didn't. But I was tempted. And I'm telling you because it led to a realisation."

Alister wants to share his quest to find Deshi with Su Yin. He wants to relive his love for Fleur with her beautiful young niece. What I thought we just shared downstairs has shrivelled to a knot in my chest. I don't want to hear any more, but my throat's so dry that I can't find the words to stop him.

"Look at me, Selkie." He lifts my chin with his finger. "What I'm trying to tell you is I was tempted ... by a mirage. Su Yin didn't know it, but in that moment she gave me a gift. She reminded me that I can love. She reminded me that I loved Fleur—and Fleur's gone. It's time for me to love again."

I'm too choked up to speak, feeling like such an eejit for doubting him. Then his kiss makes speaking impossible.

"I know who I want to be with," he says when he gets his breath back. "You, Selkie. I want to be with you."

Getting the words out at last, I say, "That ... makes two of us."

The only thing I'm wearing under the robe is my glass heart and we both reach for it and giggle.

"Time to renew our fingerprints," I say.

We press our little fingers into the locket, pour more wine and let one thing lead to another.

* * *

My fear of intimacy with Alister goes the other way and I can't get enough of him and his king-sized bed. Derek notices that something's changed over a bowl of noodles at the Pearl. He stops halfway through ticking off the stages in my hero's journey on his fingers.

"Judging by the colour in your cheeks, you've got yourself a lover."

I grin. "After a little passion on the parquetry."

"Let's all fly over to Dublin when you go back for the funeral and have a double wedding."

I almost choke on my noodles.

He closes his eyes and visualises. "Tuxes in black for Nigel and Alister. White whatevers for you and me. If we make it a long weekend, the world will fly in for the party."

"Things haven't progressed that far, DD. Alister and I are still playing 'shag, eat, repeat'."

I'm making it sound shallow, which it isn't, but it's the most fun I've ever had lying down and I don't want to spoil it with commitment.

"Has he asked you to move in yet?"

When I don't answer, Derek puts down his chopsticks and looks at me.

"It's complicated," I say.

"Really? Doesn't sound like you."

"Moving into his penthouse isn't my idea of the next step, DD. It's his space, not mine."

"Too much *luxury*?" he asks, mimicking Monty Python. "You could always live in a shoebox on the Lunalilo Freeway, I suppose." Then he gets serious. "Living out of a suitcase, and racing backwards and forwards between Waikiki and Kaka'ako and your office will kill the magic, Selkie."

Derek knows this from experience, from what he used to call his 'crash site' days when no stranger's couch was immune to his surfing. Then he met Nigel and they made a home together.

"I'm applying the Chinese philosophy," I say. "Wait for a solution."

He grunts. "Just don't wait too long."

* * *

The inquest gets delayed twice and when it finally takes place in Tralee, Mikey calls me with the highlights. I can barely contain my impatience, but he takes his time to get to the Coroner's finding so I'm guessing he's pleased.

"The courtroom was packed. The pathologist got up and said that a small bone in Ciara's throat indicated strangulation. And the bird brooch says it's Ciara and the approximate date.

"They let me speak about the attitude towards the tinkers at the time and why Bridie and Brendon felt they had to hide the body. A statement from the Rathbones said they never visited the rath. Then Dermot got up—he's sobered up since you were here—and explained that the builders never looked in the souterrain because they were scared of the faerie folk. That got a few titters.

"Your statement was read out even though it wasn't evidence. But an analyst confirmed that the vial in the tin in Ciara's shoe contained digitalis: a tea brewed from foxglove. No longer a lethal dose, but it might have been in 1896."

So my vision about Bridie's darkest moments was right.

"Then the Coroner adjourned to think about it overnight and this morning he told us that his report won't be ready for several months. There was a lot of hooting and calling to order, so he gave us a summary." He pauses for a moment. "There's not enough evidence to pardon Brendon, Selkie, but he's going to change the victim's name from Bridie to Ciara and find an open verdict. Ciara Fey O'Connor was murdered by assailants unknown."

I swallow. "It's good isn't it?"

"The best we could ever have hoped for. And it's all down to the faerie from Down Underworld."

He's been talking to Dermot.

* * *

We're going to bury Ciara. The Church has confirmed that the whole ring fort is consecrated ground; it was never deconsecrated after the church building was abandoned. It means that Ciara's soul was safe after her interment in the souterrain so Bridie can finally rest in peace about that. But Ciara needs the send-off she never had—a funeral, and a grave with her name on it.

The Rathbones have agreed she can be buried in sight of the infinity symbol. Dermot Donnelly will do the headstone, and Mikey and another Traveller will dig the grave.

I fly back to Ireland, and call in to the Dingle Garda office because the superintendent has a parcel for me—what's left of Ciara's clothes, the hair comb and the bird brooch.

"Ciara O'Connor's effects go to the next of kin," he says.

I just need to sign the paperwork.

Stella is unlikely to want any mementos of the great-aunt she never knew, but I'll keep the rest, except for the brooch which is going to my own sister. Gretel.

* * *

An early flurry of snow keeps the gawkers away. Our intimate group gathers at the graveside and a suitably ancient priest says some Latin over her coffin. After being entwined in the lives of the twin sisters in such a powerful way, I can't stop crying. Mikey puts his arm around me.

This is a special moment in more ways than one. In spite of their tragedies, Bridie and Brendon left their mark—through their children and their stories—but Ciara has remained a child forever, lost in folklore and denied even her place in history. It's why she became the nightingale.

They lower her into the ground, and we toss in handfuls of freezing soil. Then there's something extra for me to sprinkle: the gems from both sisters' names. As I toss in each tiny button of colour and murmur its name and quality, the twins born eight days apart are reunited in spirit. It's a kind of prayer to them both—to Ciara for dying in Bridie's place, and to Bridie for never giving up on her sister: citrine, cleansing; beryl, creativity; iolite, clairvoyance; ruby, spirit guides; amethyst, intuition; ivory, the East; aquamarine, fearlessness; diamond, innocence; emerald, hope. They wink up at me from the rich brown of the earth and I lose myself in their magic.

Ciara needed an epitaph, and when Derek heard the whole story he found an old poem by William Cowper: 'The Nightingale and the Glow-worm'. Through the prism of my tears I read the words carved on her headstone:

*For 'twas the self-same power divine*
*Taught you to sing, and me to shine,*
*That you with music, I with light,*
*Might beautify and cheer the night.*
Mikey touches my shoulder. It's time to say goodbye.

* * *

As Mikey and his mate get busy with the shovels, I turn down the hill towards the house. It's the view that brings this journey to a close. And begins another journey: mine. As

I look towards the well, I reach for my red heart and wrap my fingers around it.

While I searched for answers to Ciara's murder, my life took on a surreal quality as history kept repeating itself until I unravelled the answers.  Now that my ancestors are laid to rest—physically and symbolically—I'm able to get fully grounded in the present. And I can see how history has been repeating itself in a good way.

I've got my man and he's waiting for me 'at the well'. I just need to pack my bag and meet him there.

# Epilogue

I t's my first Irish wake and they sure know how to honour the dead. Every downstairs room in the Rathbone house is buzzing with tears and laughter.

"How did you get the Rathbones to agree to this?" I ask Josephine as she scoots around taking photos for the ghost tour website.

"They're hoping they can finally stay here," she says, "that Ciara's ghost won't bother them any more. I told them that a wake will release her spirit." She winks.

It makes me think of the tangle of ghosts down near the well. I haven't been back to check if they're still stopping sensitive individuals in their tracks. Perhaps the truth has released their spirits. Either way they won't bother the ghost tour. Josephine is planning to switch it to the faerie fort. She's just waiting for official permission before she buys a bigger bus.

Nola has created mourning cards in the Victorian style for everyone to take home, with the photo of Ciara cropped from the family portrait and her name printed in gold letters. She's also made a little shrine with a candle, incense sticks and flowers around a photo of both Bridie and Ciara.

In the living room, Finn's band Tinker's Cuss strikes up songs both poignant and joyful. They've brought a striking black singer with them and she launches into a folksong called The Tinker's Poteen which puts everyone in the mood if they weren't already.

Until tonight I haven't met anyone else from Mikey's clan but they insist I try the drink that inspired the song. One sip hits my throat like a virus, and the fire renders me so breathless I can't even cough. To hoots of derision, one of the women rescues me by pouring my shot glass into a tumbler of orange juice. It's an ice-breaking introduction to more of my long-lost cousins. When I can speak again I try to get my head around the family tree, and wish Gretel was here.

Dermot introduces me to his wife who's heavily pregnant with their first child. She's shy about meeting me after her infamous use of a dead cat—to keep me out of this very house. I haven't caught up with where the former feline is now but if it had driven me away as intended, the myth about the faeries wouldn't have been busted and Dermot wouldn't be beaming. But after his terror that I might have designs on their first-born offspring, I dare not ask too many questions about the baby.

As I try to think of something to say to her, she knocks me over with their news. "It's a girl we're having and we're going to name her after Ciara."

"Ciara's the most popular girl's name in Ireland," Dermot adds, but his wife won't have any of it.

"It's like an omen, what's happened," she says. "The faeries giving her back after all this time. Dermot is a new man."

I smile and nod. She's right about Dermot but I don't think he's out of the woods with his superstitious wife, not to mention the prospects for poor baby Ciara.

Josephine has even invited Sister Bernadette from Abbeymare and as the medicinal refreshment pinks her cheeks—and doesn't rob her of breath—she tells me about their resident seal, Merrow.

"The rest of the pod won't be back till the spring," she says. "But Merrow never leaves."

"Why? Doesn't he have a family?"

Then she floors me. "He thinks we're his cousins."

I almost choke again. Merrow must be the seal that blinked at me. And here was I thinking his 'hello cousin' message was just for me. Selkie Moon, Seal Whisperer. Dervla doesn't have exclusive rights to hubris.

Pixie and Rory are here—I've discovered they're a couple—along with other fishermen from the pub. The fishermen are arguing about which one of them was the first to debunk the cliff burial theory that sent Brendon to the gallows. Rory is dining out on his notoriety as the great grandson of the man who *didn't* kill Ciara, and I decide not to tell him how James terrorised Bridie after his sexual gratification was delayed. On top of losing the baby, it's the reason she ran away—a cloistered life steeped in grief wins over daily brutalising by a monster.

Pixie thanks me for the sudden interest in acrostic jewellery that's keeping her shop full of customers. "After one woman asked for bracelets for her daughters, named Deirbhile and Eibhleann,"—she spells them for me—"I'm now specialising in Irish spelling."

And selling more gems in the process.

It's my turn to thank her for helping me on the night of the solstice. "It was your advice about breathing that made me play the thin note."

"The thin note?"

"I had three goes at playing the penny whistle and when I breathed out, the third note was thin—to align itself with the *rath* and the solstice."

"Ah, I forgot to tell you about the power of three, but you found that out for yourself."

She makes me feel homesick for Derek.

A man in a wheelchair arrives late, muffled in a shawl and unrecognisable. He's helped through the front door by some of the fishermen, with Widow Winsome behind him. When he's unwrapped, I see it's Vincent from the brewery. Someone whispers that he's had a stroke and Widow Winsome is looking after him.

"I told her just to send the *sheehogue*," he jokes. "With his long arms, this contraption would be no problem at all, at all. But would she listen to me? I'll not be telling her what to do."

She's moved in with Vincent and left the *sheehogue* to run amok at the old gatehouse.

I get Vincent a glass of *poteen* and he uses his good hand to sip it.

"So you found her, lass," he says. "Ciara O'Connor wouldn't be giving you the slip. I could see that when I met you."

I laugh. "What did I do?"

"You're the kind of woman they used to call a faerie back in Bridie and Ciara's day. Clever and hard to handle."

Like Bridie. What did Sibby Dolan say? *She was very determined was Miss Bridie.*

Vincent winks his good eye, then turns serious. "They say it's why Michael Cleary burned his wife Bridget—she was too independent and he wanted to control her."

Luckily there's a hush to end this conversation. The singer with Finn's band is getting ready for a solo. Everyone's read the channelled words of Ciara's version of Two Sisters, after they were published in *The Kerryman*, and now they soar through the house, a fitting farewell to all the departed souls in this tragedy.

Finn keeps his distance all night, but when daylight is peeping over Dingle Bay and everyone's finally leaving, Mikey calls him over to me and gives him a nudge. Like a shy teenager Finn presents me with a gift.

"We thought it was time you made it your own," Mikey says as I open the parcel. "Brendon passed his skills onto Finn his great-great-grandson, so it's right that Finn made them for you, Bridie's great-granddaughter."

"I had one hell of a time finding them all," Finn grumbles. "Kyanite of all things."

I wasn't sure who owned the pendant, now that its job has been done, but on my palm I hold out six acrostic gems. A whole new set for the whistle to spell SELKIE.

# Dear Reader ...

Thank you so much for joining Selkie Moon on her Irish adventure in *The Third Note*. Her great-grandmother Bridie was right about a lot of things.

Where to next for Selkie — and Alister?


*Thirty years ago, a baby boy was kidnapped ...*

*When Selkie Moon travels to Hong Kong to discover his fate, she has high hopes of using her psychic twinges to find him and reunite him with his father, Alister.*

*Until the tea leaves on her flight make a chilling prediction ...*

*Some is going to die. Someone close to Selkie? Or Selkie herself?*

You can start turning the pages of *The Fourth Door* right away.

http://www.selkiemoon.com/

# About the Author

When a voice wakes you up in the middle of the night and tells you to write a fiction series what's a writer to do? That's how Virginia King came to create Selkie Moon.  After this nocturnal message, she sat down at the keyboard until Selkie Moon turned up.  Soon Virginia was hooked, exploring far-flung places full of secrets on Selkie's personal journey of self-discovery.

Before Selkie Moon invaded her life, Virginia had been a teacher, an unemployed ex-teacher, the author of over 50 children's books, an audio-book producer, a workshop presenter and a prize-winning publisher. These days she lives in the Blue Mountains west of Sydney with her husband, where she disappears each day into Selkie Moon's latest adventure.

# Also by Virginia King

Follow Selkie Moon's journey to Hong Kong ...

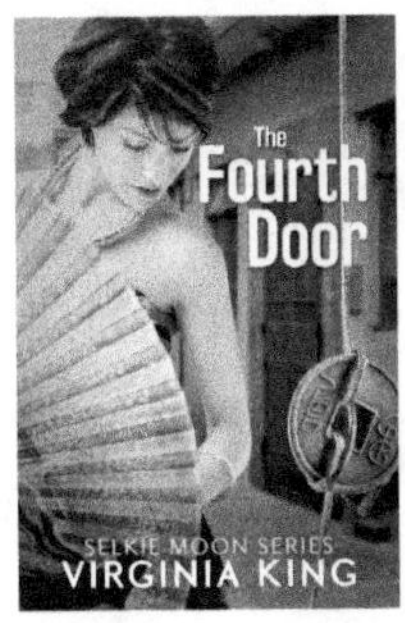

**The Fourth Door**

Thirty years ago, a baby boy was kidnapped. When Selkie Moon travels to Hong Kong to discover his fate, she has high hopes of reuniting him with his father. Until the tea leaves on her flight make a chilling prediction.

Then in a Kowloon night-market she witnesses a child abduction—and the echo with her quest suddenly raises the stakes.

As the strange events escalate and reach back into Chinese folklore, Selkie is forced to confront the powerful force that's hell-bent on stopping her. The omens are unmistakable. Someone is going to die. Someone closest to her? Or Selkie herself?

http://www.selkiemoon.com/